D1002110

A Lake of Feathers and Moonbeams

Dax Murray

Copyright © 2017 by Dax Murray

All rights reserved. This book or any portion thereof may not be reproduced or used in any manner whatsoever without the express written permission of the publisher except for the use of brief quotations in a book review.

This is a work of fiction. Names, characters, businesses, places, events, locales, and incidents are either the products of the author's imagination or used in a fictitious manner. Any resemblance to actual persons, living or dead, or actual events is purely coincidental.

Printed in the United States of America

First Printing, 2017

ISBN-13: 978-1521970621
ISBN-10: 1521970629

Second Edition

Moon Cat Books
P.O. Box 8074
Silver Spring, MD 20907

daxmurray.com

Cover Illustration Copyright © 2017 by Laya Rose Art
Cover design by Louisa Smith, Juneberry Design
Cover design by Dane Low
Book design by Aurelia Fray, Pretty AF Designs
Chapter opening illustrations © 2018 Aurelia Fray
Editing by Jen Anderson of Clearing Blocks Editing

Also By Dax Murray

The Resignation Letter

Birthing Orion

A Lake of Feathers and Moonbeams

For the three wise women who taught me how to survive this world;
Stevie Nicks, Carrie Fisher, and my mother.

A
Lake
of
Feathers
and
Moonbeams

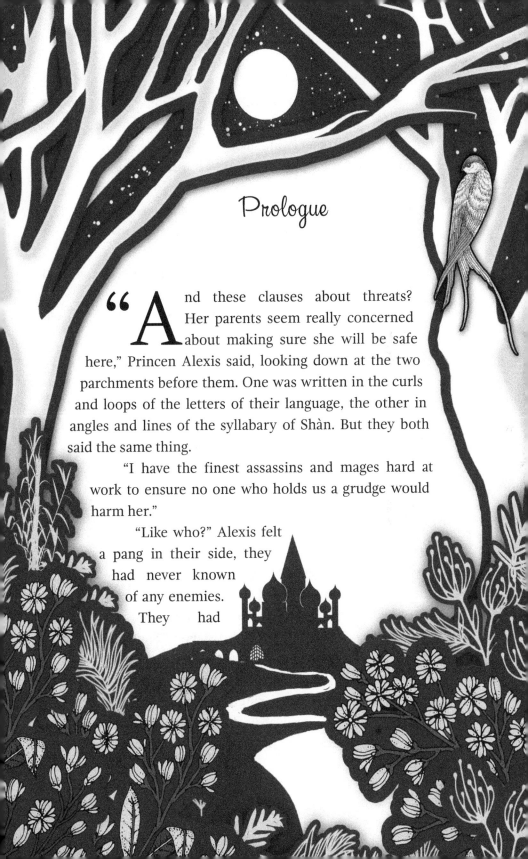

Prologue

"And these clauses about threats? Her parents seem really concerned about making sure she will be safe here," Princen Alexis said, looking down at the two parchments before them. One was written in the curls and loops of the letters of their language, the other in angles and lines of the syllabary of Shàn. But they both said the same thing.

"I have the finest assassins and mages hard at work to ensure no one who holds us a grudge would harm her."

"Like who?" Alexis felt a pang in their side, they had never known of any enemies. They had never heard of plots on the lives of their family, the royal dungeons were empty, and their parents were loved as some of the kindest monarchs Lebedia had ever had. Who would wish them ill?

"Leave that to me, I am still Czar. It is my task both as ruler and your father to make sure you and your bride come to the throne secure. It is mostly a formality." Alexis' father stood up and waved his hand, dismissing the notion and Alexis' anxiety.

"I do not think I am ready." Alexis sat back in their chair, letting out a sigh.

"I was not ready either," their father said, reaching his hand across the mahogany table and laying it on his child's.

"But you got lucky. You and mother, you understand each other. You love each other."

"You will be lucky, too. This marriage is important, Alexis. We need to settle this dispute, it's been too many generations. Your marriage to Princess Yi Zhen will bring peace."

"I know, but—" Alexis pulled their hand away from the Czar. They needed to do this for their country, for their people.

"Is there someone else? Someone here at court?"

There were dozens of "someone else's"; kisses behind curtains, hands held a second too long during dance practice, sidelong glances when attending lessons. But there was nothing serious, nothing that was worth troubling their parents with. Nothing that had ever lasted more than a few fluttering weeks.

"How did you feel when Lady Natalya came home?"

It was not the question the Czar was expecting, his jaw dropped and he stared at his child. He sighed. "She had been sent to be a lady-in-waiting to Queen Elizabeth, her parents wanting her to be in the kingdom of Ahrian. Their family were distant cousins to the Queen Elizabeth, and wanted to support her. Natalya also wanted to undergo the magics she needed for her transformation away from Lebedia, away from the court, especially after Maria was engaged to me. She is your mother's first love. I knew that. I knew that she loved Natalya as my parents lay out the betrothal agreement before me, just as I am doing now. But Natalya was gone, far away on the other side of the continent, and your mother had the most beautiful eyes."

"She came back though."

"She did," he said, nodding. His hands were interlaced in his lap, and he kept looking down at them, as if they held drawings of these days gone by. "Your mother loved me. We adopted you. Named you heir. But I knew she still loved Natalya, and it was with Natalya that she had always wanted to have a child. I could have let it break my heart. I could have let it break hers. I could have locked her in her rooms and banished Natalya. She could have ran away in the night and traveled with Natalya. It was the hardest time of our marriage. We cried, we said mean things to each other. We threw compromises long settled back in each others faces."

He stood up, grabbing his cane and walking from the office and into his sitting room. Alexis followed, unsure if they should bring the paperwork with them, but decided to leave it there.

"Your mother is more passionate than I am, which is to say, I am not. Which is why you were adopted. I kept waiting for her to throw that in my face, to lump it in with the way she hated how I slurped my soup, or how she got so annoyed by how I would bite my nails sometimes. I kept waiting for her to scream that I did not care that she longed to give birth and how she gave that up for me." He went to the fireplace and rested his arm on the mantle, his forehead on his arm.

"That's when I knew that she loved me, truly and deeply. She was not asking to leave me, rather, she was asking if she could bring Lady Natalya into our family. I love her so much, Alexis, I would give her the world if I could. How could I deny her another partner? How could I not want her to have as much love as she could?"

"I did not know. You three make it look so easy to love, to be kind to each other. I do not know if I can take on the responsibility, the duty—"

"We were not ready either. Which is why we made a mess of it at first. We messed up, we had to learn how to communicate. We had to learn how to ask and how to tell and how to understand. You will not feel ready to rule when I die, no matter when that is. I did not feel ready, then, either. I still do not, honestly. You will not feel ready to parent when you look at your first child. But you will learn. Bring the paperwork here. We can sign these and send off the envoy to go fetch your future wife."

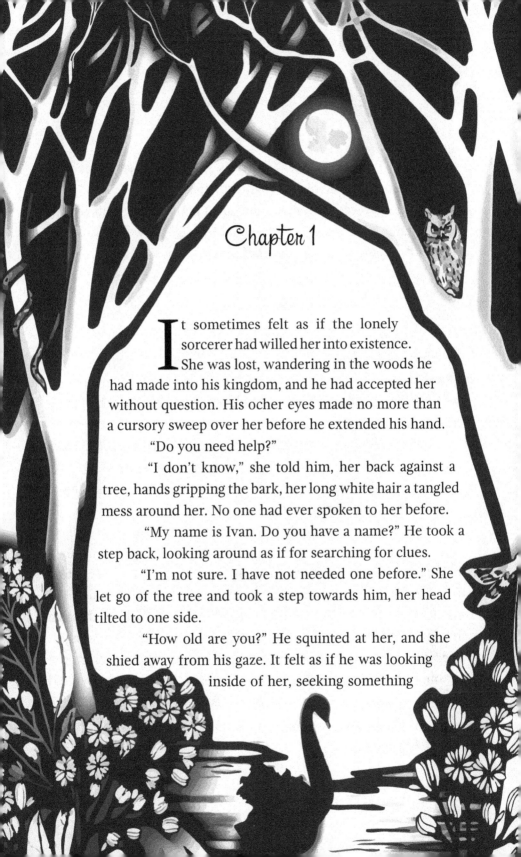

Chapter 1

I t sometimes felt as if the lonely sorcerer had willed her into existence. She was lost, wandering in the woods he had made into his kingdom, and he had accepted her without question. His ocher eyes made no more than a cursory sweep over her before he extended his hand.

"Do you need help?"

"I don't know," she told him, her back against a tree, hands gripping the bark, her long white hair a tangled mess around her. No one had ever spoken to her before.

"My name is Ivan. Do you have a name?" He took a step back, looking around as if for searching for clues.

"I'm not sure. I have not needed one before." She let go of the tree and took a step towards him, her head tilted to one side.

"How old are you?" He squinted at her, and she shied away from his gaze. It felt as if he was looking inside of her, seeking something unseen.

"I don't know."

"What *do* you know?" He shoved his hands in the pockets of his too-large robe.

"I woke up in the lake a few days ago." She looked behind her and pointed to the only lake the forest held.

He furrowed his brows, and ran a hand through his shaggy brown hair. "You seem to me to be a little shy of two decades old, you do not remember anything before a few days ago?"

"Should I?" She shook her head.

"I suppose it does not matter. You can stay with me, if you would like."

So she followed him. He carried himself through the woods as though he expected the dawn-poppy, ferns, and orchids to bow before him, and the towering oak and maple trees to move out of his way, an easy smile on his face and his hands clasped loosely behind his back.

His castle was a large thatched cottage with a stone chimney, and he invited her to live with him inside of its moss-covered walls. She fell into his life easily enough. She claimed a small room in the east as her own, and then claimed a name of her own—Katya— from one she read in a book. She accumulated charms and trinkets to solidify her sense of belonging. This arboreal king kept his own belongings in some sort of order, but she could not differentiate it from chaos. Despite the lack of discernible organization, she soon found a trove of books and journals. She loved to look through his journals detailing the creatures in his kingdom, marveling at the accompanying hand-drawn illustrations. Everything from the looming *leshy* to the irritating mosquitoes indexed and accounted for.

If there was a strangeness to living with a sorcerer, she did not at first recognize it as such. She never noted that neither of them seemed to age, nor that both of them had some affinity for the animals in the forest. She never wondered what he had thought of her when he came upon her. Somehow, years passed. During that time she never truly encountered another human and had no standard against which to measure her own life.

"These insects make a sweet substance," she said one day. They were both seated at the oaken kitchen table, one on either side. Ivan was either sorting his ceremonial dagger collection or hunting for one that was missing, Katya could not tell which. He nodded in what passed for a response.

"Do you think we could construct a home for them?" Her words came out all in one breath, and her eyes were wide as she shoved the open book in his face. "Here," she jabbed her finger at an illustration. "We could build it in the back garden, the book says this 'honey' is good for baking, in tea, and to keep wounds from festering."

"Katya, I am busy!" His shoulders tensed and he tapped one of his knives on the table with slow *thunks*.

She raised an eyebrow as she looked at his dagger collection and then back up at him. "With what?"

"You are impossible." He threw the dagger down and grabbed the book from her, "let me see the book. Should be simple enough to build a hive for them, the problem would be getting a queen to relocate."

"Could you use... well, you could do that with magic, right?" She tried to keep her voice light. Despite living with a sorcerer, his magic made her uneasy. She could never place why. At least, not in a way she wanted to verbalize, even to herself.

He put the book down and squinted at her, frowning. "I could, of course."

"We could try to coax a queen without magic first, but maybe I would ask for a small bit of magical help if it has been a few weeks and there are no bees."

He leaned back, rubbing his chin. "But with the seasons changing, you would want them established sooner rather than later."

Her shoulders sagged. "We could wait for next year."

"You asked about magic, but now you seem to want to avoid it. What is going on?" He leaned forward again, resting his elbows on the table and his chin on his fists.

"Nothing." She grabbed the book back, clutching it to her chest. Her face felt like it was on fire, and she suddenly wanted to be anywhere but here.

"All right, I will not pry, but if you want to talk about whatever is bothering you, I am here."

She was glad when he made no comment the next day when he found her taking a saw to the woodpile. The construction of the beehive distracted her for a little while from the pile of books she still had to get through, and the joyful arrival of a queen and her workers prolonged that diversion. She screeched when she went outside that morning to check for new inhabitants.

"What happened? Are you all right?" Ivan said, standing disheveled and out of breath in the doorway.

"I think I have bees!" She beamed, not taking her eyes off of the tiny entrance.

"You scared me! I thought you were hurt!"

"I'm fine, come look at my bees!"

She felt his arm settle over her shoulders as he kneeled down to peer inside. "You did it! We should celebrate tonight."

He went into town that afternoon and came back late. Ignashino was outside the woods, a fair bit of distance away, and Katya had never been there, though she often wondered what it must be like. He was frowning when he came back home, his brows knit together in worry. Katya was about to ask what was wrong when he dropped a pouch on the table.

"You can make a better garden," he explained. "I think there is about 30 different types of seeds in there. I hear the honey tastes different depending on what sorts of flowers the bees pollinate."

"Thank you!" She opened the pouch and sorted out the smaller pouches inside, each containing seeds of different sizes and shapes.

"I am probably going to be busy a lot these next few days." He sank into a chair, leaning back and closing his eyes, his hands interlaced in his lap.

"Oh? With what? You looked worried earlier, is everything all right?"

"I do not know yet, worrisome news from the capital. I overheard some conversations today. I want to look into it."

"What sort of news?"

"I should not have said anything, I will keep us safe." He pulled a crumpled paper out of his cloak pocket and uncrumpled it in his lap. Katya craned her neck to try and read it, but he tore it up and threw it in the fire, then stormed into his room and locked the door behind him.

Katya did not linger long on his dour mood, instead she threw herself into gardening and reading while he was gone most of the time over the next few weeks. She returned to her neglected pile of unread books. As the pile dwindled, she asked Ivan if he had any more hidden in a cranny she had not noticed. He stared at her for a long time, as if she was a puzzle he was trying to solve, rubbing his chin. She was beginning to think he would not answer her when he got up from his desk, and headed into his room, motioning her to follow.

She hesitated, her stomach in knots. She'd never been in his room before, and her eyes leapt from one corner to another as she entered, taking in all the odds and ends, tools and instruments, he had collected. He heaved a trunk out from under his bed, reached into his pocket, and pulled out a key. He held it in his hands, scrutinizing it. He took in a quick breath and then opened the trunk. "If you are interested," he said as he stood back up and backed away from the trunk, allowing her to approach and look inside.

All the books held inside of this trunk were on magic. She backed away, but she wanted to lean closer, she wanted to pull out each book linger on the title, her fingers tracing the inlaid gold lettering. Her heart was racing, the desire to flee from or dive into the trunk twinned and paralyzed her. Ivan looked at her and frowned, his brows knitting together. He let out a sigh and closed the trunk.

Katya wanted to yell, to tell him to wait, but the words would not leave her mouth. Instead of locking the chest, he dragged it out of his bedroom. Katya followed him, one uneasy step after another, her heart still pounding in her head.

"I'll leave these here, so you can get them if you are interested."

For days she resisted, glancing at the books in the trunk while holding one of the better worn, but mundane tomes in her lap. Magic was *his* thing. But there might have been more to her hesitation than that. "Katya," he said to her one day, "I can tell you want to read them, why not just read them?"

She turned to stare out the window.

"Are you afraid? I do this sort of thing every day."

She glanced at him, his shaggy brown hair falling over his thick eyebrows and covering his eyes, and then returned to her intense study of the insects milling outside. She was afraid. She was afraid that the books might contain the answers to the questions that had lodged in her heart and scratched at her core every time she took a breath. *Where did she come from?*

She did not want to be preoccupied with that question, she

A LAKE OF FEATHERS AND MOONBEAMS

was here now. She was here and happy, and that should be all that matters. Looking into magic might mean finding more questions instead of answers, it might means years of desperate searching and crushing heartache. It was better not think about it at all.

It was frightening, too. Ivan seemed exhausted after larger spells, and when he got something wrong, a rare occurrence, it could be catastrophic. It was a reasonable choice, she told herself, to stay away from magic.

Except.

He out running an errand the day she opened the first book. She learned magic in the hours he spent away from the cottage, stealing away a text and secreting it back into the trunk when she thought she heard him approach. She learned that all magics required a source of power that you could not create something out of nothing. Each form of magics had laws or rules or ceremonies, but most of the books suggested that regardless of the form of magic, all required a small bit of life as the sacrifice, be in the caster's own well of aether, or that from the earth, or trees, or creatures.

Some darker texts suggested that great feats could be accomplished by using all of the life of a creature. Illustrations accompanied these somber spells, knives being pressed to the throats of birds or goats. She did not linger on these pages.

She read about conjury, witchery, thaumaturgy, celestialism, and sorcery. All different forms of magic, each with their own styles, instruments, and accouterments. She read vociferously, a magpie stealing spells and styles and stratagems to make for herself a nest of daggers and crystals and wands. Soon, the magic she had feared came to her easily, and soon she was doing simple magics without error. She could light a candle, conjure a wind, and call a storm, and summon earth golems. She could make a healing tonic, or brew a pot of poison, and she could identify both by smell.

She thought she kept this learning to herself, but she

was caught. She had stayed up late the night before, reading by candlelight in her room, her door closed. But she still needed to wake at dawn to tend to the chickens Ivan had purchased for her from the nearby town a few weeks prior. After that, there were even more chores to be done. Ivan, disguised as always, left after lunch for an afternoon of bartering his teas, charms, and tonics at a market. She was exhausted by the time she settled in at the kitchen table for more reading that night.

"Katya, go to bed."

"What?" She sat up, the candle burned out, and looked around.

Ivan snapped his fingers, and several of their wall torches sprung to life. "I said, you should go to bed. I cannot imagine a book to be a good pillow."

She looked down, the book still open to a page on using the stars to divine the future. "Oh, you're right." She tried to slam the book closed, hiding it as though she were a child caught with an extra sweet.

"Wait!" He called. Katya turned around, sure she had been found out. "I got you something while I was out," he said. He pulled a ceramic mug out of his bag. "This should keep your tea warm much better than the one you have now."

"Oh! Thank you!" She took it from him with her freehand, keeping the book's title still out of sight by clenching it to her chest. The mug was hefty and glazed with a beautiful blue paint. She always appreciated the small gifts he brought back for her when he went to town.

"Were you thinking of invoking the Boar?" Ivan gestured at the book that Katya clung to her chest. *He* had *seen*, she thought. *He saw the exact page the book was open to.*

She acted as though she had not heard him as she gathered her skirt and stood up, placing the mug on the counter in the kitchen, and then turning to head into her bedroom.

"Celestialism was never my strong point, maybe we can go the lake tomorrow night and see which stars are out, make some charts?" She paused in the doorway, her one hand braced on its frame as she tried to quiet the war in her head. He could teach her a lot, but if she took him up on his offer of mentorship, what might happen next?

"We can do that, but I would want to learn at my own pace, this feels like a private and personal journey for me. It's not that I don't trust you, but that I want this for myself."

"I understand," he said as he headed to his own room.

The following night they headed for the lake, scrolls and ink and quills bundled in small bags thrown over their shoulders. Ivan meticulously set ups his supplies, neat stacks of scrolls, quills laid out just so. Katya plopped to the ground and scattered her materials in a mess that was more of Ivan's style than hers normally.

"Have more care, Katya!" Ivan said as he unfurled a cloth star map in front of him, smoothing out the edges. "This is very complicated, and you need to get the measurements precise."

"You're one to talk, who was it that lost their reading glasses this morning?"

He sighed, shoulders sagging in defeat.

"And, where were they, Ivan? Your glasses? Where were they?"

He rolled his eyes.

"Weren't they in with your candles? No! No, they were inside one of your empty candle jars."

He held up his hands. "You win! You win! It's getting dark, we should be set up already."

Katya grinned and began re-organizing her tools. They each approached the craft in their own way, but their excited squeals were near identical in their enthusiasm as the night passed and they charted the heavens in search of answers.

"Look!" Ivan cried, startling Katya from the math equations she was scratching into the ground with a stick. "A falling star!"

Katya leapt to her feet, determined to give the star chase. She raced through the clearing and into the wood, and a coven of crows followed behind, drawn to her laughter. She felt each leaf beneath her heel and smelled each flower in bloom as she passed by. Further behind, she felt Ivan's presence, unsure if he was chasing the star or her.

She neared the edge of the woods, watching the star fly past the horizon. Just ahead of her was the edge of the forest, and beyond that open fields. She could keep chasing, but as the thought crossed her mind, she felt a wave of dizziness and nausea. Ivan's hand found her shoulder and pulled her close. "Go and catch a falling star," he said, a smile on his face.

She let out a laugh, the moment of unease passing. "What does it mean?"

"Change. I think it means that everything is about to change. And I am very ready for what that change may bring."

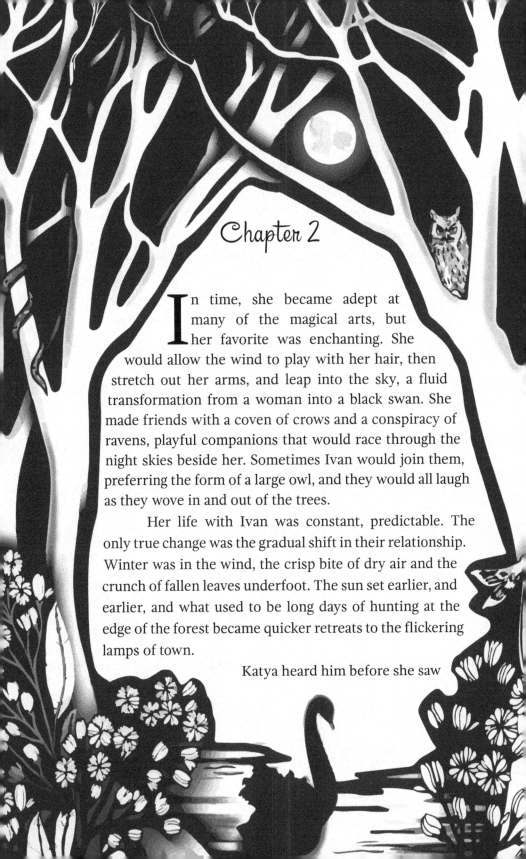

Chapter 2

In time, she became adept at many of the magical arts, but her favorite was enchanting. She would allow the wind to play with her hair, then stretch out her arms, and leap into the sky, a fluid transformation from a woman into a black swan. She made friends with a coven of crows and a conspiracy of ravens, playful companions that would race through the night skies beside her. Sometimes Ivan would join them, preferring the form of a large owl, and they would all laugh as they wove in and out of the trees.

Her life with Ivan was constant, predictable. The only true change was the gradual shift in their relationship. Winter was in the wind, the crisp bite of dry air and the crunch of fallen leaves underfoot. The sun set earlier, and earlier, and what used to be long days of hunting at the edge of the forest became quicker retreats to the flickering lamps of town.

Katya heard him before she saw

him. She'd just joined her crow-sisters, but a cry tore her from her path of flight. "Where'd you go? This isn't fun anymore!" A small boy was trying to run, his head sweeping back and forth, his hands flailing as he tried to dodge branches and brush.

His momentum was too much, and he tripped, flying face first to the ground. Katya couldn't let him continue to wander the woods, lost and hurt. She swooped down, her webbed feet rustling the leaves beneath her.

"Who's there?" The boy called, his eyes wide as he tried to search the woods for monsters or bears, his breathing shallow and heavy.

She stepped forward, a woman once more, hunched over and her hand outstretched. "I'm here to help you," she said.

He pulled away from her, getting up and stumbling backwards, not letting her out of his sight. "My ma told me not to talk to strangers. I need to get home." He straightened his back, his lower lip quivering as he tried to keep it still.

"I can show you the path out of the forest." She got down on her knees, her gown settling on the forest floor with the faintest of whispers. "I'm not here to hurt you. You're bleeding, let me see your hands."

He took one tentative step towards her, and then paused, looking around as if he expected something more sinister to spring from the dark. He gulped, and then took another step.

She grabbed his hand, and without even thinking, used conjury to re-knit the skin he had scraped away on the rough bark of roots. He shook the entire time, equal parts fear and wonder, trying to put on a brave front. She finished, and he pulled back his hands with a start and then shoved them in his pocket.

"Thank you, lady, I got to get home now, though."

"I can show you the way." She stood up and held out her hand. He took it with trepidation, and followed. She knew the quickest path, the one that would lead him to the field that became Ignashino. He wasn't the first child to wander into the woods, but he was the first one who'd gotten this lost.

"So, d'you live here, lady?" He asked after some minutes of silence.

"Nearby," she replied. She didn't know how much Ivan let on of their living in the woods when he went into town for supplies, or much at all about anything outside of these woods, but she felt the need to be circumspect.

"Do you live alone or with your parents? I live with my mom and dad and grandmas and my brother. He's only four years old, but I just turned eight."

"You're almost all grown up," she said.

"That's why my parents let me come here today! But my cousins ran off home without me. Only older kids can come in here."

"That makes sense, don't worry, we will be out of the woods soon."

"Oh, I see it!" He dropped her hand, running forward and pointing to the light in the distance, where the trees parted and the last light of the sun was still visible. He turned back to her. "Thanks, lady!"

He was gone before she could reply.

She thought she had rescued a small boy from a terrible nightmare, but the people of Ignashino did not see it that way. She never knew what he told them, or didn't, about their encounter, but soon the forest was full of farmers with shovels and makeshift weapons. They were looking for a witch. Her crows told her of hunting parties, of men with revenge and fear in their eyes and women with fierce determination. The monster they sought was her; the fae creature who had bewitched a child. Their torches sought her flesh for kindling, and their axes her bones.

But Ivan stopped them. She hid in their cottage, frightened, as he went outside to confront them. She could not watch. She did not want to see them drag him away to be burned or beheaded. She paced in front of the fireplace, picking up her mug and then putting it back down. She wrung her hands as she imagined every horrible scenario. She had never truly known a life without him, and she did not want to find out what that might look like. She tried to ignore the distant sounds, telling herself that he was confronting them at the edge of the woods, far from their cottage. The screams she thought she heard were phantasms, she assured herself.

But he came back, no worse for wear. His robes torn and dirty, but no injuries. He stood, breathing heavily, in the doorway of their cottage. She ran up to him, throwing her arms around him and pulling him close. As he tried to disentangle himself from her, she asked, "May I kiss you?" She did not know why she had asked him that, but she had read about it in some of his books. It seemed like the thing she should do at that moment. He nodded, and their relationship changed.

This was the life she lived, gladly. Friends, and then more, living together yet undertaking their own individual pursuits. It seemed as if they had always lived like this, and she thought they always would. But the changes a star had once foretold were not done yet and had not even truly begun.

The night was still young, a gibbous moon hanging low over the forest, illumination enough for Katya and her coven of crows to weave in and out of the trees in their ever more elaborate dances. But something was not right. Katya could sense something in the air, something heavy that weighed her down. She landed, becoming human once more.

There was a glow in the distance, bobbing up and down, making its way towards her from the south. Torches. Her trembling hand came to her stomach, clutching at it while she tried to make her feet move. Another party of scared villagers, here for her? Where was Ivan?

She tried to will herself back into a swan, but she could do nothing but stare.

The torches grew closer, and she saw what looked less like a mob and more like an escort party, guards or soldiers leading a carriage. She let out the breath that had become lodged in her throat. They were not here for her.

But then, what were they doing?

"Hold! Who goes there?" they called to her. She stepped from the shadows of the trees, cautiously approaching their torches. She slowly smiled as she saw Ivan on the other side of the escort party, a shade in the shadows, the soldiers and their bright torches between them. In the silent language they shared, he asked her to try to gather information.

"I'm no one, sir, I'm just out walking."

"It's late, my lady," the tallest soldier said. He glanced back at his companions, a question clear in his eyes.

"I could say the same to you," she replied. She looked past the leader, taking in the other soldiers as they halted. There were about two dozen of them. Nearly half were wearing long chain mail armor that extended down their legs in a robe-like fashion, with a belt around the middle, the buckle an intricate dragon head. Over their heads they wore helmets accented with a plume of red tassels on the top and ear plates that brushed their shoulders. The other half of the party were dressed in long double-breasted doublets, with long fur-lined jackets hanging over top. They wore felted hats on their heads, and fur-lined boots covered with sturdy greaves. Behind them, she could see another line of torches making their way toward their halted companions.

"We're an escort, my lady. Are you lost? If you would like, we can take you to the nearest village."

It was the easiest answer, and Katya could still feel her heart beating quickly, her body lagging behind in the realization that she was not in danger. She nodded.

"There is room enough in the carriage for you. You don't have to be frightened."

She looked past the soldier and saw Ivan lingering in the shadows. His eyes gleamed with mischief, a smile making its way across his face. Then he winked, and an owl replaced him, taking flight and heading toward the second line of torches. Even without words, she knew exactly what he wanted her to do.

"I appreciate it, thank you" she said, as the carriage came into view. It was finely furnished, trimmed with molding and frills, though it appeared someone had tried to make them appear plainer than they were by smudging mud onto the sides and trying to cover up some of the golden flecks in the paint. Or perhaps they had traveled a great distance with little rest.

"Commander Alexei, why are we stopped?" A young woman leaned out of the carriage's window. Her features and accent gave away she was not Lebedian. Her face was pale, with thin eyebrows and rosy lips. Her black hair was pulled back in an elaborate bun held in place by glittering rods from which glistening jewels dangled.

"We're almost there, my lady. I promised to escort you safely to your destination, and I shall. But we've run into someone who is lost in the woods."

Katya curtsied to the lady in the carriage, and then boldly looked her in the eye and smiled. She caught a small movement above her—an owl perched on the carriage—and told the woman, "I'm sorry to trouble you on your journey."

"Well, do you need help? There is room in my carriage for you. I would be glad of some company."

"My lady, if it's no bother to you?"

"None at all." And with that, she leaned back into the carriage.

A soldier opened the carriage door for Katya, and she got in the carriage, marveling at the silk curtains and velvet brocade cushions.

"I'm Katya," she said, sitting next to the lady while taking in the white and yellow silk *aoqun* the woman was wearing. It was not ornate, but it still exposed her as someone who was wealthy. No one of more humble means could afford silk of such high quality, nor such detailed embroidery.

The lady gave Katya a small smile, a blush creeping into her cheeks. She lowered her lashes and said, "I am Yi Zhen."

"Where are you going?" Katya asked, curious about the enchanting woman.

"The capital of Lebedia, Kristallicheskiy. I am on my way to meet my betrothed." Her excitement was genuine, but Yi Zhen picked at an imperceptible spot on her skirt.

"Congratulations on your engagement, that's exciting. Are you traveling from far away?"

"From Shān, we've been on the road for some time now."

"Are you tired of traveling?"

"A little, I have little to occupy my time except reading or embroidery."

"I love reading! Do you have a favorite book?"

"So many, but I think none of them have been translated to Lebedian. There's one I love about a girl and a *qilin* who save the Emperor, and one about a brave archer who rescues a goddess. What about you?"

Katya felt her heart racing. She had spent little time in other people's company before, but she definitely wanted to spend more time in Zhen's. There was a buzzing just under her skin, she wanted to reach out and touch her, smooth away the creases in her skirt, move a stray strand of hair out of her face.

She blushed thinking of the books she enjoyed, romances with fluttering eyelashes and pounding hearts. It felt intimate to discuss this, and a part of Katya worried that maybe Zhen would take it as an invitation.

But then shouting erupted outside, Zhen peaked her head out the window and Katya grabbed her by the shoulders and pull her back in the carriage.

"Stay inside! The soldiers should be able to handle whatever disturbance is out there." Zhen nodded while she bit her lower lip, tears pooling in her eyes. She clutched herself, haunted by whatever she had witnessed taking place outside.

The shouts became more frantic, more fearful. Katya did not know what was going on outside, but she did not think it could be thieves. She knew that she and Ivan were the most fearful of creatures in the woods. She did not think it could be Ivan, as she was sure she had the information that he might want about these travelers in their woods. They were not loggers or miners or hunters, they did not threaten the forest. Ivan would not resort to this kind of intimidation for a party of travelers, people merely passing through.

Time passed oddly, elongating and contracting as seconds or years passed, the only way to pass the moment was to count the wails of the dying soldiers. The shouts became muffled cries, some quick, others prolonged in agony.

"Who do you think it is? We were so careful!" Zhen said, holding back tears through shallow gulps of air.

"I don't know." She heard awful gurgling noises and watched as the glow of torches outside the carriage dim as their bearers fell and the flames drowned in spilled blood.

"We sent my handmaidens along other routes. I hope they are all right." Zhen wrung her hands, placed them in her lap, and then wrung them again. Where Zhen was anxious movement, Katya had settled into terrified stillness.

"I'm sure they are, and we will be, too."

The last torch went out. Katya could hear nothing, not even her crows. Silence was not the word for what hung in the air, silence could be shattered. The surrounding miasma was that of finality, not the lack of noise but the state where no sound could even exist.

"Is it over?" Zhen asked Katya. Slowly, she let go of herself, tension releasing just a little from her neck and back. Alert, but no longer consumed by terror.

"I'm not sure. I'm going out. Stay here."

"It might not be safe!" She tried to grab Katya by the sleeve.

"I will be fine," Katya said, placing her hand over Zhen's. "Just stay here." Zhen nodded, pulling her hand back, and Katya gave her one more glance before she opened the carriage door. She took a few steps into the dark of the woods, scanning for the source of the threat.

Ivan stood a few paces before her, taking the form of a giant black owl, arms as wings with a mane of feathers around his neck. He stood over the scattered corpses of the guards, his chest heaving. He made his way to the carriage, passing Katya without sparing a glance. Wrenching open the carriage door, he peered in. Katya heard a strangled scream come from the carriage, a shriek that pierced the night and ricocheted off every tree, looping back on itself, growing fainter but no less haunting.

He reached in and pulled Zhen out, the shriek dying in her throat as she lost consciousness. He hooked an arm under her knees and another around her upper back. Her head dangled as he brought her toward Katya. Katya stared, trying to make sense of what she was witnessing. Her throat was dry, the only sound she heard was the beating of her heart, blood rushing in her ears. She tried to count his feathers as they floated to the forest floor, she tried to count her breaths. She tried to focus on the feel of her dress against her skin, she tried to focus on the smell of the leaves. All her attempts at re-establishing a connection to her body and the world failed, though. She did not want to be there.

As he walked, his form became less owlish, shedding feathers and tufts, the effect making him seem like a king with an expensive cape, marching in his throne room.

"Katya," he said, voice low but harsh. "I know what this looks like, but I've known this day would come. This was not just any escort, any noble lady. There is something threatening us—you and me, our forest—and she is part of it."

"What are you doing? How, what do you mean?" Katya did not understand what he was talking about. She had known him all her life, and while he treated these woods as his arboreal kingdom, he had never been this cruel to those who trespassed. He used fear and intimidation to chase out thieves who wished to hide here, or hunters who tried to take too much. He instilled fear in the hearts of those who had come after Katya, but he had never harmed anyone. He had never resorted to murder.

And Zhen. Zhen did not seem like someone who could ever harm them.

"I will explain later, love. Will you help me?" His voice quavered, but Katya was not sure if it was from nervousness in asking her, or because of what he was about to do.

She looked at the dirt on her toes, then back at him, and nodded.

Chapter 3

The lake was not far from the path that Zhen and her retinue had been traveling. The trio made it there about an hour before dawn. Ivan set her down near the edge of the lake, still unconscious. "This might take a while, love, get comfortable."

"What will take a while?"

"Protection. I need to keep us safe." Without elaborating further, he set his tools and instruments out. A small tiger snake slithered up to him. He jerked back, but then leaned closer. The snake did not seem to notice him. After a few moments, he threw up his arms and stood up.

He circled the lake, placing his hands on the ground every few steps. He walked the edge of the clearing around it, doing the same thing again. He came back to Katya, but paid her no mind. The snake continued on, back into the night. Katya hoped that the snake would find whatever dinner it sought.

Watching him from her perch on a log, she tried to follow along with what he was doing. He reached into a pocket and drew out a knife. Drawing circles on the ground, he chanted in a language that sounded familiar but Katya could not comprehend. He plunged his knife into the ground, but while Katya was versed in many forms of magic, she could not make sense of what he was doing. This spell was complex, with components she had never seen before. It seemed to incorporate many styles of magic. She could feel the spell around her, the magic hummed just above the ground, but she could not read it.

"Katya." The sound of her name startled her out of her musings.

"I'm sorry. What is it?" In a fluid swirl of silk, she raised herself to her feet and took a tentative step toward him.

"I need your help with this part." He bent over the circles he had drawn in the ground with a stick, focused on some small detail.

"My help? I haven't even been able to follow along." His faraway look and strained voice disturbed her. He had always been self-assured and grounded while working his magic. Sure, sometimes he was too focused, lost in the intricacies, riding the currents of aether and ephemeral streams, but always himself. Always *here*. This set her on edge; something was off.

"That is not what I mean. Come here." He looked up, eyes smoldering with a desire Katya had never seen before.

Katya approached him. She looked down at Zhen, unconscious and sprawled in the center of the largest circle, her hair swirling on the ground, seeming to become part of the spiraling patterns around her. She did not look like a threat that they needed protection against. She had looked like a friend, she had looked like someone Katya wanted to know more about. Even earlier, when she had feared the men with the torches marching through the forest were coming for her, she had not seen Zhen as a danger.

"Stand next to her," he demanded.

Katya rubbed her forehead and then did as she was told. Without warning, he grabbed her hand. Before she could protest, he pricked her ring finger with a knife, squeezing the blood onto the ground. She yelped. "Would you mind warning me next time?"

He didn't seem to hear her.

"Ivan, there had better be an explanation, and *soon*."

Ignoring her, he mumbled the end of a spell. Nausea overwhelmed her. As he said the last word, they both fell to their knees. Katya tried to catch her breath, confused as to why she was so exhausted so suddenly. Bigger spells could take a lot of energy, but she had done no magic. Beside her, Ivan was grimacing and holding his side, not making any movement to get off of the ground.

A battle raged inside of her. Even if she could have found the energy to get up, she was not sure if she would help him or hurt him; comfort or confront him. So she did nothing.

"I am sorry, love." It was almost inaudible. "I am so sorry there was not time for me to explain. I have unfinished business from before I met you. It seems it has caught up with me. I have tried to keep it from you because it is not your battle. But I promise, I will protect you from it. Katya, I am so sorry."

"What are you talking about, Ivan? What is happening?" Her voice cracked. She gasped, panting, and tried to bring the words of her confusion to the surface.

"I need you to help me. I need you to be my ears, my eyes. I am holding her here, so that she can not harm us. But I need more information in order to keep us safe. I need to find out how large this threat is. She cannot leave this lake. I need you to feign captivity with her, pretend that you are just as much my prisoner as she is." He rose to his feet, at first unsteady, but soon straightening fully, shoulders back, it was as if the exhaustion that followed his casting had never happened.

"Ivan, why? I want to help you, I do, but what does she have to do with whatever business you have?" Still drained, still dizzy, it took great effort to form the words, embattled rage and concern a giant pit in her stomach.

"I can not tell you now. The sun is rising, but soon. Can you pretend to be my prisoner with her? At night, when she is sleeping, find me, and give me any information you have."

"What information are you looking for? What's important? What do you need? How is she a threat, aren't I in danger staying here with her? How do I keep myself safe from a threat if I know nothing about it?" She hoped she could coax enough information to help her understand the road he was traveling down now, along with the ones he had walked in the past. She stood up, moving towards him, hoping to entreat with him. Her legs wobbled under her. She felt herself falling, her vision spinning.

She felt his arms wrap around her, catching her before she hit the ground. She sagged into him, letting him bear her weight. She stayed there, letting him hold her and caress her hair. She closed her eyes, hoping that when she opened them they would be home, and all of this would be a nightmare.

But there was still an unconscious woman on the ground, and she could still smell the blood on Ivan's boots. She was still scared.

"Please, I need your help, Katya."

"What do you want me to find out?" She pulled away from him, crossing her arms. Angry that he was asking her to do this, angry that this was even happening.

"Anything and everything." His unhelpful response inflamed her—she shook and clenched her fists—her skin on fire and her face flushed. But she bottled it, saved it for the acting he was demanding.

As the sun rose over the horizon, the forest glowed. Ivan shifted, becoming the half-man, half-owl monstrosity. He shoved

Katya to the ground and hurried away.

She landed badly, twisting her ankle beneath her. She reached, instinct and pain coursing through her, for the magic inside of her, her hands grabbing her ankle. But movement beside her caught her eye. Zhen was waking up.

"What happened?" She got up on her knees and looked around, searching for her escort. She tried to get up, but fell right back to the ground beside Katya. Zhen looked back up, but then her eyes went wide, her mouth opening as if to scream, but no sound came out. Without a word, Zhen lifted her arm to point at something behind Katya. Katya's turned her head, gaze following Zhen's outstretched hand until her eyes found Ivan, his feathers puffed out, grinning like a man gone mad.

It was an act, Katya told herself. An act. He was playing a part and she would talk to him about it later. For now, she had to pretend to be afraid, to cower and panic. She did not need much coaxing. He was frightful, and she was angry.

He approached with a sense of slow purpose, the early morning light shrouding him in brilliant light and foreboding shadows, casting him as an otherworldly being. He paused a few feet from them. He looked them up and down, his face passive until his eyes met Katya's. Katya swore she saw hesitation run across his face, hesitation and fear. She looked away in disappointment when she realized she would not be seeing guilt.

"What do you want?" Katya asked, louder than she had intended, unsure if she was addressing him as herself or as his fictional prisoner.

"Do not leave the clearing. Take one step into the forest and you shall regret your choice." He crept towards them, one slow set at a time. "But I can be kind, and so long as you return, whatever predicament you find yourself in shall be reversed when the moon rises over this lake."

"What are you talking about, you *monster*?" Zhen's voice was barely more than a whisper, but each word was sharp enough to cut ice.

"Do not despair, I am not a cruel jailer, your needs shall be provided for, so long as you stay put." He swung his arm out and twirled on his foot, metamorphosing into an owl in a flurry of feathers and launching into the embers of the night.

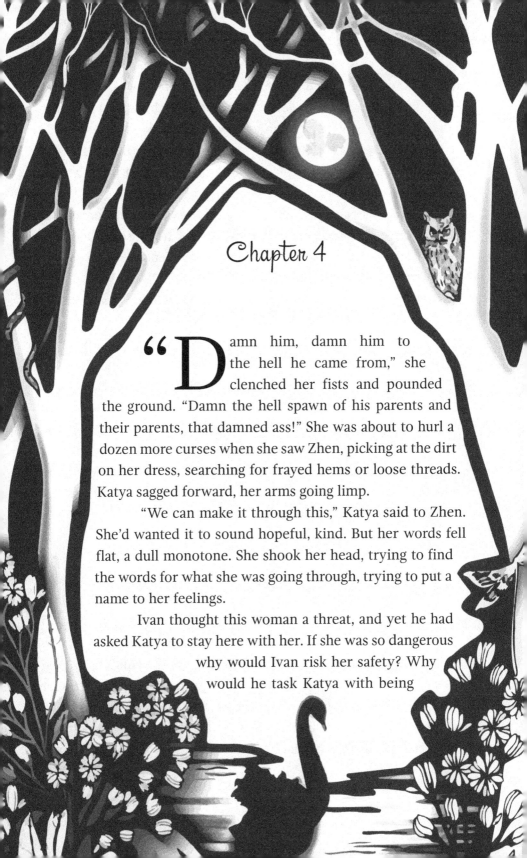

Chapter 4

"**D**amn him, damn him to the hell he came from," she clenched her fists and pounded the ground. "Damn the hell spawn of his parents and their parents, that damned ass!" She was about to hurl a dozen more curses when she saw Zhen, picking at the dirt on her dress, searching for frayed hems or loose threads. Katya sagged forward, her arms going limp.

"We can make it through this," Katya said to Zhen. She'd wanted it to sound hopeful, kind. But her words fell flat, a dull monotone. She shook her head, trying to find the words for what she was going through, trying to put a name to her feelings.

Ivan thought this woman a threat, and yet he had asked Katya to stay here with her. If she was so dangerous why would Ivan risk her safety? Why would he task Katya with being a spy? Katya didn't even know how dangerous she was, how could Ivan expect her to stay safe? Did he not care about Katya getting hurt? Was the spell he cast earlier supposed to keep her safe?

Her chest was tight, she wanted to run away from this lake, she wanted to find a quiet place where she could just think, where she could just sort this out.

She bit her cheek. But what if Zhen wasn't the threat that Ivan thought she was? What if he was wrong? It was so hard to look at Zhen's kind eyes and see anything but innocence.

"Do you know what he was talking about?" Zhen asked. "He was cryptic, and I do not understand what he would want with me. Or you."

"Are you someone important?" Katya fidgeted with a strand of her hair.

"Are you?" Zhen asked.

"No, I suppose I'm not." Katya's throat swelled, she could feel a lump growing there and she could not get rid of it. Was she not important enough to Ivan to be let in on what was going on? Was she not important enough to trust with the whole of this? Even if he had no time to explain today, why did he not trust her earlier?

"Then it's probably me he is after."

"What makes you say that?"

Zhen stood up and paced, wringing her hands before throwing them out. "I'm here to marry the Princen."

Katya might have guessed, if she had been paying attention, that Zhen was a princess. Was it a coincidence that he had found her? Random chance that it was Ivan's woods through which the escort party passed? Or was it deliberate? Was she coming through these woods to harm them? Did Ivan guess them to be a threat when they first stepped foot in the woods, and was it confirmed when he figured out who she was? He had been listening to their conversation in the carriage, and unlike Katya, he must have recognized the name for the royal it belonged to. What plot might a princess have against Ivan? What threat was a princess to their home?

"I didn't know. I didn't realize—."

"You might as well know, now, I suppose. I am a princess from Shān, sent here to marry the czar's heir, Princen Alexis. I do not know if it has been announced in Lebedia, yet."

"I have not heard word of that yet, no."

"It is still a fragile agreement," she said, looking away from Katya. She slumped down, a bitter smile on her face.

"I don't talk to other people much, there could have been an announcement, and I hadn't heard it yet."

"That must be it," Zhen mumbled.

"You seemed excited about the engagement earlier, are you not?"

"I am excited about the Princen, but, I suppose it is complicated." Zhen turned away from Katya, staring at the water as it rippled against the shore.

Katya got to her feet, heading toward the edge of the clearing that surrounded the lake. She plucked some almost-ripe berries, not caring that she plucked some of them too firmly, or that the red juices were staining her fingers and dress. She didn't care that they would still be tart, or that they were not her favorite. She counted each one that she pulled from the bush, but she couldn't figure out how many she should have.

"I found berries," she said as she plucked the last one on the bush and turned back to Zhen.

"Are they safe to eat? Is this what he meant by our needs being provided for?"

"I don't think this is what he meant, but yes, they're safe to eat."

Zhen took a handful, but soon crinkled her nose. "They

aren't very sweet." Zhen looked at the berries pooled in her hands and closed her eyes. "I wish—."

A wave of dizziness washed over Katya, and she threw her arms out to regain her balance. Spots of darkness crowded her vision and her fingers tingled. She tried to keep her breathing even, steady. When the spots cleared, Zhen was no longer next to her.

"I found breakfast," she heard Zhen call from behind her. Katya turned around and saw Zhen sitting at a table that had not been there before. Still shaky, she stood up and approached with caution, not sure where the vertigo had come from, but determined to not aggravate it into coming back.

"It is not as good as I would have had at home, but I suppose that was asking too much," Zhen said.

"Where did this come from?"

"I am not sure; I thought of how hungry I was, wishing for a breakfast like I usually have at home, and then this appeared."

"And you suspected my berries?" Katya said wryly.

Zhen shrugged. "The berries I've never seen before, I don't think they grow where I live."

Katya sat down next to Zhen and picked at the food, none of which she recognized. "How far away is your home from here?"

"I am not sure. We have been traveling for a few weeks now. How close are we to the capital?"

"A few days' ride on horseback. Probably longer, though, at the pace your carriage was going."

"Have you ever been there?" Zhen asked.

"No, I've never left these parts."

"This is not my first time traveling a long ways, but the first time I have left my country. My parents love me, but they do not see me. Sending me so far away? Just one more example. They made sure I was educated. I know seven languages aside from my own. I can calculate distance using the stars, but I did not learn a lot of disciplines that I wanted. I wanted to learn magic. But all I know is simple thread magic, usually used to create illusions on already embellished dresses, sometimes to give glimmer to art. A magic of fanciful illusions."

This was not a magical art Katya was familiar with, and while she longed to ask her more questions about it, she felt that this wasn't the information Ivan wanted. So she asked, "they did not let you learn magic?"

"No, they had a firm idea of who they thought I was, or am. I took an early interest in art, and suddenly I was their artist. They gave me a broad but shallow education in all the other subjects, but hoped to refine and hone my artistic side. But as I learned thread magic, I shifted in my wants, and their vision of me did not follow suit. I would steal away to the kitchens to escape. The cook and her assistant would let me watch them, and, sometimes, the assistant would let me help. We would make simple moon cakes together and then gobble them up as if we were hiding evidence of some crime, licking the crumbs off each other. I miss her so much, but one of my tutors caught us. I was a princess, and what life could a princess make with a cook's assistant? I was not an heir, but I was valuable for alliances. Soon after, my parents matched me with Princen Alexis."

"So your parents sent you away? To a place so different, when you're still so young, and to a person so very not to your tastes?"

Zhen laughed. "I would not be so sure on the last point. I have never met the princen. I hope that we like each other. I hear they are attractive, sweeping maidens, men, and those in between off their feet with equal grace."

"I wouldn't know. I have not met them either, I assumed..." Katya trailed off.

"I understand. But one fling with a pretty girl covered in

flour does not mean that I am only attracted to people with culinary expertise. Although I hear Princen Alexis can make a good roast deer."

Katya laughed.

"Can you keep a secret?" Zhen asked, a coyness in her voice and eyes, clasping her hands together in front of her chest.

"Sure."

"We did exchange some letters, Alexis and I. They seem really nice, very caring and sincere."

"How is that a secret?"

"Our parents did not know! It was Alexis' idea, they managed to send a letter slipped in with one correspondences back and forth between our parents. We wrote through each others cooks after that! They would give theirs to their cook, who would send it out addressed to mine! Hidden in with recipe exchanges. Our parents thought the cooks were just trying to find ways to prepare a fitting feast for all the ceremonies surrounding our engagement and wedding."

"Would your parents not have approved?"

"Oh, they may have, but they would have been read by a dozen lawyers and advisors first, making sure we were perfectly respectful and diplomatic. This way we got to really have a chance at knowing each other."

"That's really cute, so are they your type?"

"Maybe! They seem like they might be. I hope they are. And what would your type be, Katya?" An opening, a distraction. Zhen was biting her bottom lip, her left hand rubbing her right arm.

Katya raised her eyebrow at Zhen.

"Do you like helpless damsels alone in the woods?" she asked as she clasped her hands together and held them to her chest.

"You want to know my 'type'?" Katya ran a hand through her hair.

"Or do you like the cold silent type?"

Katya laughed and shook her head.

"I know! You like the sword-wielding adventurers who would leave you alone for months at a time, but then come home bearing the heads of dragons!"

"Dragons?"

"Yes, dragons!"

"You're wrong," Katya said, a small grin on her face. "I do not have a type. I *am* a type."

"Is that a threat?" Zhen asked, raising an eyebrow.

"It is." Katya replied, smirking at Zhen. "I am the mysterious maiden who will let no one get close, who tempts people and yet holds them at bay. I'm the siren who leads people toward their doom, the swan song of a love that never could be. I am the beautiful Fairy Queen, the entrancing witch in the forest who is lethally beautiful and forever out of reach. And you better be careful, I have found the next victim to enthrall."

Chapter 5

"Do you know any stories? My sisters and I would tell scary stories around the hearth when we were little. Lin would always end hers with a *qilin* slaying the monster."

Katya knit her brows.

"I do not think she really understood the point of scary stories," Zhen added.

"You want a scary story? I think we're already in the middle of one."

Zhen had imagined a cottage for them, a small one with a stone hearth and a sturdy roof with plenty of supplies, but she wanted to keep a fire going outside, hoping someone would come looking. Hoping someone would see it. So they sat there, Zhen looking into the fire, wrapped in a shawl, and Katya staring up at the stars. They might have been two oracles, trying to divine the future.

"Do you have any scary stories, Katya?"

"No, I'm sorry." Katya fought to keep her eyes from closing, hiding yawns behind her hands.

"What about happy ones?"

Katya took a long breath, closing her eyes and holding the bridge of her nose. "No. I don't know any stories."

"What about songs, then?"

"You want to sing songs?" Katya said, squinting at Zhen

"Yes. Music, dance, stories, anything." Zhen mumbled, shrinking away from Katya gaze.

Katya opened her mouth to say something, then shook her head and said nothing.

"What?"

"Trapped in a forest, waiting for a rescue, and you want to sing?"

Zhen threw down her hands and pushed herself up, stomping the ground. "Yes, we are trapped. Yes, we are waiting for someone to save us. That doesn't mean I want to dwell on the fact!"

Katya threw her hands up. "Fine, fine. You sing."

"No, I'm going for a walk." Zhen nearly ran away, clutching a shawl close, a star-filled ocean receding from the ground, as she left the warmth of the fire.

"Dammit." Katya said to herself. She was tired, but her pulse was still racing. "Dammit!" she said, getting to her own feet and chasing after Zhen. She needed to make friends with this princess, not drive her away. "No, wait, come back! Zhen!"

She caught up quickly. But Zhen did not seem to hear her. Or maybe she didn't *want* to hear Katya.

"Zhen, please, I'm sorry. I'm tired and I shouldn't have taken that out on you!"

But Zhen kept walking. Katya reached out and grabbed Zhen's shoulder, trying to stop her.

But Zhen flinched away, glancing back at Katya before

tripping.

She fell to the ground, a scream tearing from her throat.

It was not the princess that hit the ground though. Katya watched in horror as the princess's sleeves grew feathers, her neck lengthened, and her cries were replaced with the bleat of a swan.

Zhen fell forward, her feet no longer the human ones she had been running on moments earlier. Katya was knocked back by a blast of wind, landing, badly, near the edge of the lake. An owl swooped in front of her and landed between her and Zhen. The owl changed, grotesquely mirroring the transformation of Zhen, until he was the half-man, half-owl from the attack. Katya stared at Ivan, not sure what to expect.

"I thought I had told you both to stay put," he said, his voice hurting Katya's ears. It was not the gentle voice she had known all her life. She had not even known he could ever raise his voice from the sweet tenor he used with her.

Zhen flapped her wings, trying to take off. Katya stared in horror.

"Do not worry, little princess. This is not permanent, unless you want it to be. All you need to do to change back is to let the reflection of the moonlight in the lake touch your feathers. Come, see." He beckoned to Zhen toward the lake.

He stepped into the calm waters, shattering the crystal surface. Zhen took a few tentative steps before she reared back, throwing her head up, then flapping her wings until she took flight, swooping into the water beside him. Katya held her breath, waiting. She had no clue what Ivan was doing. She had been so in-sync with him for as long as they had been together, but now his entire being seemed alien to her.

Zhen searched the sky, a blanket of stars, but the moon had not crested the trees. Katya stood, favoring her left leg. She tried to approach the lake, to reach out to Ivan. She wanted to hold him, she wanted him to hold her and tell her this was a nightmare, that this never happened, that there was no shadowy threat lurking in the heart of a princess and he did not need to take on this harsh mantle to protect them.

She stopped as her feet sank into the cool water, the cold waves draining away the swollenness and pain in her ankle. Katya closed her eyes, letting her magic meld with nature and ease the results of her bad fall. Maybe she could let the water take away this phantasm.

But when she opened her eyes, there was still a monster at the center of the lake. If she had looked beyond, she might have seen a faint specter, an older woman watching with eyes unblinking. If she was paying attention, she would have heard the forest go silent, and then explode into a haunting song, crows and crickets lending their voice to a Phrygian sonata.

She tried to determine what she could say, what could convey that she would follow him down this road, but only if she knew why he needed to travel it. She did not understand this side of him, but she knew there must have been a reason. She wanted to trust, but she needed to know the extent of the threat before them. A threat so great, and yet he left her here clueless and defenseless.

Her lower lip quivered, and she could feel the hot tears on her cheeks. She looked away, unable to watch anymore and unwilling to let Ivan see how upset she was.

But the moon overtook the tops of the trees, and shone down on Zhen. The water rose around the princess, swirling in a mix of moonbeams and feathers. There was nothing Katya could compare to the spectacle before her. There was no music that could accompany this sight without seeming flat, there was nothing in this world that could challenge swan to a match of elegance and win. And yet, as Zhen emerged from the cocoon, it was as though a goddess had appeared.

The moonlight settled over a now-human Zhen as a gown might, with feathers flowing behind her as its train. Her hair was in a pristine bun, but the jewels were replaced with white feathers. Her tattered gown gone, and instead she was adorned as though she were a swan queen.

"See, my dear. No harm has come to you." Ivan stepped toward Zhen, melting into human guise. The crown of black feathers on his head became the disheveled hair that Katya loved to run her fingers through.

Zhen held her head high, a stark contrast to her show of fear the night before. She crossed her arms over her chest and looked away from him. She turned her whole body away from him. He put a hand to her shoulder and tried to turn her toward him. She grabbed his wrist and flung his hand away.

"Princess, I apologize for putting you in this position. But I must protect what is mine. Help me, and no harm will come to you."

Zhen turned away from him.

"I see." He stepped backward and bowed to Zhen before turning on his heel, feathers wrapping around him as he once again took the form of a great owl, sweeping his wings out to take flight. Katya watched as he gained altitude, gliding over the treetops toward their home, the only home she had ever had, without her.

Fixated on Ivan's flight, she jumped when she felt Zhen wrap both her of hands around hers, tugging her back toward the fire.

"Are you all right, Zhen?"

"I am trying to be. I want to be. If I pretend hard enough that none of this is happening, it will not be happening. If I let it be real, I will fall right where I am and sob until the lake becomes an ocean. The salt of my tears will stick, harden, and I shall be a maiden at the heart of a statue, looking over the vastness of the sea of my sorrow."

Katya led her back to the fire. "We can keep the fire going all night. I can stay out here and shout if I see anyone coming for us."

The words had barely left her mouth before she stumbled forward, her vision going black.

She felt heat, the caress of fire near her face, and then arms around her. She almost cried out for Ivan, hoping it was his arms around her, setting her down. The dizziness made the world move around her though she knew she was on solid ground.

"You can't stay out here, we can keep the fire going but we should go inside."

"All right."

"It will be all right. Let us get you to bed." Zhen stood, offering her hand to Katya. She helped her up, and together they walked to the cottage. She sat Katya down on one of the beds. Katya collapsed into it, sinking into sleep. She didn't see Zhen shred the swan dress, nor did she see Zhen toss the tattered remains into the hearth and set it ablaze. She did not see Zhen fall to the floor, her body shaking as sobs tore out of her chest.

If she had not been awake for so long, she might have settled into a dream of soaring the skies with Ivan at her side. If she had not been awake for so long, she might have paused to worry about the episodes of vertigo she had had throughout the day. But she had been awake for far too long, and even if she did wonder about it, she might have chalked it up to exhaustion. She drifted off to sleep, her dreams a tangle of shadows and invisible enemies.

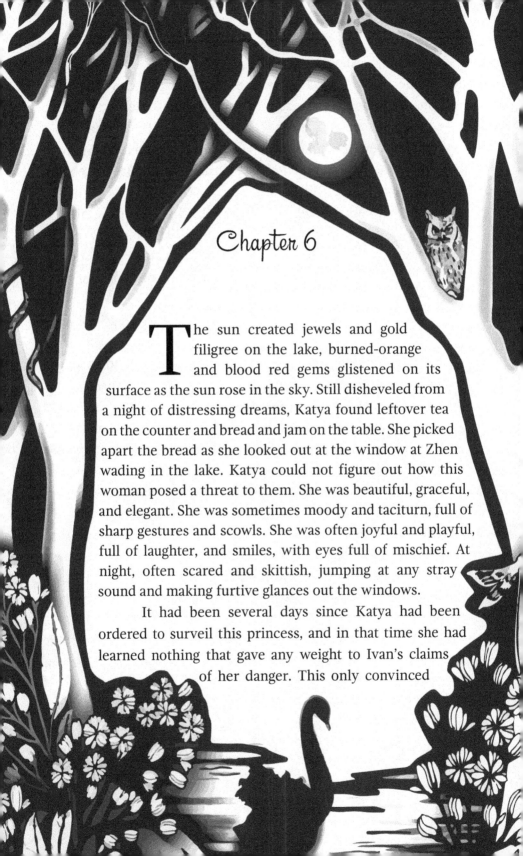

Chapter 6

The sun created jewels and gold filigree on the lake, burned-orange and blood red gems glistened on its surface as the sun rose in the sky. Still disheveled from a night of distressing dreams, Katya found leftover tea on the counter and bread and jam on the table. She picked apart the bread as she looked out at the window at Zhen wading in the lake. Katya could not figure out how this woman posed a threat to them. She was beautiful, graceful, and elegant. She was sometimes moody and taciturn, full of sharp gestures and scowls. She was often joyful and playful, full of laughter, and smiles, with eyes full of mischief. At night, often scared and skittish, jumping at any stray sound and making furtive glances out the windows.

It had been several days since Katya had been ordered to surveil this princess, and in that time she had learned nothing that gave any weight to Ivan's claims of her danger. This only convinced

Katya she was more dangerous than imaginable, clever enough to conceal weapons or magic of unknowable cruelty. At night, these fears consumed Katya's dreams. She fretted that Zhen was a powerful sorceress, sent to kidnap Ivan and take him away. She was a thaumaturge who wanted to destroy their forest. Maybe Lebedia had re-instituted their bans on magic, and Zhen was here to lure them to trial. Perhaps she was sent by the village, having hired a clever assassin after realizing their pitchforks were ineffective, still determined to destroy the witch who had cursed their children.

The dreams almost always ended with her sobbing, and alone.

Except sometimes they ended with her sobbing in Zhen's arms.

Katya hurled a chunk of bread into the fire and marched outside, not wanting to stew in her confusion over these nightmares any longer. Zhen was no longer splashing in the waves, a water nymph making friends. She now held a *dizi* to her mouth, her fingers finding the holes in the bamboo with the agility of someone who had been playing for a long time.

Katya stood behind her, not daring to move any closer. She had read about musical instruments, but hearing one was entirely different. She'd read about the timbre and the buzzing sound that was unique to the *dizi*, but Zhen made it sing. The air turned heavy, the hair on Katya's arms stood on end and she felt the almost-familiar rush of magic. It was magic, but not any kind she had known.

This is it, Katya thought. *This is the start of her plan.* She wanted to lash out with her own magic, to fight back against whatever spell was falling over the lake.

The lake became hazy, the trees blurred together. She could no longer hear the water or the bees or the birds. In its place, unfocused but there, was a younger Zhen playing in a garden. Katya watched as scenes played out before her, illusions written over the lake entwined with the melancholic twittering of the *dizi*. Zhen scraping her knees in a garden, Zhen sneaking into the kitchens, Zhen practicing music on string instruments, percussion, and this very *dizi*. All accompanied to the joyful, nostalgic music Zhen was playing now.

Katya watched Zhen and a girl, both covered in flour, running off together. A stern older woman, eyes like Zhen's, arguing with her. An older man, a chin as defiant as Zhen's, pleading with her. Zhen sobbing in a bed covered in silk, wiping her tears on a pillow.

The edges of the images faded, the scenes taking on a strange transparency. The lake and forest again came to the foreground. A knight approached, superimposed upon the scene, quiet as a ghost and just as ethereal. A spectral Zhen greeted the knight. The knight jumped off the horse and lead the phantom Zhen in a *pas de deux*. They twirled and sashed across the lake, graceful and elegant. *Tondues* and *grand jetés*, *pirouettes* around the lake. And then they walked hand in hand, the horse following behind, out of the clearing and into whatever future Zhen imagined for them.

The song died, and Zhen dropped the instrument from her lips.

"That was beautiful," Katya said, approaching Zhen.

"Oh, thank you," Zhen said with a small blush. "I did not realize you were up."

"What was that? I've read nothing about that."

"Memories, wishes. I did not mean to take it so far."

"Is that yours?" Katya asked, pointing to the *dizi*.

"Yes. I brought it with me. I had it in a case in my pocket when we were attacked. I had another one, a traditional one. I suppose it's lost now. This one has a joint, so I can tune it. My other one was one whole piece of bamboo."

"You're so accomplished."

"I'm a princess, I have to be. I am also skilled in fiber magic, using thread or yarn or cloth to channel magic." She listed off her accomplishments as though she had rattled them off hundreds of times, rote and monotone. But then she sighed and looked up past the tops of the trees. "I wanted to be skilled with herbal magic, with teas and tisanes. I was always clumsy with that art, though; there was so much more I wanted to learn. So many books on different forms of magic I saw listed in the library catalog, but which I could read." Zhen laughed and looked out across the lake.

Katya listened, parsing each word, considering each syllable. She listened for any slip, anything that would not be part of a princesses standard education, something that would give Zhen away as a saboteur. She chewed the inside of her mouth. "Was that the princen coming to rescue you?" Katya was not sure what to make of the rescuer in the final illusion.

"I have not met Alexis, nor seen a portrait of them yet. So the illusion was not as solid. I suppose anyone will do, in terms of someone coming to my rescue, but ultimately, I will have to marry Princen Alexis. It is a very perilous peace that Lebedia and Shān have. The best way to secure this peace is through our marriage, according to our parents."

"I had no idea," Katya said. The books she had access to were not the sort to reference modern history or politics. Katya pursed her lips, again trying to tug out any clues about what sort of danger she might be in with Zhen. It was rather difficult when she did not even know if the political situations Zhen was describing were true.

"I am expected to arrive in Kristallicheskiy in a few days. I fear if I do not get there by the then, search parties will be sent out, and if I am not found, my parents might believe Lebedia played them false." Zhen stood up and paced.

Katya needed more information, not for Ivan, but for herself. "I'm sorry, Zhen. I don't really know much about this sort of thing.

Why are relations strained between Lebedia and Shān? What would happen if your country thinks Lebedia has done something terrible?"

"No need to apologize for not knowing, it is rather dry reading for the most part." Zhen took out a bit of silk from her pocket and used it to wipe off the outside of her *dizi*. "There is a territory dispute going back generations. The founder of the current dynasty in your kingdom claimed parts of my country's northern territories were actually Lebedia's southern territories. The area is sparsely populated and the people who live there have never really cared. They speak both languages, sometimes in the same sentence, and save for the river that runs through those lands, there are few valuable resources."

Katya frowned, trying to visualize the borders and regions in her head, realizing that the forest she lived in was just to the north of this contested region. She was still raking through each word for a hint of a threat, some detail in this story that proved Ivan's suspicion.

"The Czar found documents that supposedly proved the region was Lebedian," Zhen said, moving on to cleaning the inner parts of her instrument, "and that Shān had stolen it a century before. He was a young king who felt insecure on a throne that he had gained through battle. His eldest son volunteered to lead a team to take the lands back. I am sure you know this part, but that prince then betrayed the czar and the invasion never happened. His second son took the throne, and was not as interested in claiming those lands. Rulers have come and gone, and Lebedia has been threatening an invasion for years now, but time and time again, it has not happened."

"Did the papers actually prove who the lands truly belonged to?"

"I do not know, I do not think anyone has produced them

since. Some say they do not even exist."

Katya chewed on her lip. Was this the threat? Was the princess here on false pretense? Claiming to be here for a wedding but part of some effort to fortify and secure the contested land? Maybe using her glamour and illusion magic to hide soldiers, or to set up a magical spy network, undetectable?

"But a few summers ago," Zhen continued, pulling out the case for her *dizi* and putting it away with great care. "A merchant from Shān and his pet dog traveled there on business. A soldier from Lebedia was also there—a high-ranking general, I believe—who claims to have been there for personal business. But, everyone was mistrustful, fearful that the simmering tensions were about to escalate. The merchant's dog got loose. The merchant chased it all over, not realizing he had chased it out of the disputed territories and into lands that were firmly Lebedian. The general followed him, and once he was squarely in Lebedia, he drew his sword and killed the merchant. Soldiers from both countries have slowly been gathering on the borders ever since."

Zhen placed the *dizi* in a large in-seam pocket, and cast her eyes toward the sky, searching for something. Katya followed her gaze. She waited for Zhen to continue.

"My dowry is that plot of land." Zhen cried, with seemingly all the care and restraint that she could call upon.

Katya pulled Zhen into an embrace. It seemed like the right thing to do. She still had so many questions, but knew it was not her place to pry.

Except, that was exactly why she was here.

Chapter 7

Although Alexis was not expecting their future bride for another few days, one of her escorts rode into the courtyard at a pace that was sure to leave the horse exhausted for days. Princen Alexis sprinted from the lookout tower they had been hiding in—their father was insisting on dancing lessons, again—and raced to meet the rider.

They took the steps four at a time, heart racing as they narrowly avoided servants and court members. They had a pit in their stomach telling them something was wrong, and they needed to talk to this rider now. They were almost there, but skidded to a halt at the landing on the main floor, almost colliding with their father. Their father remained upright—back straight, chin up—resting his hands on his cane, unperturbed by their child's flustered entrance. "Oh, Alexis! *There* you are! Come, your sister and cousins are waiting! We are going over a new style from Shān so you can dance it with Princess Yi Zhen!"

"Not now, not now! One of her escorts is here!" Alexis tried to move around their father, but the Czar caught their arm in his hand and they were spun around to face their father.

"What? They are not expected for a few more days!"

"I know! I am worried something has gone wrong." Alexis pulled their arm away and began their flight again, eager to get to the rider. They threw open the doors that lead to the courtyard and hurried out, knocking the doors' guards out of the way.

"Alexis!" The rider dismounted before the horse came to a stop, a stable-hand already reaching for the reins. The rider threw off her riding helmet; her black, finely curled hair, no longer restrained, went everywhere.

"Tatiana! What happened?" Alexis took her by the shoulders, searching her face for any clues about why she was here, and why she arrived as if death were on her heels.

"Alexis, I rode ahead to scout, but when I returned the carriage was turned over. There were signs of a struggle, and I could find neither survivors nor bodies. I searched all night."

"How long ago? Where were you when this happened?"

"About a week ago, I rode straight here, barely stopping except to trade out horses. It was in a forest just south of Ignashino."

"We need to tell my parents," they said, turning back to the tower. Tatiana followed them, calling over her shoulder, "Inna, you better make sure that horse is taken care of!"

"Missed you, too, sweetheart" Inna replied, still checking the horse's feet while Alexis and Tatiana hurried to find Alexis' parents. They did not have to go far, for Czar Mikhail had been on his way out to follow his child.

"Well?" he demanded, leaning on his cane. The princen glanced at Tatiana, anxious for her to repeat what she had found.

She got down on her knee. There was no getting out of this obeisance with her friend's father, no matter the present circumstances. She placed one hand over her heart, the other behind her back. "Your Grace, I was sent to scout ahead, and, upon returning, I found the carriage overturned. Our soldiers and her guards were missing, as was the princess. I searched for as long as I could. I found no one, and then returned here to bear the news."

She was composed and steady, save a nervous twitch in the hand she held behind her back, her thumb spinning the small ring on her pinky finger. The czar took in a long breath, his shoulders rising, chest expanding near the capacity of his doublet as he inhaled, and then expelled it, shoulders sagging.

"Did you find remains of any enemy forces?"

"No, your Grace, I couldn't tell what happened, beyond a struggle."

"No footprints of an enemy army? No signs of an ambush? Nothing *unusual*?"

"Unusual?" Alexis asked.

"Your Grace, the only oddity was that there were some rather large feathers, scattered on the ground." Tatiana said.

"A scouting falcon?" the czar asked.

"No," Tatiana said.

"Then what?"

"Perhaps a large owl?" She chewed her bottom lip.

"Get up, Tatiana," he said, and then walked towards a library, gesturing for them to follow. "Were there any signs of magic or sorcery?"

"Sorcery, your Grace?"

"Nevermind," he said, waving off his suggestion. "Did it appear as though the struggle was against another force, or could it have been her guards against ours?"

The princen protested. "Father! Our marriage is to create peace. Neither country's soldiers would so deliberately go against orders!" Alexis did not want to consider what their father was implying.

"Ours would not." The biting edge in the czar's voice would have told anyone else that this was the end of the discussion. But Alexis did not care.

"Neither would hers! And did you yourself not suggest sorcery? It could have been bandits, too!"

"How do you know that?" The czar stopped mid-stride and pushed his index finger into Alexis' chest.

"They have just as much of a reason to prevent this war as we do. Last word we got was that they were nearly here. Why would they betray us now?"

The czar looked them up and down, unsure whether to keep the argument going. Alexis could feel the tension in their air, heavy and charged. "We must talk with the council. I will send word, and we will convene after dinner. I shall have my advisors gather information until then." He strode away from them, entering the library, but then paused, craned his head backward and said "You should still go to your dancing lessons."

Alexis clenched their fists and then turned to Tatiana. "Was there any signs that her escort might plan to betray us? To slaughter our soldiers?" They didn't want to consider what their father was suggesting, but they wanted as much proof on their side as they could get before the council meeting.

"No, none at all." Tatiana said while her and Alexis headed to Alexis' rooms. "We met them at the border, rode together to the royal families' winter home in the north. There was a feast that night, a farewell for the princess. They accommodated us with the best rooms, food, and took excellent care of our horses. There was tension before we arrived at the palace, but once we had all eaten and drank together, it vanished. We all set out in high spirits the following morning. I would honestly not be surprised if your wedding were not the only one this summer between our countries if you catch my meaning."

"So what do you think happened?" Alexis said as they entered the princen's rooms. Alexis tore off their doublet and removed the belt from their skirt, the heavy golden epaulets clattering on the marble floor.

"I'm not sure," Tatiana said as she collapsed into a sofa in front of the fireplace. "It was me and another Czarina's Guard hopeful doing the scouting. Neither of us had seen any signs of bandits or smugglers. We'd encountered a few protests on each side of the border, people superstitious or mistrustful, but not many. The woods are not common hunting grounds, the flora and fauna in there have been less abundant as of late."

"Protests. I know there are more conservative people even amongst my fathers advisors, but I did not think-"

"I know, Alexis."

"Could there be more to it than just grouchy old people? Could they have a well hidden plot?"

"A plot that would lead to war over a piece of land we are already about to secure with a wedding?"

"There might be more to it than that. But we have to find her, we have to save her."

"We will."

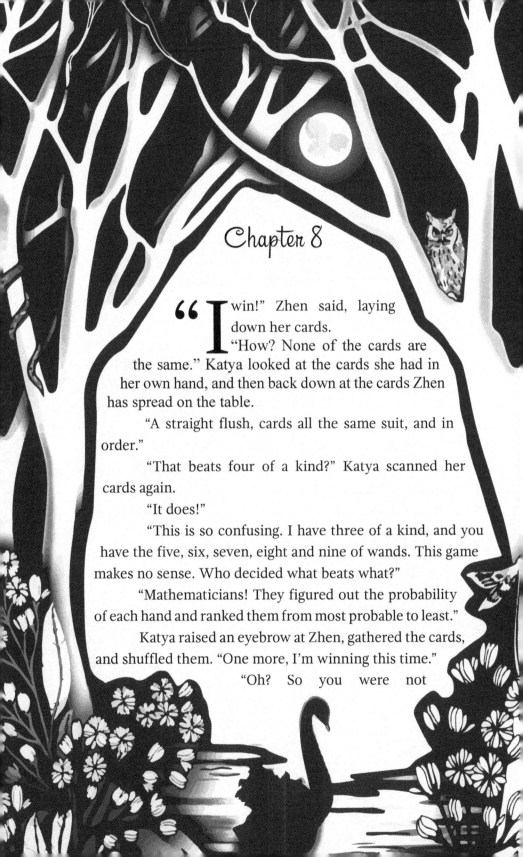

Chapter 8

"I win!" Zhen said, laying down her cards.

"How? None of the cards are the same." Katya looked at the cards she had in her own hand, and then back down at the cards Zhen has spread on the table.

"A straight flush, cards all the same suit, and in order."

"That beats four of a kind?" Katya scanned her cards again.

"It does!"

"This is so confusing. I have three of a kind, and you have the five, six, seven, eight and nine of wands. This game makes no sense. Who decided what beats what?"

"Mathematicians! They figured out the probability of each hand and ranked them from most probable to least."

Katya raised an eyebrow at Zhen, gathered the cards, and shuffled them. "One more, I'm winning this time."

"Oh? So you were not

pretending to not know the game? You were not letting me win?" Zhen lowered her eyes and pouted.

The past few days had been full of little moments like this, moments where Zhen teased or flirted with Katya. Sometimes Katya reciprocated, sometimes Katya stared at her in confusion.

"And why would I let you win?" Katya cocked her head to the side and grinned at Zhen.

Zhen winked at Katya.

The moment disintegrated when a strangled and terrifying sound reverberated through the cottage. Zhen jumped, her hand going to her heart. Katya whipped around, her chair flying, as she got into a fighting stance. She raised a hand, magic sparking from her fingers, looking for a target.

Katya jerked her head back and forth, straining to listen for any clues as to where the scream came from. She crept to one of the windows, her one hand still full of magic, the other pulling back the curtain. She willed the candles' flames to die, and then looked out.

There was nothing outside.

She stood there for several moments, scanning the darkness for threats.

Was it some monster out there? Maybe something Zhen had conjured when Katya was lax? Had she somehow missed some summoning ritual? Was this the threat that Ivan meant?

"It might have just been a deer, someone out hunting late at night," Zhen whispered. Her eyes were wide, and Katya could tell her breath was shallow but quick. She was terrified, or an excellent actress.

Katya sagged, releasing the pent up aether and letting the curtains fall. She nodded, and sat back down at the table.

Zhen gathered up the cards and put them in her bag. "Where did you learn magic? You never told me you could."

"Oh. From books." Katya looked away from Zhen.

"Do you think you could use it to help us escape?"

She met Zhen's eyes and saw in them questions. Doubt. Hurt. Katya knew she needed Zhen's trust if she wanted to learn what she needed to know to keep herself and Ivan safe. "I've been trying. This whole time."

"Why did you not tell me before?"

Katya bit her lip. "I didn't want to get your hopes up."

Zhen looked down at her laps, her hands clasped. "I suppose that makes sense. We could maybe try together tomorrow. I wish you had told me, though."

Katya looked away, unable to find another lie. Not wanting to.

Zhen looked back up at Katya, her eyebrows knit in confusion, a plea waiting on her lips. She slumped down, then. "I am going to bed now."

Katya wanted to follow her, wanted to find something she could say to bridge the gap that had formed between them. Part of it was she knew she needed to have trust in order to get information. But another part? No, she didn't want to think about that.

She knew she had put off a visit to Ivan for too long. She did not have much to report, but she needed reassurances. She wanted to know if he was safe, she needed to know if he had any more information he could share with her. As soon as she heard the deep breathing of sleep from Zhen, she crept out of their cottage.

Once outside, she took several long strides, stretched her arms, and in one fluid movement leapt into the woods, becoming a black swan as she took flight. Her crow-sisters found her instantly, and she soared toward the glade where she and Ivan lived.

Ivan was waiting for her as she descended. A small pirouette completed her metamorphosis back into human form, and she ran into his embrace. She inhaled the earthy smell that seemed to cling to his skin and lapped up the warmth that radiated from his chest as she listened to his steady heart.

"I am so sorry, Katya," he said. Gently, he ran his fingers through her hair and stepped back, searching her face. "Are you all right?"

"Yes, I am. Did you hear that noise earlier? Do you know what it was?"

"I took care of it. Do not worry about it, we are safe."

She sighed, sagging back into him.

Ivan took her hand and led her into their cottage. She settled into the sofa by the hearth, taking in the familiar scents and sounds of her home. Ivan handed her a mug before seating himself next to her.

"You did not answer me earlier, my love. Are you all right?"

"I'm fine. I'm glad to be here right now. I've been so scared. You haven't told me anything about the threats we are facing. And that terrifying sound earlier—"

"I am sorry, you are right."

"How much longer will this go on?"

"I suppose that depends. Do you have any information for me?"

She told him everything. It came out in a torrent, jumping back and forth in time, skipping parts before circling back. Her stomach knotted whenever she divulged something intimate about the princess. She talked too fast, and swallowed too much, as she told him about Zhen's fears and hopes. She owed the princess nothing, and yet.

"Is there anything else?"

"Not really. I didn't really know much of the current situation, so I wasn't sure how to ask questions that might get her to open up about it. I don't know what is important or if she told me anything that is wrong. Do you have any books on the history of the relations between our countries?"

"There is little reason to know what came before. We live here and they do not bother us." His nostrils flared, his tone deepened with a forced evenness.

"I know! I just need to know more so I can be more effective." Katya shifted away from him, hugging herself.

"Do not worry about that, just bring me whatever information you can. I will sort through it."

Katya clasped her hands, wringing them over and over. She still had so many questions, but she did not want to fight with him. "Do you know any more about this conflict or this marriage arrangement?" she asked.

"I honestly cannot tell you much more than what you know already." He let out an exasperated sigh, his irritation clear in the way he tapped the table next to him.

"Do you know what happened with the treasonous prince?" she pressed.

"She told you that prince betrayed the czar? And his second son became the heir?"

"Yes, but not what he did, or what happened to him." She twiddled her thumbs as she held her mug between them, not able to meet his eyes anymore, instead glancing between her tea and the fire.

"That is really all there is to know."

Katya straightened her back, lifted her chin, and took a deep breath. "So how is she a threat, then? What kind of threat is she? Am I really safe there, with her, without knowing what she can do? Every second I worry that she is about to unleash something on me. And how is keeping her not even more of a threat to us? If she does not make it to Kristallicheskiy, there will be a war. And then we will probably not have a forest anymore. Is whatever threat she is larger than the threat of two armies marching through our forest?"

"Do you trust me, Katya?"

"Of course, but right now I don't think you are thinking this through."

"It is complicated."

"I figured that out already." She rolled her eyes and slumped back into the chair, slamming her empty tea mug on the table.

"I promise I will tell you as soon as I can, and you know I will not let harm befall our forest. Or you. Ever. You are a treasure, and I love you."

"I love you, too, but I do want answers. I can't keep doing this without them. I need to know I am safe there with her, if she really is such a threat."

"I know. It will only be a few more nights, I promise. That is all I am asking. You are safe, I promise, I will never let any harm come to you." When he looked into her eyes, his expression was a plea. He never begged, but Katya understood that this was as close to begging as she would ever seen.

"I can do a few more nights."

"Thank you." Ivan took her into his arms, and she rested her head on his shoulder. They spent the rest of the night enjoying each other's company.

Chapter 9

Dawn was just beginning to break, and the soft glow of red kissed the golden teardrop-shaped domes on the palace, reflecting and refracting in a stunning spectacle. Alexis loved their room for its view of the spires, the way that the morning sun reflected from them made their room seem ablaze.

There was a knock at the door. They knew it was Tatiana, come to get them so they could head down together to the training grounds for their morning workout with the Royal Guard.

"Come in," Alexis said, not bothering to look at the door as Tatiana entered, their eyes trained on the horizon.

"Good morning," Tatiana said, sounding more awake than any human should be at this hour.

"Do you remember when we first met?" they asked, still staring out their window.

"Yes, how could I forget throwing you to the ground and touching my wooden practice sword to your throat while you cried that it was unfair?"

"I was more thinking when we first talked to each other."

"Well, you refused to do that for a while. Something about how I never stopped kicking your royal ass during every practice. I never knew that an ego or an ass could so easily bruise."

Alexis blushed, heat creeping up their neck. "Yes, after that."

"After you got over yourself?" Tatiana crossed her arms, raising an eyebrow at them.

"Yes." Alexis could almost feel a bruise forming on their arm, could almost hear the whack of a wooden sword slapping the leather armor they wore for those earlier trainings when they were still kids.

"I remember you begging me to help you, pleading with me to teach you tricks and give you advice."

"You said yes, and then immediately went on a family vacation! I had to go *two more months* of being humiliated while you went off with your family to Nribo!"

"That was not a 'family' vacation, it was a business trip for my father. It was only a vacation for my mother and I. But it was a good time, I got to spend time with my grandparents and cousins, and it was gorgeous! Always sunny. I didn't miss the snow at all. I brought so many wonderful things back with me, I even gave you trinkets from some artists my father brought back with him!"

"Whatever you want to call it, fine. *Anyway,* you came back and went right back to kicking my ass!"

"Because you yelled at me! I came back, and you asked where I'd been instead of saying 'thank you' for the gifts, going on and on about how I lied to you!"

"Maybe that was out of line, but you *did* omit that your mother was the head of the Czarina's Guard!"

"I still fail to see how that was relevant. You were all, 'how was I supposed to know' and, 'that is unfair' and, 'you had extra practice' and, 'you have the best teacher in the kingdom' and I did not see how any of that was relevant. I was better, that was that!"

"Yes, you were. I deserved every trouncing you gave me."

"I still am better."

Alexis raised an eyebrow. "Maybe. You pull your punches now, so I guess we will never really know."

"I've gotta, patriotic duty or something to not harm the heir. Although, you had some pretty unwise plans over the years that definitely could have jeopardized your life."

"Only because you were not with me! I asked if you wanted to come along, protect me, defend me, but you would just roll your eyes and go back to your push ups."

"I wasn't risking my life for some scheme to sneak out into the city, to steal pie from the kitchens, to ride your uncle's horses, or whatever other ploy to get in trouble you concocted!"

Alexis leaned back in the window frame, looking out at the dawn again. They frowned, wondering how to bring up what they wanted to ask.

"I hope when I meet the princess, it's like your parents." They looked down at their hands. Tatiana moved towards them, her lips tight in confusion. She sat down in the chair next to the window, facing them.

"What's going on?" Her voice was soft, concerned. She reached out a hand and put it on top of Alexis's own hands.

"Your father falling for your mother the second he laid eyes on her; him peddling his wares at the bazaar, her making her patrol." Alexis looked Tatiana straight in the eyes. "Language and culture and birthplace melting away as he tried day after day to draw her to his booth. They are both so respectful of each other, so understanding, so indulging. Until you told me the story, I thought my own parents were the greatest love story of all time. I hope-" They broke eye contact, shrugged off Tatiana's attempt at a hug, and paced.

"She is all right. She is not delicate." Tatiana got up from the chair and placed her hands on their shoulders, forcing them to look her in the eye. "I spent weeks on the road with her. She is a survivor."

Alexis nodded, they remembered all the wild schemes they had cooked up over the years. All the ones that Tatiana had said no to. They could have used their position to demand her help. But a relationship of any lasting durability must have perfect trust. Alexis would never betray that trust, constantly aware of how much power they wielded by virtue of nobility alone.

They were about to propose the most dangerous scheme to date. They expected no help from her, but as her best friend, they owed her at least the chance to laugh in their face and call them a complete fool. They took a breath, backing away from her. They threw their shoulders back in what they hoped passed for confidence.

"I do not care what my father says, I am going out." They'd rehearsed this in their head, it all came out too fast, though.

Tatiana crossed her arms over her chest and leaned back, a small grin playing on her lips.

"I will find her. Those woods have a reputation for a reason. He said last night he would convene a committee to discuss an official search party. I think he wants to find a reason to launch an attack. I can not let that happen. There is an enemy, yes, but I do not think it is from our neighbors to the south. It is so strange. My father was always bringing up how important it was that we trust them, and now? I am not asking for your help, Tatiana. You've already risked your life once for my future bride. I want to ask you to come along, but I know you will not. So, please, I am asking you to cover for me. I understand if you do not, but I needed to ask."

"Alexis, I do not need you to explain this to me again. I heard exactly what you heard in that meeting last night." Tatiana laughed and plopped down in a chair, clasping her hands behind her head as she reclined.

"So, you will not stop me, Tatiana? Can you tell my parents I am ill? At least long enough for me to be far enough away they cannot stop me?"

"You think I would stop you?! I'm going with you!" She rose from the chair and pointed at a packed bag near the door.

"Oh. I did not think—" Alexis stared at the bag, wondering how they missed it before.

"That your best friend would be willing to go with you on a search for your bride? I was wondering if you were just going to go without me, with all the reminiscing you were doing. I would have followed though."

"It is just that you have never—"

"I've already given Inna her goodbye kiss. We're wasting daylight. Our horses are waiting around back."

"I am so glad you came back safely, Tatiana."

"Daylight. You've wasted enough of it already."

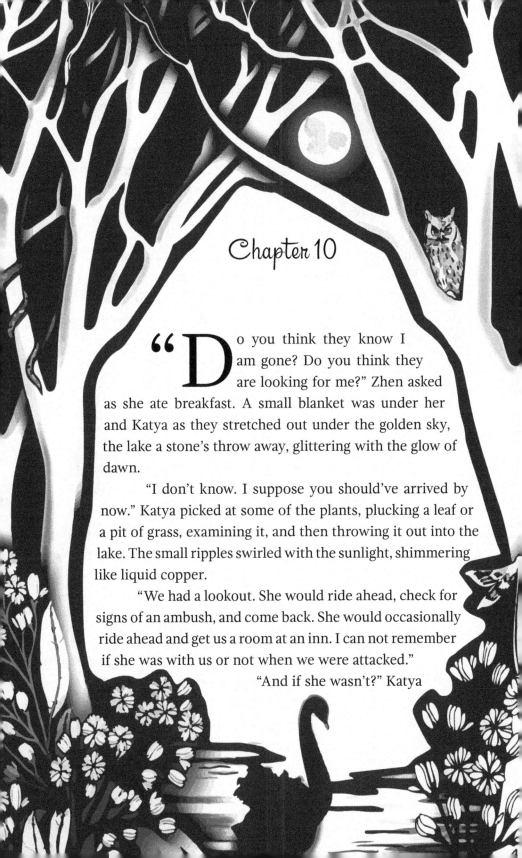

Chapter 10

"Do you think they know I am gone? Do you think they are looking for me?" Zhen asked as she ate breakfast. A small blanket was under her and Katya as they stretched out under the golden sky, the lake a stone's throw away, glittering with the glow of dawn.

"I don't know. I suppose you should've arrived by now." Katya picked at some of the plants, plucking a leaf or a pit of grass, examining it, and then throwing it out into the lake. The small ripples swirled with the sunlight, shimmering like liquid copper.

"We had a lookout. She would ride ahead, check for signs of an ambush, and come back. She would occasionally ride ahead and get us a room at an inn. I can not remember if she was with us or not when we were attacked."

"And if she wasn't?" Katya

continued her idle inspection of the flora.

"She would have come back and found her fellow guard slaughtered, and no princess."

"What do you think she'd do?" Katya laid down on her back, covering her eyes with her hand, trying to distract herself from the headache throbbing behind her eyes. She had never felt this ill so constantly before.

"Probably ride straight to Kristallicheskiy to let them know; they would come looking for me straight away."

"If that was the case, they might be close." Katya sat up again. The conversation was turning toward something she might find useful, something she could use to figure out what was going on. Much as she wished she could go back inside, drink chamomile tea, and sleep away this pain, she had a job to do.

"But, if they had found us, we could not just go with them." Zhen sagged.

Katya said nothing, though her stomach churned as she knew she needed to find something to say.

"But we could go looking for them," Zhen said, perking back up. "We could see if they are close, and try to lead them back here as night falls."

"How would that differ from waiting for them here and then trying to leave?" Katya closed her eyes and massaged her temples, trying to follow Zhen's logic, trying to find the threat that must be there. Soldiers in the woods, again, protecting her while she carries out some complicated spell that obliterates everything.

"I do not know. I just want to do something, I guess."

Zhen pulled her knees to her chest and hugged them. Katya opened her eyes back up, looking at Zhen, searching her for giveaways and tells, inspecting her for deceit. But all she saw was a frightened and hopeless princess.

Katya felt an ache in her throat, and she knew it had nothing to do with her headache. She felt heavy, weighed down. Some part of her wanted to reach out to Zhen, to touch her, to take away whatever pain she was going through right now. Another part of her wondered if this was some masterful manipulation on Zhen's part. Coerced empathy, some spell undetectable to Katya. But Katya pulled Zhen into her chest as she cried anyway. Zhen's body shook against Katya, heaving and heavy sobs torn from her chest. Tears pooled on Katya's clothing. Katya allowed her to drown in her sorrow quietly. Snot and tears mixed, both being wiped away with the same drenched sleeve.

When no more tears came, she coughed and wailed. The gulps of breath lessened, the increments of time between her dry sobs increased, until she sat upright and took one final wipe of her nose with the hem of her shirt. "I think I am all right now."

"I didn't mean to upset you. I'm sorry I did," Katya replied.

"I know, thank you. I hate feeling so helpless." She picked up pebbles and threw them one by one into the lake, the ripples overlapping and overtaking each other.

"That's understandable," Katya said, leaning back and looking up at the sky. The clearness of the sky was now interrupted by clouds, heavy ones further on the horizon.

"I do not think I have ever been so helpless before. I am a younger daughter, but I still could use the sway I had as a member of the royal family to right minor injustices. I could plead with my parents to intervene in one matter, or another. I once tried to get better working conditions for the horses. Nothing could have prepared me for this. Lives depend on my being at the royal palace, and I can do nothing to get there."

"I can imagine," Katya said. "I'm feeling lost myself right now."

"Have you felt this way before?"

"I'm not sure, I've never been responsible for anything aside from my bees. But they mostly take care of themselves."

"Do you think they are all right without you?"

"I'm sure of it."

"I hope I can meet your bees someday, I would love to try their honey."

"I hope you can meet them someday, too. Do you want to find something to do to distract ourselves while we wait for someone to rescue us?"

Zhen gave a strained smile and nodded.

"No more cards, please, I can't keep losing to you."

"We can skip stones on the water."

Katya did not know how to do this, but Zhen took her hand and held it, moving it back and forth as she showed Katya how to hold the stone, how to grip it and let go flying. Katya shivered each time Zhen touched her, heat rushing to her face as Zhen corrected her form. She remembered when they first met, the buzzing she felt just below her skin. She had not wanted to acknowledge it ever since Ivan told her Zhen was a threat. But she let Zhen touch her, and she tried to ignore the part of her that started to long for those small touches.

"You are doing better! That was three skips in a row!"

"But you can do over ten! This game isn't fair, either!"

"All right, what do you propose?"

Katya put her forefingers over her lips, thinking back to the days and nights she spent playing with her crows and with Ivan. Her stomach churned, not wanting to put Ivan and Zhen in the same place in her thoughts, rebelling against the comparison. She settled on just thinking of her crows.

"We could climb those trees, see who can reach the highest!"

Zhen frowned. "I am afraid of heights."

"Oh, I didn't know, we can think of something else."

Katya sat down, and Zhen joined her, resting her head on

Katya's shoulder. Katya thought about moving away, adjusting her position so that she could break contact. The game Katya was playing now was dangerous, a knot grew in her stomach but she ignored it. Zhen was a threat, an enemy, a force of destruction that could tear her whole world apart and bring everything she loved to dust. But the spark she felt whenever her skin touched Zhen's was so enticing.

As if in answer to Katya's thoughts, the clouds that had gathered on the horizon broke loose, the downpour drenching them before they could even jump up in shock. They ran toward their cottage, tripping over the soaked hems of their dresses along the way.

"Help me! I will help you after," Zhen said once they were inside, reaching behind her back and motioning to the twisted ties. Katya unlaced the ties holding Zhen's dress in place, unlooping the drenched strands of ribbon one by one.

"Is something stuck?" Zhen asked as she twisted her neck to get a look.

"Yes, there is a knot. I have made a mess of it."

"Well, it can not be anything like the knot in my stomach."

"What?"

"Oh, never mind."

"No, why is your stomach in knots?" Katya tugged once more and the knot came out. Zhen sighed as she slipped out of her dress and began draping her outerwear over a chair near the fireplace.

"Zhen! You can't just say stuff like that. Come here, help me out, too, please." Zhen's face flushed as she stepped behind Katya. Katya moved her hair out of the way and began fidgeting. She had been consumed by her task before, but Zhen's nearness was hard to miss. Her heart fluttered. She stifled shivers as Zhen's fingers brushed across her back. Katya's bodice comprised several panels that spanned her broad back and wide waist, each cinched together in complex knots.

"You are the reason my stomach is in knots."

"Oh."

"Oh?"

"I just wasn't expecting that."

"Neither was I. I am engaged already!"

"There is that, yes." Katya turned around, her dress falling to the floor as Zhen let go of the last ribbon. Zhen tentatively put her hand on Katya's shoulder. When Katya did not pull away, she took another step forward, closing the gap between them. Zhen tilted her face upward and leaned into Katya, balancing on tiptoes. "May I?" she asked, her intentions clear.

Katya wanted to say yes. She hated that she wanted to say yes. She had not considered that would even be a debate in her head until just this moment. This had to be a trick, a spell, some sorcery that Zhen had cleverly woven. "No, I am sorry, I can't. I can't! I have someone, and you, you're getting married!" She pulled back and turned away from Zhen.

"You have someone?" Zhen sagged. "I did not know. I am sorry."

"I never mentioned it before."

"So, who is this person? Are they coming to find you, too?"

"Well, my going missing is not likely to start a war."

"That is not the only reason to search for someone. This person probably misses you and is worried about you."

"It is complicated." She pulled out a chair that did not have wet clothing draped across it and sat down near the fire.

"Do you think this person misses you?"

Katya picked at a loose thread at the hem of her camise. "Yes, I think he misses me."

"Do you think he misses you enough to be worried that you did not come home?"

"It is complicated."

"You have mentioned that already."

"I know, but, I can't really tell you more than that, because I honestly don't know how he—"

"I am so sorry. I will not pry anymore. I am going to try to make a lunch," Zhen said, as the table magically filled with spices and ingredients.

Exhaustion hit Katya, making the world spin. "I think I'm going to take a nap." Katya said, unsteady as she lurched toward her bed.

Zhen did not wake Katya as the afternoon settled into evening and faded into night.

Chapter 11

Alexis and Tatiana left the city before anyone but the merchants and priests awoke. They took four of the fastest horses in the Czar's stables and swapped them every few hours. They took almost no breaks, keeping the horses going at a pace that would have gotten them yelled at by the Mistress of the Horses if she knew.

They rode for several days, making camp where they could, staying at inns when they, or the horses, needed a good night's rest. At first, Alexis rode with one eye to their back, certain that their parents would send guards after them. This wasn't the first time Alexis had made rash decisions, and there were probably spies at every village, sending word back to the Czar.

Good, Alexis thought. *Let my parents know that I intend to act in a way that honors the peace treaty, not jump to conclusions. I am not the impulsive one.*

"We're close." Tatiana said. Night neared, and they soon had to decide. "We need to sleep and the horses need rest, Alexis. We can make camp and sleep in shifts, but we won't make it at all if we do not give them a rest."

"I know, I know you are right, but we could be—" Alexis held the reins tightly, looking ahead, squinting as if they could see their destination if they just looked hard enough.

"We're soaked, the horses are tired, and we need more than bread and cheese. There's a small village just ahead. I know you don't want to trust your horses to an innkeeper, but we could get dinner, let the horses eat in the inn's stables, and then be on our way."

"But if we just kept riding—"

"Then we would arrive tired, overworked, and in no condition to fight whatever we may encounter."

"I suppose so. Fine, let us do that." Their shoulders sagged and they looked down at their hands. They knew Tatiana had a point.

They rode slower as they neared the village. While the additional horses gave them away as wealthy, their travel-stained attire would do enough to make even the more cunning of thieves think twice about the actual amount of valuables they had on them.

The inn that Tatiana pointed out was bustling. Alexis dismounted from their horse and handed the reins to her. "You take them to the stable. I will get us settled with a meal inside."

A small band was trying to play over a raucous gambling match as Alexis stepped inside the inn. They pushed their way through a crowd of onlookers and made for the bar. The bartender approached and gave Alexis the once-over before asking, "Room for one?"

"I am sorry, no. My traveling companion and I would like a hot meal apiece and spots in the stable while we dine. She is already leading our horses that way."

"There should be room enough in the stables for your horses. Tonight, we got some great *shchi*, and we just got a fresh batch of vodka from my in-laws' distillery up north. Seems you've ridden hard today. Surely you want a good night's rest."

"Aye, my friend, we have ridden hard, but we are close to our destination. A good meal is enough. And discretion."

"If you insist, take a seat, I'll have something nice brought around for you."

Alexis handed the bartender a fistful of coins, more than enough to cover the costs and the innkeeper's silence. They felt a tap on their shoulder as Tatiana slid into the chair next to them.

"Horses are taken care of; not in the best shape, so we should be careful after we head out. What's on the menu?"

"Stew, and apparently a fresh batch of vodka from up north."

"The best kind, if you ask me. I care little for the pot distillery that is common at the capital now."

"Welcome," the bartender said to Tatiana as she set some rye bread down before the two of them. "I couldn't help but overhear. Have a drink, on me. I want your opinion of it."

She poured a glass and set it before Tatiana, who graciously raised it up. "To the only true way to make vodka," she said with a grin before throwing it back in one big gulp. "That is good. A hint of berries, but not overpowering."

"I am glad you enjoy it! The *shchi* should be right up." The bartender went back to making the rounds while they waited for the stew to come out. A tall man with a hard face caught Alexis' eye, and before Alexis could look away, he ambled over, sitting next to Tatiana.

"What's a fine pair of kids like you doing out so late?" he asked.

"We are just trying to get food, sir," Alexis said, an edge creeping into their voice.

"No need to get defensive," the man said raising his hands. "Just trying to make conversation. I haven't seen you two around before."

"We're just passing through," Tatiana said, picking at her bread.

"We do not get many people traveling through these parts. The next village over is on the edge of some spooky woods. So, you're either from there, or you are going there if you are passing through Kasimov."

"Are you from Kasimov?" Tatiana asked.

"Born and raised," the man said as a brawny girl served them their stews. Alexis started prying the rye apart and dunking it into the broth.

"What do you do?" Alexis asked.

"I am a tanner, mostly. So, you've got family in Ignashino?"

"Distant family," Alexis supplied. "But we have never been there before. Have you?"

"Aye, a few times, mostly to do trading."

"What should we expect?" Tatiana asked.

"The townspeople are all very generous, but a bit superstitious."

"Superstitious of what?" Alexis asked, leaning forward.

"The woods, what lives in them."

"What do they believe lives in the woods?" Tatiana asked, raising an eyebrow.

"I don't hear too many of their stories, but they definitely believe a young boy was enchanted by a strange woman who lives in there. He went into the forest one day and claimed he saw a black swan turn into a lady. He was climbing a tree and fell out in fright. He claimed she healed his cuts; when he got back, he had no marks at all."

"Well, if she healed him that was to be expected," Tatiana said.

"He apparently had a birthmark that also disappeared."

"Children create stories all the time," Alexis replied. They wanted to roll their eyes, but then they remembered how their father had asked about signs of sorcery.

"Apparently a bunch of them believed the child was swapped and went looking for the sorceress who stole him. They found a cabin there, and a giant beast attacked them. Killed one of the child's grandparents who had gone with them."

"A beast? Or a large bear?"

"This is just the story I heard. *They're* superstitious. I'm not. But, they will be kind as can be to you. Good food, good vodka. But not as good as here," he finished, pointing to the counter as the bartender walked by. The bartender sauntered over at the gesture.

"Another round, my friends?"

Alexis and Tatiana shook their heads, but their new friend gave a lopsided grin. "Always, Vika. Always."

Another man came up behind them and tapped their new friend on the shoulder. "Boris, Boris! Vlad's lost the round and wants you to take his spot for him while he drowns his sorrows." Boris nodded and doffed his cap to Tatiana. "It's been a pleasure talking to you. I hope you stop by here again after your business in Ignashino is over."

"We will see what we can do," Tatiana said. Alexis nodded.

"Well?" Tatiana said to Alexis after Boris rejoined his friends.

"I am ready to get back on the road. Let us get our horses."

They rode until they could no longer see the lights of Kasimov and then dismounted to make camp. "I wonder if my parents have sent anyone to look for us," Alexis mused.

"I think they have a good idea of where you are and why."

"Am I so predictable?"

Tatiana snorted.

"You are probably right. Thank you for coming with me, Tatiana."

"What's that you say? You owe me? You will gift me lands? And a title? And enough money to keep Inna happy for the rest of her life?"

"Yes, yes, yes. But first you have to help me make sure I can keep Yi Zhen happy for the rest of her life."

Chapter 12

As Katya was learning, Zhen was unstoppable when she was on a mission, and today's mission was finding the beast who had trapped them. Katya had tried to talk her out of it multiple times, but Zhen could not be convinced otherwise. She had heard her explain the plan multiple times, and had offered so many reasons not to go along with it. All this while her stomach churned in fear and she tried to keep the quivering out of her voice.

This had to be it, this had to have been Zhen's plan all along, though she could not figure out why. She had planned to come to this forest with a small army united to take out Ivan. But Katya could not figure out why, and when pressed, Zhen gave the expected answer: because he was holding them captive. All she could do now was try to make her pleas based in logistics, and not an objection to killing the sorcerer.

"The curse he has us

under could be an advantage. We could go back to the carriage, find materials, and bring them back. We could fly weapons back and hide them. Then we could locate his abode, fly there, and come back as night falls. He will chase us, but by then we shall be human again—and armed. Between magic and weapons, surely we can take him on."

"We can't carry weapons as swans."

"We can make straps or bags we would attach to ourselves-"

"Neither of us have enough experience flying unencumbered, let alone with satchels."

"I could see if I could use some of my magic while transformed."

"Maybe. But how will we find his home? We don't have a ton of time, what if we get lost?"

"I am good with directions, and he flew off to the north both times he left us."

"Okay, but say we do find him. This plan relies on him chasing us. How do you know he will do that?"

"He will want to catch us and bring us back."

"But why? He knows that we will have to come back. Our alternative is to remain swans for the rest of our lives."

"Not necessarily! When I cast a glamour on a dress, if I should take it off and send it to another province for repairs or alterations, it loses that glamour. I cannot sustain a glamour at a long distance. I am sure there are limits to his power, too."

"Then why should we come back to fight him? Why not just keep flying until we reach the limits of his power?"

"Because it would be quicker to kill him."

"Kill him? How would that help us?" Katya already knew the answer. This had to have been Zhen's end goal all along. Ivan was right, she was a threat and a danger to them and she was still determined. *But why*, Katya asked herself again. *Why have two nations united and sent a princess as an assassin? Or maybe she isn't a princess at all.*

"Most forms of magic draw on the life force of the caster, should that life force be extinguished—"

"The curse would end."

"Exactly."

"I don't know." Katya stood up from the table near the fire and fiddled with the tea pot. Swirling the dredges, she scrambled to find a reason that this plan might fail that Zhen was not sure to try to counter. The plan was not great even if she were honestly attempting to escape Ivan.

"I know he is scary. I know he seems so much stronger than us, but if we plan this right, if we are determined, we can do this."

"What if we get the weapons and find his location today, but we do not lead him back tonight? What if we do that tomorrow?"

"It is too close. I need to be in the capital soon."

"When you do not arrive, don't you think that the royal family would assemble a search party? We could wait for them. Maybe just go to the wreckage and scrawl a note for them, a drawn arrow to our camp? Once they find us, they'll surely come to rescue us, bringing sorcerers of their own, ones who could take on Ivan without our help."

"Ivan?" Katya heard the edge of suspicion in Zhen's voice, but did not understand why it was there.

"Our captor."

"He has a name? How do you know it?"

"You don't?" Katya tried to deflect, turning away from Zhen.

"How would I?"

Katya bit her lip. If Zhen were sent to assassinate a sorcerer, wouldn't she have been told his name? If she had been told his name, why hide that from Katya now?

"Please, Katya, what do you know about him? I know

absolutely nothing, and every bit of information might help us."

"Your guards, they did not know about him?"

"No, if they had, we would have taken another route. They would have stayed far away from here. They would not jeopardize my life like this knowingly."

"There are rumors. Living near this forest, you hear stories." she said, being truthful while concealing her own involvement. "Once, there was a little boy who returned from the woods bespelled. The villagers went into the woods to find the source of the enchantment, and they found a creature that was part man, part beast. 'Ivan' was the name the villagers said he gave. I didn't believe them. I was wrong."

"You were not fearful of this sorcerer when you were out picking flowers?"

"No, I have never feared for my safety while in these woods." If Zhen was not a threat, if Ivan was wrong and holding her here on faulty pretense, then maybe she should tell Zhen the truth. Tell her it was a mistake, and she would talk to Ivan.

Katya twisted her hair, trying to think about how she might explain this to Zhen without making Zhen mad at her. Maybe she felt sorry for possibly keeping Zhen here, maybe she wanted to keep up the pleasant lie that Zhen was something close to a friend.

"A name is a good thing to know. A name means he has a thread on this loom and we can pluck it."

"My question still stands. Why must we be the ones to cut him from this loom? Why not wait for your betrothed's army?"

"My escort from home was sending word back every so many days, informing my parents of my progress, just as surely as the Lebedians were riding ahead. I fear that when no word gets back to my border, my family will think they have been played wrong. The war that has been simmering will boil over."

"But the Lebedians will find us, surely, before any army from

Shān could get across the border."

"I do not want to take that chance."

Katya gave a defeated shrug and paced back and forth.

"I will go alone, Katya, if you do not want to help. I understand. You have nothing really at stake."

"Zhen? Do you think we are friends?"

"I would like to think so, yes."

"Do you think, if we had met under different circumstances, happier ones, do you think we would be friends?"

"I do not know. I would like to imagine so."

"It's not that I don't want to help you, Zhen. I want to. I want you to be free. I want you to have a happy life with your princen and not have to worry about a war or battles or sorcerers. I want nothing more than that right now."

"But?"

Katya hesitated. She should probably talk to Ivan first, before getting Zhen's hopes up. She did not know how she would manage this, how much acting she could do to satisfy Zhen and protect both Ivan and Zhen from each other while they still thought of each other as threats. Katya could not pinpoint the exact second when she stopped pretending to be Zhen's friend and had started to truly care for her. She did not want to put words to it and admit that the job Ivan had given her had become complicated.

"I guess there is no 'but.' I shall help you."

"Thank you, Katya."

Zhen finished the last of her tea, then stuffed the last of a bread roll in her mouth, crumbs tumbling down her chin. She held out her hand to Katya, and they walked hand in hand outside.

"Can I ask one more thing?" Zhen said, looking up at Katya.

"Sure, what do you want to ask?"

"May I kiss you?"

There was still a hesitation this time, a lingering sense in the back of Katya's mind that this was dangerous. But it was swept aside, Katya nodded and wrapped her arms around Zhen, tilting her head down to meet Zhen's lips. *I will make sure to sort this out,* Katya thought. *It's just a misunderstanding.* But the thought melted away as Zhen grabbed at Katya's collar, pulling her closer. Katya and Zhen stayed like this, exploring each other, for several moments, neither of them noticing the large black owl launching from its perch overhead.

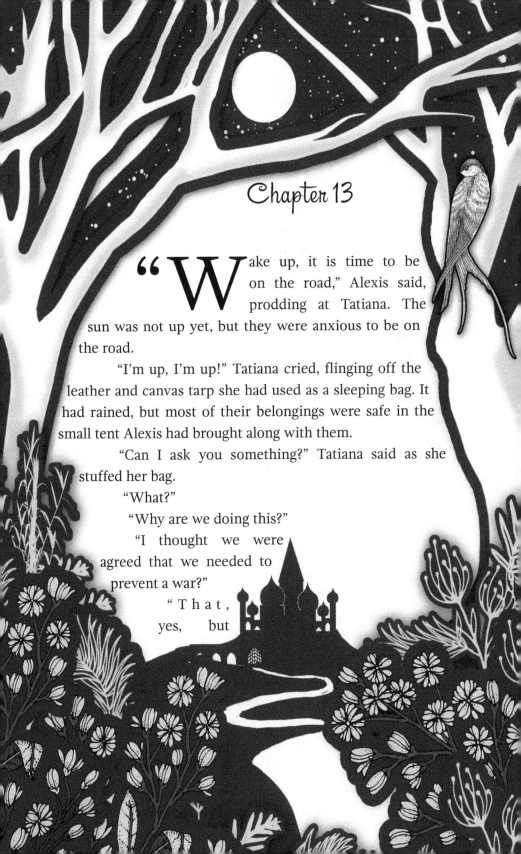

Chapter 13

"Wake up, it is time to be on the road," Alexis said, prodding at Tatiana. The sun was not up yet, but they were anxious to be on the road.

"I'm up, I'm up!" Tatiana cried, flinging off the leather and canvas tarp she had used as a sleeping bag. It had rained, but most of their belongings were safe in the small tent Alexis had brought along with them.

"Can I ask you something?" Tatiana said as she stuffed her bag.

"What?"

"Why are we doing this?"

"I thought we were agreed that we needed to prevent a war?"

"That, yes, but

you've never met Zhen. You seemed less than pleased with the news of your upcoming nuptials. Have you come around? Is this just about proving your parents wrong?"

"The princess and I, we corresponded secretly, sending messages like star-crossed lovers and not two people in a political marriage."

"You never told me."

"I never told anyone, I did not want my thoughts filtered through the legal lens of an advisor, nor the worry of a friend. I wanted to be wholly myself, unaltered. I wanted those first few correspondences to be just between her and I."

"So you're not just a flirt, you can be romantic when you want to be."

Alexis pinched the bridge of their nose. "This is why I did not tell you."

"All right, all right. So, do you like her?"

"Yes, she is quite funny, very playful. I think we will get along."

"So you care enough for her to mount a dangerous and unsanctioned rescue?" Tatiana finished stuffing her bag and pulled the canvas off the tent.

Alexis blushed while taking apart the rods of the tent. "If that is what you want to take away from my response, sure."

"I know you were afraid of this marriage, and I am trying to be serious here," she said as she put away the last of their supplies and jumped on her horse.

"I was afraid. I still am. I do not think I have ever loved someone before, but I think I could love Zhen. I am still terrified of messing up, of doing something wrong. I had nightmares about being in a marriage where we hated each other. My parents, yours, they make it all look so easy. Is it easy with Inna?"

"Sometimes it is very easy with her, sometimes it is incredibly difficult. It started out all—"

"I remember how it started, you did not talk about anything else for a week and I managed to almost beat you at our daily sparring session."

Tatiana smiled. "I was very smitten with her. It was so easy at first, we never fought and I never thought we would. But I was rising through the ranks, and she was spending more time with the Mistress of the Horse and we were sometimes grouchy, sometimes at the same time. I cannot remember why we had our first fight. I had seen her mad at some of the stable boys, I had seen her tear into them for being lazy or careless. When we started fighting that night? I thought we were done for."

"Wait, when I found you sleeping in the arms room, was that because—?"

"We fought, yes. We had to work really hard after that, on forgiving each other and forgiving ourselves. We still mess up, but we get over it quicker now. And sometimes the making up part is a lot of fun." Tatiana grinned.

Alexis hopped up on their horse. "I hope I can make it work with Zhen, I hope we can learn how to talk to each other."

"First we have to save her. Shall we?"

They rode even harder than they had the day before, making it to Ignashino before breakfast. Half the town was still in bed when they arrived. The keepers of the small inn, an older couple who had run it longer than they had been married, were awake but still bleary-eyed.

"This morning's bread is still baking. Would you mind leftovers from yesterday or would you rather wait?"

"Ma'am, whatever you have is fine," Tatiana told the one innkeeper, a plump woman with white hair she kept braided and pulled up.

The other innkeeper, a taller man with gray hair who favored his left leg, soon brought them some bread and cheese and told them that their horses were being provided with fresh grains.

"How do you want to do this, Alexis?" Tatiana pulled out her knives and inspected them, testing the edges and searching for knicks while absently picking at the bread.

Alexis shoved bread and cheese into their mouth, hoping that their lack of words could be attributed to their eating and not their lack of plans. Maybe they could come up with something quickly.

"Alexis?"

"I did not think that far ahead," Alexis said, lowering their head.

Tatiana sighed, and Alexis expected her to begin her lecture. She had lectured them on their impulsivity hundreds of times before.

"No, I am not going to lecture you. But we should have a plan. Let's discuss one. Together." She put one of the knives back into its sheath in her boot.

"All right. You know the path they were taking. Do you think you could lead us there, and we can look around see what we might find? Circle out from there?"

"I could probably lead us back there."

"Do you think there would still be footprints after all the rain from yesterday?"

"I'm not sure." She chewed her bottom lip, closing her eyes.

The white-haired innkeeper set a dish of berries in front of them. "Here you are. I picked some fresh fruit in my garden for you. So, what brings you to town?"

Tatiana looked to Alexis for guidance, but they shrugged.

"We are on a hunting trip. Heard there was big game to be had in those woods." She put away the rest of her knives and moved the dish full of berries squarely in front of herself, grinning at them.

"That's not a good idea." The innkeeper shivered.

"There isn't any game in there?" Tatiana wiped away some of the berry juice staining her lips.

"Something lives in there. Something evil."

"Superstitions," Alexis said, trying to sound confident. They could not squash the rumble in their gut, though.

"No, it's more than that. We can't even plant crops too close to its edge. They shrivel up and die."

"It's been a harsh few winters, and our summers have not been so great." Tatiana said, waving her hand in dismissal.

"I'm telling you, something evil lives there."

"Have you ever seen this evil thing?" Alexis asked.

"No, not with my own eyes, but my sister's grandson was attacked by it!"

"Was this a black swan?" Tatiana asked.

"No, that was another boy. This time the great beast took the form of a giant owl. Chased him out of the woods, and he came home crying and screaming. His moms had to mix some chamomile in with his milk to get him to calm down and sleep for the next several weeks. They were both very scared they would wake up to find their son gone, stolen back by the evil forest."

"How horrible. Is he doing better now?" Tatiana asked.

"Mostly. The nightmares still come but are less frequent. Do not go near them woods—there is something old and angry in there."

"Children sometimes exaggerate, is it possible what he saw was a burly thief who has made the forest their home?" Alexis asked.

"You've heard about the black swan and still you are skeptical?"

"Pardon me, ma'am, I mean no disrespect, but I am not easily convinced." Except, they had been convinced. Something had been nagging at them since their father first asked Tatiana if she had seen anything *unusual*.

"A few people, my husband included, saw it, too. We went into the woods to root out the evil and were confronted by it directly. A giant monstrous owl."

"We will be careful, ma'am." Tatiana said, glaring at Alexis.

After breakfast, they rode to the outskirts of the village. The woods loomed in front of them, dark, but not unnaturally so.

"So you believe them, then? About this monster?" Alexis asked.

"I'm starting to. Remember what I said about finding large feathers?"

"I do. I am starting to think there is something strange going on. I had been hoping for something more mundane. A gang of bandits who wear a disguise could explain those feathers. Remember that band of thieves who wore deer horns in the forest just north of here?" They sighed. "But now? I am not so sure."

"Let's just be careful. I want to be proven wrong, but I don't want to be dead because I wasn't."

There was a hazy glow as dawn mixed with the heavy fog that clung to the air. Without a word, Alexis and Tatiana turned to face each other, nodded, and entered the forest.

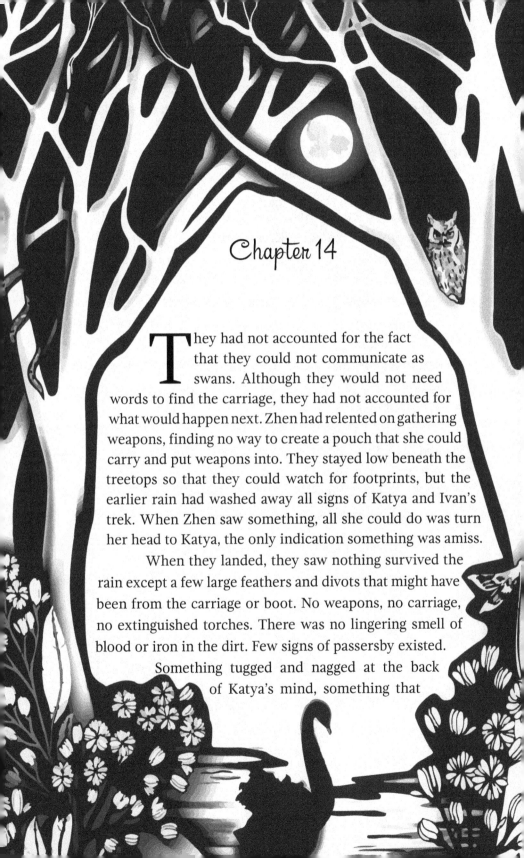

Chapter 14

They had not accounted for the fact that they could not communicate as swans. Although they would not need words to find the carriage, they had not accounted for what would happen next. Zhen had relented on gathering weapons, finding no way to create a pouch that she could carry and put weapons into. They stayed low beneath the treetops so that they could watch for footprints, but the earlier rain had washed away all signs of Katya and Ivan's trek. When Zhen saw something, all she could do was turn her head to Katya, the only indication something was amiss.

When they landed, they saw nothing survived the rain except a few large feathers and divots that might have been from the carriage or boot. No weapons, no carriage, no extinguished torches. There was no lingering smell of blood or iron in the dirt. Few signs of passersby existed.

Something tugged and nagged at the back of Katya's mind, something that felt a little bit like doubt and tasted like revulsion. She pushed the thoughts aside. Her eyes locked with Zhen's, and Katya knew they were both thinking the same thing: they would not have gotten the weapons even if that were still the plan. No Lebedian soldiers would recognize this as a site of battle. A search party would have nothing to go on.

Katya tried to find a way to communicate with Zhen, wanting to offer comfort. Katya's crow-sisters gathered around them, perching in tree branches and circling in the air, swooping down to pick up a twig or leaf before taking off again.

Zhen paced, her long neck craning to look at all the crows at once. There was a small nervous tremor in her wings as they moved to expand, then suddenly contracted back into themselves. She scratched at the ground, trying to leave marks or signs. Katya could not tell if she was trying to leave arrows to point to the lake or some sort of message in a language Katya did not recognize.

Her efforts were without reward, though, as the still wet ground would not hold the shapes Zhen was trying to impress into it. Katya decided that they had spent enough time in the empty ruins of the doomed voyage and reared back to take flight again.

Zhen followed suit, and they took to the skies once more. Once above the treetops, Katya let Zhen take the lead. They flew in circles, Zhen navigating without purpose. Katya tried to hold her nerves at bay whenever they came close to the cottage she shared with Ivan. She was terrified not only of confrontation, but also of the fact that Zhen might learn Katya was an instrument of Zhen's captivity.

As twilight descended upon them, Zhen swerved toward the direction of their lake, and Katya, resigned, followed. They descended from their height, several meters above the treetops, and entered the forest proper.

"Tatiana! There! Do you see them? That is definitely a black swan, just like the rumors said."

Katya glanced back at the sound of voices, terrified of who they might belong to. A woman with a halo of thick black hair framing her face was following them on horseback, determined eyes fixed on Zhen. Beside her was another rider with choppy blond hair, a pert chin, and a nose that had been broken at least once. They were both leaning low over the reins as they urged their horses forward.

A thin crescent moon hung low in the sky, but moonbeams still played on the surface of the lake. Zhen landed in the waters, her wings spread wide to slow her momentum. As she swam into the reflection of the moon, the water wrapped around her, a vortex of moonlight, feathers, and water. It was a thousand diamonds in a glittering vortex, shooting stars coalescing around the swan until she vanished behind the veil of magic.

And then it stopped, and Zhen was standing before them, draped in a dress of feathers and adorned in diamonds.

Katya followed suit, imitating as much as she could but putting in her own flourishes. She wrapped herself in the moonlight, the stars becoming beads in her hair, and she cloaked herself in silver dewdrops. She stepped out of the vortex and onto the shore of the lake and took Zhen's hands in her own. She stared into Zhen's eyes and smiled. Zhen blushed, and returned the smile.

"That's her! That's Yi Zhen!" The call came from the edge of the forest, and both Zhen and Katya turned to see their pursuers dismounting from their horses and running to them.

"That woman! She was my Lebedian scout!" Zhen covered her mouth with her hands.

The scout came upon them, her blade snaking inches away from Katya's throat. Her lean muscles pulsed as she held perfectly still, the heat of anger clear in the angle of her chin.

"Stop!" Zhen cried, her hands going to her chest, clasped

tightly together. The other rider approached them more slowly, taking in the scene. They stopped a pace behind the woman, their eyes sweeping from side to side, taking in every detail.

They nodded, sheathing their own sword and then they dropped to one knee, one hand over their heart, the other outstretched toward Zhen. "My lady, my beautiful star, I had hoped to meet you under better circumstances."

"Alexis! Can you do your courtly games *after* we have finished properly saving her?" The sword against Katya's throat quivered with each word the woman spoke. Katya tried to remain motionless, certain that these people were here to rescue Zhen but unsure how she could prove her own innocence to them.

Katya's heart sped up, she could hear the blood rushing and pounding in her eyes with each beat of it, quicker than the scherzo. Her thoughts raced over each second she doubted Zhen, each moment she was complicit in keeping her here, regardless of the reasons. This scout had every right to suspect her.

The other person looked up at the woman, nodded, and circled Katya, assessing her as the pommel of their sword was clutched firmly in their hand, ready to be drawn.

"Please, please, she is a friend. We can explain!" Zhen pleaded.

"Are you a sorceress? A witch? An enchantress? Have you bespelled my betrothed? We saw you both. That was magic."

"It was indeed," Katya replied. This was the person who would lead Zhen away from her, who she was going to marry. Her jaw clenched, and something was burning in her stomach. She tried not to think of all the ways the princen and their companion were leaving themselves open to attack, all the ways in which this rescue was lacking, and the ways that this princen was proving themself incapable of protecting Zhen. She tried not to think how she could do these things better. There was no point in going down that road.

"Then you have enchanted my bride?"

"I have done no such thing," Katya said, her head held high as the words left her lips.

"I saw the way she looked at you and I hear the way she is defending you now. Truly, you have not ensorcelled her?"

"Katya has not! I swear, she is a prisoner here, just as I am," Zhen covered her face in her hands.

"Is that true?" The princen continued circling.

"It's true." Katya swallowed the lump in her throat. It was not a lie, technically. "I'm a prisoner with her. We can't leave the clearing surrounding this lake."

"But you were both flying around earlier," the woman said, her sword still at Katya's throat.

"That's the curse," Katya replied. "That's what happens when we try to leave." Another technicality, another statement on the far edge of truth.

"We can only transform by coming back here, by going into the lake when the moon is reflected on its surface," Zhen said.

The princen stopped circling and took their hand away from their sword, their eyes meeting the woman's as they did so. "Tatiana. At ease." The sword came down, and Katya's hands rose to her throat, massaging the area where the point of the sword had jabbed her.

Zhen curtsied low, her head unbowed. "Your Highness, I am Princess Yi Zhen. I am pleased to make your acquaintance at last. I have long looked forward to the day I would be meeting my future spouse, though I did not imagine it like this."

The princen took a step toward her and offered their hand. She accepted, and they gently kissed her hand. "The honor is mine, my lady. When Tatiana arrived and told me something terrible had befallen the company escorting you, I feared the worst. I am so relieved to find you alive."

"Thank you for coming to find me," Zhen replied. "I wish I could ride away with you right now, but I truly cannot leave these woods. My companion and I had a plan to overtake the sorcerer, but we could not carry it out."

"Has he tried to harm you?"

"Not at all. I believe he lives in these woods; I do not know why he wants me here."

The princen embraced Zhen, stealing a glance at Katya before resting their head on Zhen's. Katya knew the look instantly, guessing that it was the one she wore when she realized who this person was: competition for Zhen's heart. The princen had nothing to worry about, though. Katya was just beginning to admit her feelings to herself, but she knew why she had hesitated to acknowledge them at all: she could never be with Zhen. The princesses of tales did not marry the enchantress from the woods.

Especially not *this* princess. This princess had to marry the princen and stop a war. And not *this* enchantress, this enchantress had helped take her prisoner under mistaken circumstances. It would be better that Zhen leave here with the princen than face Katya's lies, even though she had been truthful about her heart.

Katya sulked over to a log, giving the princen and Zhen some privacy, and plopped herself down before burying her face in her hands. Tatiana followed her, gingerly sitting down next to her.

"I'm sorry about the nick I put in your neck."

"You were doing your job." Katya bit her tongue to keep from saying that is was poorly done, that Katya could have disarmed her with the very witchcraft they accused her of using on Zhen.

"How were you captured, by the way? Who are you?"

"I'm just an eccentric woman who lives around these parts." Katya shrugged and tried to laugh, but it came out as a high-pitched stutter. Her mouth was dry and she was fighting the urge to flee, but she kept going. "I came across the escort party and was offered a ride back home, as it was late. I accepted their offer. Shortly after that, we were attacked."

"You live in Ignashino?" Tatiana narrowed her eyes.

"Not precisely." Katya wrung her hands. "I live near it, though."

"Have you heard any of the rumors about strange shape-shifting creatures who live in these woods?"

"What?"

"On our way here, we heard these woods were inhabited by some devilish beast. In one story, the beast is a huge owl who attacks children. In another, this creature took the form of a black swan, which transformed into a beautiful maiden and enchanted a child. When the village sought revenge, a giant owl-beast attacked them. Another told me that any plants or crops they try to plant near the edge of the forest wilt and die. You have not heard these stories?"

"They sound familiar. I mostly keep to myself, though."

"Is that so?" Tatiana asked leaning back and looking Katya up and down, each word slow and fully enunciated.

"I'm an orphan, and I think Ignashino believes I am bad luck," Katya supplied, hoping that would alleviate some of the suspicion. Katya did not want to dwell on this subject, though. She did not want to think about her strange existence, her lack of a past and her desire to know where she came from. This was not the best of times to contemplate that.

"I am sorry," Tatiana said. Katya offered a small smile. "I did not know, I mean, I'm just trying to look after the Princen. I am sorry, about your parents."

"I said I was eccentric, you aren't the first person to find it suspicious."

Tatiana twiddled her thumbs, looking anywhere but at Katya.

"Are you the princen's sister?" Katya said, trying to break

the tension.

Tatiana snorted.

"Bodyguard?"

"I'm their best friend. I don't have to laugh at their bad jokes, and I get to call them a fool when they are behaving badly. But I don't get paid for all of those things, so I guess it evens out."

Katya laughed, one that was not filled with nervous tension. "How long have you known them?"

"I was eleven, they were ten. I was a second-year page when their parents decided Alexis could train, too. They were assigned to me their first day, and I showed them the ropes, so to speak. I couldn't keep them out of trouble, though."

"They look like the sort that does not need to go looking for trouble. The roguish haircut, that knowing smirk." Katya decided that she liked Tatiana, when she wasn't pointing a sword at her.

"That's true. Trouble usually goes looking for them. As for what I do when not pulling them out of trouble, I am hoping to get a spot in the Czarina's Guard."

"Why the Czarina's Guard?"

"It's not as flashy as the Czar's Guard, but it takes a subtler precision to be an assassin, a spy, and a bodyguard while wearing a dress at a state dinner. And I still get to show off at tournaments. But I'm waiting to apply until I know the next czarina better."

"What do you think of her so far?"

Tatiana looked over at Alexis and Zhen, who appeared lost in conversation, their hands joined between them. "I think she has potential. I think she and Alexis can make each other happy. I hope she will not be too..." Tatiana bit her lower lip.

"Too what?" Katya prompted.

Tatiana turned back to Katya, her eyes searching Katya's face before looking her directly in the eyes. "Too scarred by what has happened here."

Katya swallowed and looked away. "I wish for that, too."

"I'm glad we agree."

Katya and Tatiana chatted for nearly an hour, occasionally looking over to the two royals only to see they were very much still flirting with no consideration for the time. "I should probably drag Alexis away soon, if we want to make it back to the inn with enough time to rest before we head back to the capital."

"That's probably a good idea."

"Katya," Zhen called, almost on cue. "Tatiana, can you come here please?"

Katya and Tatiana approached Alexis and Zhen, and Katya could not help tried not to look at Zhen's hands as they interlaced with Alexis'.

"I really wish I could have come here and saved you two right away," Alexis started. "But based on what Zhen tells me, that is not possible right now. Zhen and I talked it over. Tatiana and I will go back and tell my parents what has happened. We will gather supplies and reinforcements and send word to Shān. When we get back, we will be prepared to take on this sorcerer. But we should leave before he discovers us."

"I think that's the best course of action, your Highness," Tatiana said. Katya nodded, placing her hands behind her back and looking at the ground, tracing small circles in the dirt with her toe.

Zhen dropped Alexis' hand and walked over to Katya, placing a hand on Katya's shoulder. "We are going to be alright. The princen will make sure that you are taken safely back to your home when this is all over."

"I know." Katya said. Her and Zhen watched as Princen Alexis and Tatiana mounted their horses. The princen saluted, a grin spreading across their face. Then with a wink, they kicked their horse into motion. Tatiana waved, and then followed close behind.

"I am going to go to bed," Katya said once their rescuers

were out of sight. "This was a little too much excitement for me."

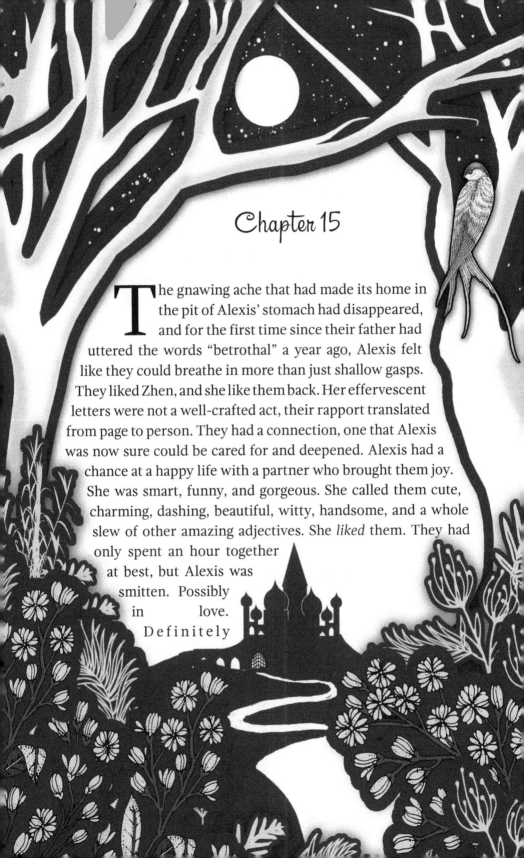

Chapter 15

The gnawing ache that had made its home in the pit of Alexis' stomach had disappeared, and for the first time since their father had uttered the words "betrothal" a year ago, Alexis felt like they could breathe in more than just shallow gasps. They liked Zhen, and she like them back. Her effervescent letters were not a well-crafted act, their rapport translated from page to person. They had a connection, one that Alexis was now sure could be cared for and deepened. Alexis had a chance at a happy life with a partner who brought them joy. She was smart, funny, and gorgeous. She called them cute, charming, dashing, beautiful, witty, handsome, and a whole slew of other amazing adjectives. She *liked* them. They had only spent an hour together at best, but Alexis was smitten. Possibly in love. Definitely over the moon.

They replayed some of those moments in their head as they headed out of the woods. "Oh, I am so bad at that dance! You will end up being better than me!" Zhen had said after Alexis explained how their father made them practice it every single day.

"I promise you, I have no rhythm at all. I can do fancy footwork with a sword, but I do not need to keep a beat to do that."

"I cannot do fancy footwork at all! And while I can keep a beat for music, that doesn't make up for being ungraceful. Your Highness, you will, without a doubt, perform better than I, and I will disgrace my country and shall have to become a recluse."

"I will not allow that. You are far too beautiful to hide away. Our future court would be much less merry without you there to lead them through revels. You will be our bright sun, and we the stars who orbit you."

"Your Highness is so eloquent."

"Being near you stirs in me the desire to impress."

But all those futures they imagined with her might never happen. They had found her, but she was still captive, and now they had to race home and put together a rescue effort against a powerful sorcerer. Alexis knew they were lucky that Zhen was not more heavily guarded, that there had no been traps and spells around the perimeter to keep her guarded. They could have been attacked by the sorcerer and the odds would not have favored them. Alexis and Tatiana bore no magic, and though Zhen could boast of exemplary glamour and illusions, they would still stand no chance.

"Alexis. Alexis! I asked you a question." Tatiana's voice roused them from their reverie.

"I am sorry, Tatiana. I was not paying attention."

"I noticed. We should stay the night here, get on the road tomorrow morning," Tatiana said as they approached Ignashino.

"The horses we left stabled here are fresh, we can take them.

We need to get back as soon as possible and let my father and his advisors know."

"Alexis, we need to sleep. These horses need a rest. We need to be smart about this."

"But we need to make sure my father and his advisors don't mobilize for war."

"Do you think your parents have figured out where you are at? What you are doing?" Tatiana raised an eyebrow at them.

Alexis rubbed the back of their neck and gave a sheepish laugh. "Probably."

"So, with that knowledge, do you think they would start anything before you came back?"

"Probably not."

"But what about Zhen, she can not just stay there!"

"Has the sorcerer harmed her?"

"Not yet."

"That companion of hers will keep her safe, if the sorcerer hasn't harmed her yet, he is unlikely to do so now."

"We do not know what he is after, though."

"No, but if he was after her death he would have done it already. So, we stay here for the night."

"You're always so responsible. I wish we had taken more time to think this through."

"What do you mean?"

"What if we had asked Lady Svetlana to come along? She's the best thaumaturge we have, she could have been helpful if we had run into this sorcerer. We were really defenseless in there against magic, if Katya had been a witch and not another prisoner? Or maybe Lairde Tanis could have come with us and broken the curse, xie is one of the best spellweavers in the kingdom. We could be riding back with Zhen right now."

"At first I thought we were up against bandits or thieves

looking to become rich with a ransom. I did not think this through much, either."

"I was so eager to prove my father wrong."

"I was eager to prove I was ready to be in the Czarina's Guard. We both messed up." Tatiana said as the neared the inn. "Would you like to go inside to make the arrangements or take these two horses to join the others?"

"The former," they said. Tatiana jumped down from her horse and waited while Alexis did the same. She took the reins of both and lead them behind the inn. Alexis rubbed their hands together and headed in. The white-haired innkeeper greeted them with a smile. "Did you have a productive day?"

Alexis tried to keep a smile on their face. "We did. For the time being, our business is finished. We could use a room for the night, some dinner, and separate baths. If it is no imposition, an early breakfast, too. We want to be on our way before the sun is up."

"I have some beef stroganoff; would that be all right?"

"That would be great for myself, but milk makes my companion sick. Do you have anything else for her?"

"I have beef pelmeni. Would that be all right for her?"

"That is perfect. Thank you so much."

"I will go warm up your dinners and send my spouse to bring up some warm water for your baths. Two rooms, correct?"

"That would be appreciated."

"Last two doors on the right." The innkeeper spun around and disappeared into the kitchen. Alexis sat down at the counter and began fiddling with the one of the rings they wore, pulling it out to the second knuckle and spinning it around and around.

They heard the door creak and turned to see Tatiana striding in. "Horses are happy. Where are our rooms?"

"Last two on the right."

"I am going to make sure they are secure. Save me some

food, will you?"

"Of course," they replied, thinking of how much they had asked Tatiana to take on. She was always looking out for them, and now they had lead her into danger.

The innkeeper reappeared. "Here you go, stroganoff and pelmeni. I found bread, too. It is a little stale, but I brought out some warmed butter if either of you want that."

"Much appreciated, thank you."

"My spouse is starting the warm water for you. There are extra blankets in your rooms, too. It's going to be a cold night."

Tatiana sat down just as the innkeeper retreated to the back, dragging the bowl of pelmeni toward her and plunging a fork into a warm dumpling. "Eat up. We are getting an early start tomorrow."

Chapter 16

Zhen had fallen asleep an hour ago, but Katya wanted to be sure before she made any movement. She crept out of her bed and tiptoed outside. She took a few tentative steps, expecting Zhen to follow her out and ask her where she was going. Once assured of her stealth, she ran. As she approached the edge of the clearing, she leapt into the air and became the black swan.

She was heading directly to her home with Ivan. Usually the wind under her wings calmed her, quieted her nervous mind, but instead, it only seemed to encourage her racing thoughts. She thought of what she would say to him, how she would explain what happened. She tried to think of his arms around her, his kisses on her forehead. She tried to think of how happy her life with him had been before the soldiers came through their forest. How easy it was before Ivan had told her there was a danger in their forest.

But Alexis' arrival this evening had surely proven that Zhen was simply a princess on her way to get married, not some malevolent threat.

She thought about all the words Zhen had used to describe Alexis. Zhen was infatuated. For hours after the princen and their companion had left, Zhen had done nothing but chatter about how elated she was that they tried to saved her and were going to try again, that they were as kind and considerate as they had sounded in their letters to her. She spent hours rambling to Katya about their many alluring qualities. Their eyes were the same enchanting shade as the forest leaves. Their hair, choppy and blonde, was as beautiful as the stars against the night sky. Their gait was confident, and they performed every action with charm. Their laugh was full and genuine. Zhen was anxious for their return with an army to battle against Ivan.

Or maybe Zhen had not been a threat before, but maybe she was now? Maybe not her, directly, but now there was potentially an army coming to avenge her or rescue her. There was no way to explain that holding a member of a royal family, soon to be a member of two royal families, was a mistake. It was treason, and she and Ivan had carried it out.

She wanted Zhen to be happy and free. Katya knew she could never provide Zhen with these things, not while she was with Ivan, and even if she left him, she had still deceived her too much to truly deserve her trust. There was no way she could be with Zhen and her captor, too. There was no way she could be with Ivan and his prisoner, too. And she had always been with Ivan. She loved him. She was falling for Zhen, yes, but she did not love her.

Maybe.

Ivan was waiting for her. She landed, her wings becoming outstretched arms, anticipating his embrace. But it did not come. He scowled, leaning against a tree, arms crossed.

"What's wrong?" Her arms fell to her sides, worry etched in her face.

"Katya," he spat out her name. "You would have, I thought I could trust you."

"Of course you can trust me. I'm here, am I not?" She took a step towards him, but he flinched away from her.

"To kill me? So you can free the princess?"

"What! No!"

"I saw you both. I watched you two kiss!" He approached her slowly, jabbing a finger in accusation.

"She asked me to! I had to play along. I tried telling her earlier that there was someone else but she asked too many questions! I could not risk her figuring me out. You said she was dangerous, what would you have had me do?" She backed away, desperate to put a tree or something else between them. Her stomach churned, and she could not ever remember him making her feel this way before: small, untrusted.

"So you did not betray me?" He stopped his approach. She was backed up against a tree, clinging to it as if it was something that could give her strength.

"Of course not! I've trusted you, even though you've given me little reason to. It's your turn to trust me. Whatever you saw, whatever you thought, it was not what it seemed. I am here." She collapsed to the ground, hunched over as tears fell to the soil, crystals being absorbed back into the earth. She clenched her fists into the dirt, determined to stop sobbing.

"I heard you plotting," he said, fists still clenched. Then he slouched, the fight going out of him. "I am sorry, Katya. I was not thinking. I was just so hurt. Can you forgive me? I will tell you everything. Please, Katya."

She gulped air, trying to stop the heaving in her chest. She tried to stand up and he was beside her, guiding her up and into his embrace. She melted into his arms. She could not stay mad at him. His anger was unjustified, even if she had told him the truth of her feelings for Zhen. The way he had acted toward her was uncalled for, but she still needed this embrace, someone to hold her.

He snapped his fingers and a sea of lanterns materialized above them. The sounds of the night reorganized themselves into something of a symphony. He stepped back from her, and she watched as his usual attire transformed into formal wear. It was still unearthly, still just this side of *wrong*, a hint of mischief and a dash of the macabre. His hair framed his face in a way that reminded her of his half-owl form, but with more polish.

He looked like an elf king, the ruler of these woods, capricious and carefree. His eyes telegraphed desire, smoldering embers veiled behind low lashes. She realized that the clothes she had been wearing were also gone, replaced by a deep red dress of crushed velvet that seemed to melt into the forest floor, and she felt a wreath of flowers on top of her head. She was his fairy queen.

He held out his hand and bowed to her. She took his hand and let him lead her. She gazed into his eyes and saw all of the faces that he had ever worn. The concern for her, the love for her, the wistful look when she caught him watching her pick flowers. But also the greedy way he looked at Zhen, the face he had worn when he had imprisoned her, and the face filled with contempt he had offered her mere moments earlier. She decided to not let those bother her. Not right now, not when all she wanted to do was forget that pain.

It made no sense to her sometimes, how he could make her feel like the only being on this earth. He had gained her trust with acts of consideration, kindness, and love. Making her favorite tea every night. Giving her a bouquet that never wilted. Setting up a hive of bees for her. Here he was, enchanting her all over again.

The lanterns were made to appear as if they were floating.

It was a dizzying effect, and Katya felt her heartbeat speed up, matching the tempo of the night music.

"I will give you the stars to wear. I will give you the night to make your cloak. I will tear the clouds from the skies to make your bed. I will make all of the animals bow before you. I will have the fish perform dances to bring you joy. Every day you will wake to the sun praising your name, and in the evening the twilight shall become your gown. Soon, Katya, when I am finished with this task, all of this shall be yours. We will live forever together, and our kingdom shall be safe."

The last word caused something to tug at her thoughts, something about Zhen and danger and Princen Alexis. But the dancing gave way to giddiness. The combination of the swimming music and dazzling lights made her forget it. The words Ivan whispered into her ears repeated themselves, floating across her mind and settling into some unconscious part of her soul. Every tender moment they had ever shared replayed in her head.

"Say you will never leave me," he asked.

The words rose to her lips before she could even think about them. "I will never leave you," she promised.

"Say you will never betray me."

"I never will."

They floated for what felt like hours, and her legs gave way, exhaustion catching up. He caught her in his arms, lifting her up to carry her, and then pressed his cheek against hers. With tenderness, he carried her into their cottage and set her down in her well-worn armchair. She curled up in it, pulling her feet up and resting her head on her knees.

"You must be so tired," he said as he put a kettle over the fireplace.

She nodded with a roteness that spoke of her habituation to her life with him. She curled up in her chair, he made her tea. There was a fondness in this routine, years of living with and caring for each other. The smell of her tea, of this cottage, made her feel as though she hadn't left it, hadn't been spending weeks in another cottage with another person.

"I am sorry I was cross with you earlier. That was uncalled for, and unfair. I let my anxiety get away from me."

She nodded, reflecting on his accusation and the glimmer of truth in it that she had denied. Her life had been in steady orbit around him, but she had been knocked off course and she was not sure how to correct it, or if she even wanted to. How had so much changed in so little time?

She let herself imagine a life she might share with Zhen, without Ivan, without Alexis, without fear of war or heartache. In this life, she did not have to confess to Zhen the part she had played in Zhen's captivity or explain her feelings to Ivan. Zhen did not have to deal with Alexis or her parents or anyone else who might ask her to consider her responsibilities. Katya imagined that the cottage they had conjured by the lake was their true home, where they kept bees and a garden and Katya would only leave, sometimes, to hunt for meat.

A warm mug was thrust into her face and she recoiled in surprise before realizing it was Ivan with her tea. She settled back into the world around her, dismissing her daydreams, letting the familiarity of her settings bring back her old habits.

"I came here to tell you something," she said. "I do not think that Zhen was actually a danger to us."

He sat down, leaning forward, elbows on his knees and his chin in his hands. "Why do you say that?"

"I think she was just passing through, I have detected no great magic from her, nor any plot. She does not behave like someone who would be here to hurt us. I think she just wants to leave and get married. Her plot to kill you earlier was just so that she could escape."

"Hmmm."

"Her betrothed came here, though, today. They planned a rescue, she told them about you. I think they will be coming back with an army."

"So she is a danger."

"She is *now*, well, her betrothed is, but I don't think she was when she came! You caused this! Neither of them would have hurt us if we had just let them pass through the woods. Why did you think she was a danger in the first place?"

He let out a long breath, leaning back in his chair, steepling his fingers in front of his face. "I have to be honest with you, Katya. I can not keep this from you anymore. I do not know how to start, though." He ran his hands through his hair. "You know, I was not born a sorcerer. I was a prince once, and I had an important mission. But more than that, I had a wife. A child. A family. My own brother murdered them, though I could never prove it. He was so afraid that my mission might turn our people against us that he took my family as a warning."

He paused, took off his glasses and setting them on the table between them.

"When my family was laid to rest, he had hoped I would bury my plans with them. I pressed on, though. I do not know how he did it, but he convinced our father that I was plotting against him—that I was working for an enemy. There was a trial, and he somehow produced evidence of my wrongdoing. I was sentenced to death, but my father spared me. Instead, I would live out the rest of my life in a dungeon."

Katya's mind reeled, the hurt and the pain palpable in the air. She had a suspicion about where this story would end, though. But had not the traitorous prince been killed? "Are you the traitor..." Katya began, but he held up a hand.

"I spent months being tortured. My brother would visit me, and upon my flesh he would carve a battlefield. I was fed spoiled meat, rotten vegetables, and sour milk. But I lived, and when the man in the cell next to mine asked if I wanted to escape, I told him yes."

He picked up his glasses again, inspected them for some blemish or spot, wiping them with his sleeve.

"He was a mage, and collected candle stubs, blood, and a knife in his years of imprisonment. I never asked him why he was imprisoned. But after we escaped, I did ask him how he had created the spell that freed us. He took me on as an apprentice, and we escaped to the north.

"I lived with him for 50 years in the frost and the cold. I learned during that time that there is more than one kind of snow. I learned how to keep warm, keep dry, and survive. But I also learned how to catch a falling star, how to call a wind, and how to translate the songs of the sirens who live among the glaciers in the northern seas."

Katya sipped her tea, wanting to interrupt, wanting to ask how this related at all the Zhen.

"One day, he told me he had taught me all that he could, and that afternoon, I packed my bags. I took all of my possessions and I created my own path. The whispers of aether took me back to the capital of the country I should have reigned over. I saw my brother's oldest daughter crowned, and then I stewed. The people had called my brother a tyrant, a king with no morals. He beheaded anyone he thought might be a political rival. Our father had been a distant claimant to the throne, and he had taken it on the battlefield. My brother was fearful of anyone with a better claim who might unseat him. His reign was a nightmare, and the people welcomed Catherine, his daughter, as a kind and compassionate ruler.

"No one recognized me. I collected gossip and rumors in

exchange for small spells and charms. I traded in books and scrolls and collected a respectable library. I watched my niece reverse the destructive policies my brother had implemented. Though she must have believed me dead, she did nothing to right my legacy, or any of the other people my brother had falsely imprisoned.

"Eventually I realized I would never get justice. That's how I ended up here, and, later, how I found you."

"How old are you?" If he was truly this prince from the past, he had to be more than a century old.

"How old are *you?*" He leaned forward, squinting at her.

Katya sat back, unsure what Ivan was trying to get at.

"Exactly," he said, leaning back again.

Katya was still confused, but decided this was not the conversation she wanted to be having right now. "I don't understand where Zhen fits into this."

"Katya, please." He looked into her eyes, and she held his gaze; unsure what he was asking her.

"Please, tell me, why is she a prisoner? Is this revenge?"

"It is not revenge," he said. "I heard about the engagement, and I found out about one of the conditions in the betrothal. Princess Zhen's parents asked that any threats to their line, anyone who might try to displace her children as heirs should be done away with. Anyone who might want to hurt the current royal family, the scions of my brother. That marriage, if it happens, well. I need to keep you safe."

"But you have done nothing to hurt them until now, and they can't know you are even alive."

"They should not, that is true. I have been looking into that. Her marriage is a threat to us."

"So what was the plan? Hold her here until the Lebedian royals give up? You had to have known they would come looking for her eventually."

"That was the plan. For them to come here."

"And then what?"

"Katya, please. I've asked so much of you. I know. Just trust me. I will keep you safe, we will be able to go back to the way things were soon. Forever."

"What were you planning on happening after they came looking for her here? Ivan, answer me. The princen came here today, with their bodyguard. Did you have a plan for that?"

"I did, I was ready to carry it out today but I changed my mind. There is a trap waiting for me, whoever the Czar has working for him is not a fool."

"What do you mean?"

"They know about me, I am certain of it, even before any of this happened. I need your help now."

"How do you know that?"

"There are whispers about us, in the nearby villages. You know this."

"But how do you know they know you are *you* and not just any other eccentric wizard in the woods? Before you kidnapped her, how would they have known you might be a threat?"

"I am not proud of this, Katya, but I have not always been so careful of concealing who I once was. I must have left clues, but they know. That day at Ignashino when I brought you flowers? There were soldiers and a mage, asking questions."

"That paper you threw into the fire?"

"The mage's orders from the Czar, I stole them. It mentioned who I was, possible spells I may have used to prolong my life, and where I may be."

"Why haven't they come here sooner?"

"I took care of them, I took care of them and made sure that no one thought this was a place I would be. But I fear that I need to ask you for help one more time, sweetheart."

"What?"

"I need you to sneak into the castle, find whatever mage they have and kill them. And then whoever might know about me, who I once was. I just want to live peacefully, here with you now."

"I can't do that, Ivan."

"They will find you, too. They will realize who you are eventually, and then you will be dead."

"I can not kill them."

"Please, Katya. Wait a few days to make sure the Princen is back home, then you can fly to the palace, disguise yourself as Zhen, and the guards will let you in. When you find the princen, you can tell them you escaped. You can find the mages who have been trying to find me, the Czar who knows I am still around. And the princen, too. And then you can kill them." He went to the bed they usually shared. He bent down and reached under the frame. He pulled out a small box, and Katya watched as he carefully lifted the lid and pulled out a slender knife, sheathed and attached to a leather belt. He carefully unsheathed it; it was engraved with symbols she did not recognize. But it seemed familiar, something tugged at the back of her mind, something telling her she should know this knife.

He came back over to her, his eyes never leaving the blade, his other hand holding the sheath and belt. He handed both over to her. "Use this when you do it."

"This sounds like revenge, Ivan," she said through gritted teeth, the knife resting in both of her palms. It felt heavier than it had any right to be.

"This is protection. Mistakes were made. This will ensure that no one will ever threaten me again, that there will always be someone to protect you."

"People will still come, both armies will still want Zhen, even if they don't know who you once were, even if there is no princen for her to marry," she stood up, stomping her foot and pointing to the north.

"I know. I intend for them to."

"How does that make us any safer?"

"Katya, trust me. Please." He put his arms around her shoulders, pulling her into an embrace.

"Why me? Why didn't you kill them when they were here?" She let him hold her, the knife warm between them. "Why can't you go kill the mages or whoever know who you are?"

"I was too distraught to be focused, I did not want to harm you accidentally when the Princen was here." He stroked her hair, winding his fingers around the ends. "And at the palace, the mages know what to look for. But you they will not recognize, you can slip in much easier than I could."

This was all too much for Katya. He promised things would go back the way they were before, but how could they when she had not known he was some ancient prince with a past of treachery and misery, and that now he wanted to spill more blood.

But who was she to hold that against him? He had not asked her to explain herself when he had found her. He had not questioned her when she said she did not know who or where she was or why. He did not probe, he just protected her. She was being honest when she said she did not know, but if she hadn't been? He probably still would have accepted her.

"If I do this, will you free Zhen?" she asked, pulling away from him, her words slicing through the heaviness that had settled in the room.

"Why?" He tilted his head to the side and narrowed his eyes in consideration.

"There will be no more marriage, no more clause that means your death, and no one left who would know you are alive. She will just know you were some sorcerer, she can go back home. Please."

"She will be released. I shall start trying to arrange for

transport back to her home. In the meantime, she will stay in my custody. No harm will come to her so long as she is in my protection."

"The armies, when they come, she can be given to them then?"

"Possibly. But she is in my protection."

Protection. Not captivity. She nodded, sheathing the knife and wrapping the belt around her waist.. She would do this for him, for Zhen, and for herself. Maybe, she thought, maybe Alexis did not know Ivan's history, maybe she wouldn't have to kill them at all. But either way, they would not be marrying Zhen. Maybe, she could protect Ivan and keep Zhen for herself. She could keep her part in all this a secret; she had already kept so many, what was one more?

Ivan pulled her into an embrace, stroking her long hair. Her cheek rested on his chest, her head fitting perfectly into the crook of his neck. She let him hold her, laying his burdens on her shoulders. "Thank you, thank you, Katya. I promise I will ask nothing else of you for the rest of our days," he whispered. Small convulsions of his body told her he was crying, and when the hot tears landed on her neck, she said nothing.

"It is late. You should head back to the lake before Zhen wakes up. You can head out tomorrow night. I am sure the princen and their companion cannot get home that quickly."

Katya made for the door, but Ivan caught her hand and spun her back around, again holding her close while he kissed her, his hand entwining with hers behind her back. His kiss was filled with a passion Katya had not felt from him since the days when they first tested the waters of their new romance.

She leaned into it, having missed intimacy and closeness since she had started this charade of being a prisoner. But before she could find what she was searching for, he pulled away. "You forgot to change," he said to her, and before she could say anything, she knew he had put her back in her earlier clothing. But the belt with the knife remained. She blushed, and hurried out the door.

She was so distracted that she almost stepped on a small tiger snake outside of the cottage. The snake reared up, its long neck coiled tightly, waiting to strike. She slowly backed away, and the orange-and-black–checkered snake eyed her suspiciously before settling back down. She kept walking.

"You can not leave here, Katya," a voice called to her from behind. She twirled around.

"Who is there?" she called, fear edging into her voice. Her skin prickled, and she felt as though there were a memory pulling at the edge of her mind, something from a dream that asked to be remembered. The snake was still there, staring at her. Tiger snakes were not aggressive, but they were venomous.

She kept walking until she was sure her transformation would not end with her becoming a meal for a snake, and then she took flight, keeping low to the tree line. Gliding downwards into the clearing around the lake, Katya saw Zhen sitting on the ground, her legs extended so that her toes touched the water.

Katya saw the very last sliver of the moon in the skies. It would be a new moon in a few days.

She landed in the water, searching for the sliver of silver moonlight reflected on the ripples of water. She swam toward it, and then her black wings flung back as she put on a show for Zhen. She emerged from a vortex of feathers and dew, a black satin dress hemmed in crimson clinging to her hips and pooling at her feet.

"You left me alone," was all Zhen said.

Katya approached her slowly, unsure what to expect. "I am here now," Katya said, a gentle plea in her voice.

"Where did you go?" There was a hint of the faraway in her words, a listlessness that scared Katya. She scrambled for an explanation that would appease Zhen.

"I wanted to make sure that the princen and Tatiana made

it out of the forest without trouble." Katya held her breath, waiting for Zhen to spot the lie.

"And did they?"

"They seemed to be safely on their way. I didn't want to wake you. I'm sorry I left without telling you."

"I do not know what to do," she said. Katya had been hoping that she had said the right thing, that knowledge of the princen's safety would bring Zhen back, ground her. Instead she seemed even further away.

"Do about what?" Katya gathered her dress and sat down next to Zhen. She crossed her legs and reached behind her to rest her weight on her palms. The stars were bright, with barely a moon to outshine them. She listened to the sounds of the night while waiting for Zhen to answer her, the same sounds that had been the orchestra to her and Ivan's *pas de deux* earlier.

"The princen is very charming, and in time I know I could come to love them. There was a current that ran between us. My dreams were reflected back in their eyes." Her voice crescendoed as she spoke each word. An air of certainty settled around her but could not quite beat back the fey mood Katya had found her in. The heaviness of that distance coalesced, and Katya knew there was something she was holding back, some part of her heart she could not bring herself to examine.

"But there is something keeping you from running to this future."

"Yes. But this is the path I must walk." She stood up and trudged to their cabin.

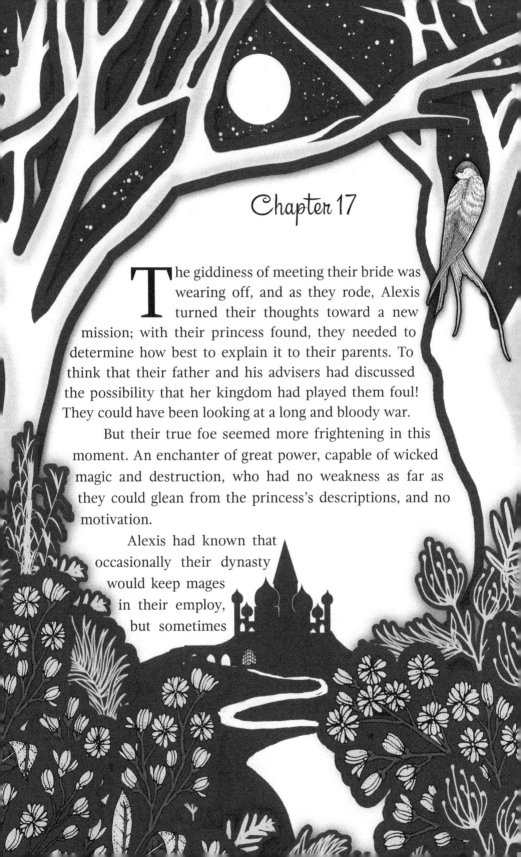

Chapter 17

The giddiness of meeting their bride was wearing off, and as they rode, Alexis turned their thoughts toward a new mission; with their princess found, they needed to determine how best to explain it to their parents. To think that their father and his advisers had discussed the possibility that her kingdom had played them foul! They could have been looking at a long and bloody war.

But their true foe seemed more frightening in this moment. An enchanter of great power, capable of wicked magic and destruction, who had no weakness as far as they could glean from the princess's descriptions, and no motivation.

Alexis had known that occasionally their dynasty would keep mages in their employ, but sometimes those mages turned traitorous and were burned. There had been ancestors of theirs that had banned the practice of magic, but it had been legal for some time now. No one alive today had been alive during those times to hold a vendetta for that. After sharing their news, they would have to scour the library for any information they could find and speak with some of the mages their father now kept on their council. Leading an army with no knowledge of their foe would be reckless. Alexis had to prove to their kingdom and their bride that they were responsible.

Tatiana held up a hand, indicating that it was time to rest the horses and to relieve themselves. Alexis slowed their horse, helping Tatiana look for a good place to rest. They pointed toward a cove of trees in the distance that would provide some nice shade. Tatiana nodded, and they both made their way over. Alexis arrived first and swung down, searching through their bag for bread.

"What did you think of the other one?" Tatiana asked as she dismounted.

"The other one what?" Alexis asked as Tatiana rolled her eyes.

"The other captive, Katya. What did you think of her?"

"I guess I had not given her much thought," Alexis admitted.

"She was odd." Tatiana pursed her lips as she opened a canteen. "She also seemed a little uncertain of you and protective of the princess."

"They have been through a lot together, it sounds like."

"Maybe that's what it was," Tatiana said, and shrugged before making her way behind some bushes.

"What was what?" Alexis asked, carefully turning their back to those bushes.

"It seemed to be more intense than that."

"Tatiana, what are you trying to say?"

"I think they might have fallen for each other."

Alexis chewed on their lip, considering this line of reasoning. Two people, trapped together with no one else. It was possible. They tried to be unphased by this. They knew that they were being genuine when flirting with her; she gave them a fluttering feeling that broke through their usual suaveness and left them bereft of words. They thought Zhen was just as genuine in her affections. Alexis and Zhen were betrothed for politics, but while their wedding was a matter of state, what lived within their marriage was entirely their choice. Alexis hoped that they could find a way to love and happiness. Zhen's affections for another should not detract from how she might feel for Alexis, but a pang of jealousy still gnawed at them.

"I am all right with that," Alexis said, trying to be convincing, as Tatiana came back from behind the bushes.

"I think she is hiding something, too."

"What makes you say that?" Alexis said.

"She seems to live near those woods. With all the locals telling us to stay away, it is a bit odd that she was in them voluntarily."

"You think she knows something? Something she is not telling us?"

"Probably."

Alexis nodded, Tatiana was rarely wrong about a hunch.

***

Zhen was already awake and dressed when Katya stirred. Katya leaned up on her elbow and craned her neck to see her sitting in a chair near the hearth, nursing a mug of tea.

"Good morning," Katya called to her as she threw off the blankets. Katya walked over to the hearth and sat on a small woven rug at Zhen's feet. "I'm sorry for leaving you alone last night. I should have at least told you I was leaving to check on the princen instead of sneaking off like that."

Katya watched as Zhen's chest rose and fell, her eyes shut tight. When Zhen opened her eyes, Katya knew that whatever she said next would not be easy to hear.

"Her name was Mei." Zhen tilted to her head to the side, focusing on some point in front of her, something only she could see. Her breathing was slow and even, her cadence clear. "She made my heart sing with adventure. I wrote songs for her. I dedicated every piece of art I constructed to her name."

Zhen looked up at Katya. "I know I can never be with her, and even if I could, I do not think we would have been able to make it work. But I can never pretend that I did not love her, and I cannot pretend that I will ever stop. I came here knowing that I would carry her with me, and one love lost is not so huge a burden to take to a marriage bed. Many people do it. But Katya, I did not want to take two." As the last words left her mouth, she bolted up and dashed from the cabin.

The confession sunk into Katya's mind. She recognized the conflict in Zhen's voice, the confusion she had about her predicament, and the battle that must have played out in her head as she sat alone on the edge of the lake, a conflict that could have no happy ending. Katya knew it because it was the same battle she fought every moment of every day since she first realized how she felt about Zhen. The part of her that longed for a life eternal full of magic and enchantment with Ivan pitted against the one that dreamed of a quiet life of love and contentment with Zhen.

But Katya knew that both of their private battles had an eventual victor. The lives of too many people relied on her and Zhen never having more than this handful of days together. She knew what she had to do to ensure she had a chance at a life with Ivan, and the same action would free Zhen of her obligation to Lebedia. Would war still come, she wondered, if the princen was dead and the princess had vanished?

She stood up, tossed a fistful of threads into the fire, and made her way outside, finding Zhen sitting in a similar position to the one she had found her in last night.

"I am sorry, I should not be putting this on you." Zhen said, hiding her face in her arms.

"I don't mind."

"I keep trying to think of ways that we could make this work. Alexis told me that they have three parents, that their mother has another partner. But she is a noble, and I do not know how well Lebedia would take take the news. Would they think I was somehow not as committed to peace? Alexis's parents are all Lebedian, with no loyalty to prove."

"I can't leave here, Zhen." Katya did not know why she said those words, but something flitted across her mind, something that elusive and slippery. The same something that was there when she thought about who she was, where she came from. The words had nothing to do with loyalty to Ivan or an aversion to castles. It was something wholly and uniquely hers. And she couldn't figure out what it was. "But I do understand, Zhen. Do you think we could try to cherish each other while we have the time?"

Zhen's face was covered in tears, and she held up an arm to wipe them away. Katya caught her arm, blotting her tears with cloth. A small smile formed on Zhen's lips as Katya assisted her, and she reached out to grab Katya's free hand. "I think I would like that," Zhen said.

Katya placed the cloth back in her pocket and pulled Zhen into an embrace. For a moment, she wondered if Ivan was watching, but she decided she did not care. They were the last days she would have with Zhen with only a tarnished conscience. That evening she would have to do terrible things to save Ivan. She should be allowed to have a small moment of contentment with the woman she loved, in exchange.

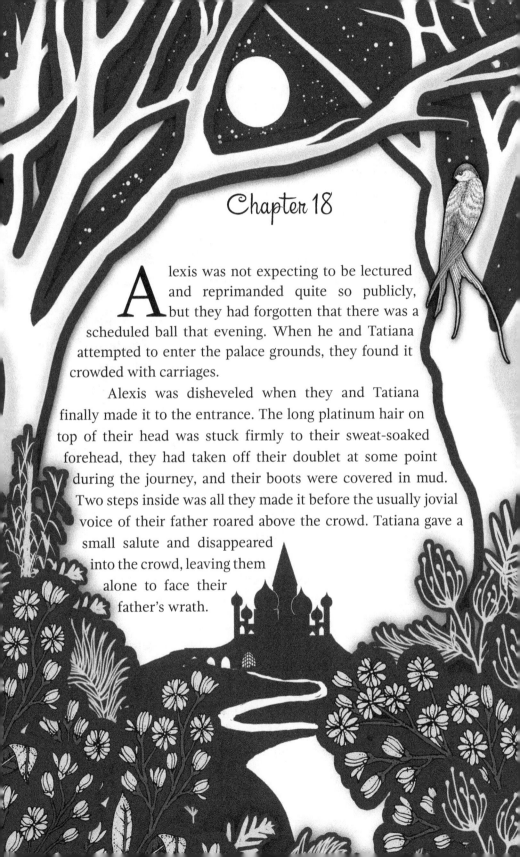

Chapter 18

Alexis was not expecting to be lectured and reprimanded quite so publicly, but they had forgotten that there was a scheduled ball that evening. When he and Tatiana attempted to enter the palace grounds, they found it crowded with carriages.

Alexis was disheveled when they and Tatiana finally made it to the entrance. The long platinum hair on top of their head was stuck firmly to their sweat-soaked forehead, they had taken off their doublet at some point during the journey, and their boots were covered in mud. Two steps inside was all they made it before the usually jovial voice of their father roared above the crowd. Tatiana gave a small salute and disappeared into the crowd, leaving them alone to face their father's wrath.

"Alexis, I know you despise dancing, but you cannot keep trying to get out of these formal events! You and I need to talk!" He laughed, an act for the gathered crowd.

"Where is mother?"

"She is with Nataliya. She will want to talk to you, too!"

"I found Princess Yi Zhen!" Alexis whispered into their father's ear.

"That's not a good enough excuse," he roared and slung his arm over Alexis' shoulder and turned to face the crowd. "Please, continue dancing! I need to make sure my wayward child is properly dressed!"

He turned back to Alexis, a crease forming on his forehead as he leaned on his cane. He called for a page. "Fetch the Czarina and Lady Nataliya and ask them to meet me and Princen Alexis in my rooms. Tell Princess Olga that she should take care of the official ceremonies and greetings in our absence." The Czar turned and walked toward the stairs, some of the crowd craning their necks to see how much trouble the wayward heir was in this time. Alexis followed behind him until they reached the stairs and their father sat down in his automated chair, a gift from a foreign wizard many years ago. He pushed a small button and the chair lifted him up alongside Alexis. They journeyed to the Czar's rooms together in silence.

"I did not sanction you going out on your own to find her. I have had to make so many excuses for you here while you were gone. We have been so worried."

"I know, father." Alexis took a seat at a large round table and ran a handkerchief through their hair to dry it and make themself look presentable. While Lady Natalyia was not their mother, she still acted just as much the part with Alexis as she did with her own daughters, Princesses Olga, Anya, Daria, and Elena. Alexis knew they were in for another round of scolding from their mothers.

A guard opened the door and announced their mother and her lover. The rustle of silk was all that was needed to alert Alexis to their presence, the guard was superfluous. The second most cherished couple in the kingdom entered hand in hand. The Czarina dropped her lover's hand and ran to Alexis, embracing them while she berated them for arriving to the ball late, for being dirty, for going missing, for dragging Tatiana into this, and for making the Lady Natalyia sick with fear.

Alexis extracted themself from their mother's arms, only to find themself looking directly into the teary eyes of Lady Natalyia. She threw herself at them, tears leaking onto their shoulders.

"I am sorry!" they cried out as they tried to duck out of the embrace. "This is really important though. The princess was kidnapped, and we need to save her!"

"Alexis," their mother said as she took a seat next to the Czar, "we have already discussed this."

"No, let them explain," their father said, taking the Czarina's hand in his own. She laid her head to rest on his shoulder, and Lady Natalyia came from behind to rest her hands on the Czarina's shoulders.

Alexis looked at his parents. They were so secure in their love for each other. Even though they annoyed them sometimes, they were glad to have them as parents. They hoped that they could navigate situations half as well as their three parents had done when they were married to Princess Zhen. But they had to rescue her, first.

They took a deep breath and recounted their adventure. When they neared the end of the saga, they steeled themself for the request they were about to make. "I would like to request an elite company of a dozen of our best soldiers to confront the sorcerer and free Princess Zhen."

"Alexis, do you remember the condition in the betrothal

agreement about eliminating any threats?"

Alexis pursed their lips, their suspicions confirmed. "Are you saying you knew about this sorcerer?"

"Mikhail, no," the Czarina said.

"They should know, we cannot keep this from them anymore. Alexis, we did know. But we did not want that information getting out. I should have let you know earlier. I did not think you would run off, and you had no idea what you were running into. You could have gotten hurt, I am so glad you are not injured."

"Who is this sorcerer and what does he want?"

"He has a very long standing grudge with our family."

"So, you did not think Shān played us wrong? You knew it was this sorcerer?"

"No, I did not think they played us wrong. I suspected it was the sorcerer, but I could not let word of this sorcerer get out, nor could I risk it getting back to Shān that I had not been successful in our end of the bargain."

"And the meeting with the advisors where you said nothing about the sorcerer?"

"The meeting with the advisors was for show. I met with the Mages' Council immediately after to discuss this. They've been working on this issue for some time now, but with no headway."

"Did they think he might be in those woods? Why was that the route she took?"

"We chose the routes for her and her decoys based on their survey of his suspected locations. They did not think he was hiding in that forest."

"If he is so powerful that he can conceal his location from our best mages, then we need to fight him with everything we have."

"You are right, I think it is time we confront this sorcerer directly. Shān has figured out that the princess has not arrived. They know we were unable to hold up our end of the bargain, not about the sorcerer, but that we were not able to protect her. They have troops lining the border now."

"So we save her and kill the sorcerer! We need an army!"

"An army will not work, I fear." The Czar shook his head and looked down at his hands.

"Why not?"

"He could kill them all very easily, he would hear their approach and decimate them before they even enter the woods."

"We could provide them with some of the Czarina's Guard, perhaps? And some of the mages who are not men? Disguised." Lady Natalyia said, glancing at her lover.

"That might work, yes. They are near silent, lethal, and cunning. I do not think they would be suspected of being a menace, especially if they were dressed as ladies, and not assassins," the Czarina agreed.

"Precisely," the Lady Natalyia continued. "You and Tatiana could pretend to be an escort for a group of ladies en route to some formal event in Shān. We can have carriages ready for you tomorrow."

Alexis nodded, making small mental adjustments to the plan to account for what they already knew of the situation. "That sounds reasonable. I would like three dozen of mother's guard, then. While they should be dressed for a formal event, they should also have plenty of concealed weapons and clothing roomy enough to maneuver on uneven ground."

"I will see to the preparations tonight after the ball," their mother said. "But tonight, you should be at the ball, dressed in your best. We can not let knowledge of this plan slip."

"Yes," the Czar said. "I will consult with the Mages' Council. The best of them shall be accompanying you. You should go dance, we do not want to raise any more suspicion among people who do not need to know."

Alexis bowed to their parents and left the Czar's chambers. Tatiana leaned against the wall outside, arms folded over her chest. She was wearing her ceremonial dress, a doublet complete with broach and epaulets, her hair in a braided crown around her head. She righted herself and followed the princen down the hall to their rooms.

"What is the plan?" she asked as they made their way from the princen's chamber to their dressing room. They pulled out their own formal attire from a chest of drawers and began to change behind a small screen.

"You and I are going to take a group of court ladies to a formal event tomorrow."

"That does not sound like a plan." She scowled at their back.

"Well, it will be an event, and those ladies are from the Czarina's Guard and a few mages."

"Ah, that's more like it. Are you in charge of this mission?"

"I am. I do not suppose you would like to be my second?"

"Not to distract from the importance of rescuing your bride, but being second in command of a mission involving the Czarina's Guard? This is the chance to prove myself. This is my chance to see how I like it, and show that my success is not because of my mother. We will save your bride!" She clasped her hands together and twirled around the room for a few minutes, thrusting a ceremonial sword as she dueled imaginary foes.

"I knew you would be enthusiastic!" Alexis came out from behind the screen wearing a shiny black double-breasted doublet trimmed in red, with flashy ruby epaulets, and a white rose corsage pinned on the left. They wore a short pleated skirt over pressed black trousers, and their hair was a mess of platinum spikes spilling over their forehead. Tatiana whistled. "This is hopefully the last ball where you'll have to deal with a line of people wanting the next dance. At least, I certainly hope so. Do you know how hard it is to maintain an orderly queue?"

Alexis laughed and went to the chest at the foot of their bed, opening it to take out their own ceremonial sword. They buckled the belt around their waist and then took one last look in the mirror, winking to themself before spinning on their heel to offer Tatiana their arm. "Shall we?"

They led Tatiana out of their rooms and around to the grand staircase. "Vladimir, mind announcing me and Sir Tatiana?" they asked the page near the staircase. The page nodded and headed out from behind the curtain to announce them.

"You look good," Tatiana said to them.

"So do you," Alexis replied.

As the page made the announcement, Alexis and Tatiana stepped out from behind the curtain in unison. Alexis raised their hand to greet the courtiers and then descended the staircase with Tatiana on their arm. They reached the bottom to a round of applause.

Alexis was immediately greeted by people of all genders vying for their attention, asking for the first dance, or the second, or the third. Alexis lost count, and Tatiana helped shoo away some of the more persistent pursuers while Alexis scanned the crowd for their siblings. They found all of their siblings save one accounted for on the ballroom floor.

As if on cue, they heard a page cry out, "May I announce, Her Royal Highness, Princess Olga of Lebedia." They smiled up at their favorite sibling and watched her descend the stairs. They caught her eye, and she gave a smile and a wink that spoke of secrets shared over many years.

"What are you grinning about?" they asked, offering their hand to her as she reached the last step.

"You will see."

The trumpet blared again, and Alexis looked up to see who

would be announced next.

"May I present Her Royal Highness, the Princess Yi Zhen of Shān."

Chapter 19

Zhen was working on small embroidery project. She had wished earlier for the supplies and eagerly began working on a design that Katya could only guess at. Katya set a mug of tea in front of Zhen and then sat down beside her, pulling her shawl over her shoulders.

"Let that cool for a few minutes," Katya instructed. "It should help you sleep, though." Zhen nodded, hardly noticing Katya's presence, squinting at the cloth she held close to her face.

Katya looked around, unsure of what to do with herself while waiting for Zhen to go to bed and fall asleep. For the last few days they had taken to pushing their two beds together, sleeping in each others arms. It was dusk, but the sky still held the warmth of the sunset. The stars were beginning to twinkle in the sky, but there would be no moon joining them tonight. Zhen absently sipped at her tea and continued to work her needle and thread.

Katya contemplated how she would know where to fly, how she would disguise herself, and how she would manage to kill the princen and several mages alone. She tried not to think of her other options. She was doing this for Zhen, and Ivan. She was doing this so that should could have a future with them both alive.

"I think I shall retire for the evening," Zhen said as she set her project down and stood up. "Goodnight kiss?" she asked. Katya obliged, leaning forward for a deep kiss. Zhen eventually straightened and took a long drink of her tea, her eyes still focused on Katya over the rim of the mug. Then she made her way to her bed, her gown trailing on the floor behind her.

Katya waited until she heard the even breathing of sleep, and then slipped outside. She bespelled the dagger, affixing it with a strap to her leg. It would still be there when she became herself again, just as her clothing and other items normally would.

A snake rose in front of her, stretching out so that half of its long body was vertical in front of her. It was the same tiger snake from earlier. The tingle of magic under her skin said the snake might be more than that, though. Katya backed away slowly, maintaining eye contact with the serpent as she did so.

"Daughter, you cannot leave the forest. " The voice seemed to both come from everywhere and nowhere. It was deep and commanding, but soft and reassuring at the same time. Katya searched for the source of the voice. The snake wobbled back and forth, taking a stance that almost looked as if it was about to strike, it's long neck weaving back and forth on itself. Katya stared back at it, wondering if it was truly a snake.

"Daughter, please listen." The snake lowered itself, still staring at her, but no longer tense.

"I am listening," she replied, looking at the snake. Precious seconds were slipping away, but she felt compelled to stay and hear out whatever wanted her to listen. The snake slithered to a tree stump, and climbed on top of it.

"You cannot leave the forest," the snake said, coiling itself into a puddle of scales on the stump. The words Katya had told Zhen a few days ago slid across her mind. *I can't leave here.*

"But I need to go to Kristallicheskiy."

"You should not."

"Why not?"

"You will die if you do." The snake coiled on the ground, its head in the middle, looking up at her.

"Who are you?" Katya squinted at the snake.

"I am the voice of the forest, for now."

"Why are you telling me this? How do you know I would die if I left?"

"I gave birth to you, in that lake."

"A snake? I am the daughter of a snake?"

"You are the daughter of the forest. Many years ago, I felt myself dying, my life force being siphoned away. You were born to find the creature that was slowly killing me. In your birth, you were bound to me, your life is sustained by me. To leave here is to cut off your veins from the blood that should run in them."

"What do you mean?" It was so much, at once. She had always wanted answers, she wanted to be all right with not knowing, too. Here were her answers, but they made little sense. Every moment of her life where she had felt that strange sense of both knowing something and not, every day she had tried to figure out where she came from and every day she tried to act like she did not need to know all jumbled in her head at once.

"You might have guessed that you were not entirely human," the voice said, laced with sorrow. "We are not entirely sure when it started, but we realized that new trees were not taking root, that our birds' clutches were smaller, that winter was coming earlier, and that young trees were dying. There is an ebb and flow to the life of a forest, but this could not be accounted for."

"So why did you think I could figure it out?"

"We needed someone who could better investigate the source of our slow death. So we created you. We birthed you in this lake under the full moon. We watched as you took your first breath, as you opened your eyes. Our first child, our most precious child. We hoped that you might find the cause of this poison and root it out. Human eyes, with the ability to communicate directly with other humans."

"Why have you not told me this before?"

"We wanted to tell you, but shortly after you were born, you disappeared. We could not find you."

"I have been right here. I've always been here."

"We see that now, but something was hiding you from us. Only recently have we been able to locate you. Something changed, and we could sense you again. We tried to speak to you a few nights ago, too."

"Do you know how much this has torn me up? Not knowing?" Katya's chest felt tight, she took several steps forward, getting within inches of the snake. "I thought I was abandoned, an orphan. I thought I was an aberration that should not even exist. And now you tell me I have some mission that I must fulfill? As if I don't have other concerns, other worries, other battles I need to fight?"

The snake stared at her.

"I don't have time for this. I have to get to Kristallicheskiy." She stormed past the snake.

"As our protector, you are bound to this forest. You can leave, but you will slowly fade away. No more than a day would you survive outside this forest."

"Then I suppose I will have to make this quick," she snapped.

"Should the forest die, so will you. We do not think we have much longer."

Katya hesitated. No matter how mad she felt, the prospect of their linked demise stirred fear in her. But, she had to leave. She had to address the matter at hand.

"I will be back," she said, leaping into the sky. She tried not to think of the conversation she had just had. She wanted to fly to Kristallicheskiy and focus on completing her task. She would come back, but not because some spirit of the forest had asked her to. She would return because she needed to be back before Zhen woke up.

She had allowed herself to fantasize in private moments about meeting her parents, being reunited, knowing where she came from. But never in her wildest dreams had she imagined a tiger snake telling her she was created by the forest. She had envisioned a sorceress for a mother, maybe a *leshy* for her father. But the forest proper?

No, she had other matters to attend to now. She couldn't just drop everything because a snake claimed the forest had birthed her and needed her help. She sped up, enhancing her natural flight ability with magic. She forced thoughts of her encounter out of her mind.

There was no moon to guide her flight, but she knew the stars as if they were embedded into her own skin, a map of flesh and fire. Ahead, Kristallicheskiy appeared on the horizon. A dark outline of the onion-domed cupolas danced against the skies as their gilt ornaments reflected the scattered starlight. The large gate of the city appeared, and she caught the attention of a guard as she soared past it.

She neared the palace itself, a spectacular structure with minarets and gold and red onion domes, around each of which was a swirl of filigree molding. She landed in a dense garden filled with bushes, vines, and small trees. There was a stone path that seemed to lead further into the garden in one direction, and towards a small pond in the other. She carefully sought the well of magic at her core to transform back into her human form. The well took longer to find, and its contents seemed shallow. But she had just flown farther than she ever had before, and attributed it to exhaustion.

She conjured an image of Princess Yi Zhen as she had been when they first met. A muted but elegant hairdo of buns and jewels and hair sticks. An *aoqun* with a pleated skirt made of white silk, hemmed in gold, embroidered with dragons dancing at the lower hem. The jacket was yellow with embroidered fiery swirls and encrusted with small burnt-orange gems.

She focused on the outfit first, letting the details settle over her, her own clothing changing to match. Her hair followed suit, darkening, straightening, and tying itself up into a high bun, ornaments appearing to adorn it. She shifted her attention to her figure. She her body tightened, becoming a little shorter and much thinner. Her thighs, stomach, and arms all shrank in circumference as she shifted focus to her facial features. Her lips became small lines, and her nose and chin acquired a pertness that Katya thought suited Zhen very well, and her pale eyes took on a deep brown that was speckled with gold.

Katya examined her magical workings, pushing aside the weakness in her knees, the tremors in her hands, and the unevenness of her breath. She had to finish this, then she could go home and recover. She grinned at a job well done as she held the fine fabrics of her disguise in her hands. She then considered that her ruse relied on her having traveled here on her own, and rubbed a few smudges of dirt into the hem of her *aoqun*, and mussed her hair a little.

Her disguise finished, she marched toward the front entrance. Her steps were awkward as she adjusted to such a small body. She was used to taking up much more space, and she enjoyed having a large presence. Now she felt as if she could easily be overlooked. The clothing was not such a huge change from what she was accustomed to, but there were several more layers than she preferred.

Nevertheless, she made it to the grand entrance without catastrophe. As she approached, the guards watched her, clearly leery of an uninvited guest. She swept a low curtsy to them, and as she rose she saw curiosity in their gazes. "Good evening. I am expected by the royal family, although they were hoping I would arrive with an escort. My carriage was attacked while we were traveling, and I was lucky to escape unharmed. I am the Princess Yi Zhen. Would you assist me?"

"Your Highness, there is a ball taking place. I will escort you to Princess Olga, who is currently overseeing its details," the shorter guard said.

"I appreciate that, thank you." She followed him through the doors, keeping her hands at her side and trying not to trip. She was soon brought before a woman with platinum hair that matched Alexis' in color, but was worn in tight ringlets that cascaded to her hips. She was taller than Alexis, but shared many of the same facial features. She had high cheekbones, a square jaw, and large steely-gray eyes; a small tiara was perched on her head, her curls woven into it.

Katya curtsied to the woman who she guessed was Princess Olga. The curtsy was returned, but with more flare and grace, leaving Katya certain her ruse would be found out.

"Welcome, my future sister. I was under the impression that you were missing, possibly captured, and would be unable to attend tonight." It was not phrased as a question, but Katya knew it was one.

"That is true, but myself and a fellow captive were able to break free. I have traveled far to be here tonight."

Princess Olga considered her words for a moment, her lips pressed together in concentration. "I am glad you are safe now.

Would you like to use my rooms to freshen up? Then we can have someone announce you for your official entrance to our court."

Katya nodded and followed Princess Olga down the hall, the guards returning to their post. She tried not to stare, mouth agape, as she passed large portraits, golden light fixtures, and crystal chandeliers. She was supposed to be a princess, born into this sort of splendor, after all.

They reached Princess Olga's rooms, Katya was convinced she could not begin to find her way out after traveling so many winding hallways and staircases. The princess threw open her doors without waiting for her anyone to do it for her.

"Here, this way," Princess Olga said, smiling at Katya in a way that was reassuring. She led Katya through a small door. A gorgeous vanity sat inside this new room, a highly polished silver mirror hanging above it. Gesturing to the chair in front of the vanity, Princess Olga said, "Sit! We can get you fixed up in no time."

Katya took a seat, her stomach a ball of angry bees. Picking up a brush, Princess Olga began smoothing her hair out, moving pins slightly, rearranging some of the ornaments. Next, she took a cloth to Katya's face, removing dirt smudges and adding a layer of light powder. "This will not match your skin tone exactly. I have blue undertones, and you seem to have pink. But I will keep it pretty sheer and blend it well."

Katya could not even nod in acknowledgment, fearful that the brush would end up in her eyes. She did not know what the princess was talking about, anyway. Princess Olga kept applying different powders with various brushes, and Katya watched as her friend's face disappeared and something different emerged. The powders created the illusion of rounder cheeks, fuller lips, and a thinner nose. She was not sure she liked the effect.

Princess Olga then had her stand up as she took a wet cloth to the hem of her *aoqun,* trying to get the dirt out of the hem.

"I am an entirely different size than you—taller and wider. You would drown in one of my gowns, otherwise I would offer one of mine. I am a handy seamstress, but I could not get one fitted for you this quickly. Just have to make do, I suppose."

"I would prefer to wear this, anyways. I would like to remind people of where I am from, what this marriage symbolizes." Katya said the words, hearing Zhen's voice behind her own. She knew Zhen would want to face the new court as herself. As much as was possible.

Princess Olga nodded, a smile lighting up her whole face. "I knew I would like you. I hope that if I end up in a state marriage, I am half as brave as you."

Laughter welled up in Katya's throat, and she let it explode out of her.

"I am being serious!" Princess Olga put her hands on her hips, taken aback by the outburst.

"My apologies, I just do not see how I am brave."

"You rescued yourself from brigands or bandits and came all the way here on your own. That must take bravery."

Katya looked away, shame burning on her face. She was not brave. She was taking the cowardly way out. She was using magic and deception to secure what she coveted. But her shame was mistaken for humility and modesty.

"I really am not, but I know you will be," Katya replied, realizing that this princess might be the one to become the new heir apparent when this night was through. Katya stared at herself in the mirror, Princess Olga standing behind her. "I am ready now."

"Come with me. I shall have you announced officially."

The princess and the pretender made their way through the deserted halls, not even an errant maid or servant to acknowledge them as they made their way to the grand staircase. Katya tried to memorize the faces staring back at her from the portraits in gilded frames that hung on the walls and tried to follow the weave of the tapestries that took up the space the portraits did not occupy. Depictions of maidens welcoming creatures of myth and magic, knights engaging their foes, elven kings presiding over revelries, marches of the forest *leshy*, and many other scenes stopped in time to adorned the walls.

Katya stared at some of them intently, trying to discern whether the imaginings of mortals matched the true magic. The *leshy* were not nearly so tall as these weavings portrayed them, and the sirens were a thousand times more beautiful. The dragon of the lake was smaller, but with longer teeth. The *qilin* was actually a two-horned beast, and burned a brighter blue.

"Beautiful, are they not? I am supposed to be working on one of my own with the help of my ladies-in-waiting. I do not have even the slightest idea of what I want to portray yet. Maybe you can help me?" Tilting her head, Katya looked up at Princess Olga, pondering what the Princess Yi Zhen would say. She was certain what her friend would say, but not how she would respond in an official capacity.

"I should like that," Katya responded after a brief hesitation. Her smile was genuine, if weak, as she made eye contact with Princess Olga.

"Excellent!" Princess Olga clasped her hands together and nearly jumped with excitement. Katya wondered if Princen Alexis was actually related to this princess, as their natures seemed opposed to each other. The quiet reserve of Alexis made them seem aloof, whereas Princess Olga wore her emotions freely.

"I believe your princen has already been announced. I cannot wait to see their face as you make your way down the staircase. The whole court is waiting for you."

Katya realized they were in front of a large red curtain of crushed velvet. A small guard, probably actually a page or squire, stood next to it, braided gold cord in hand. "This is Her Royal Highness, the Princess Yi Zhen of Shān. Please announce me first, and she will follow behind." The guard nodded, and then walked in front of the curtain.

A trumpet blared. "May I announce, Her Royal Highness, Princess Olga of Lebedia." The curtain parted in the middle and Princess Olga stepped out in front of it. Katya tried to watch her form, her step, how she held her head, how she seemed to float as she took a few steps forward. She gave a small wave and then descended the stairs. Craning her head to watch, Katya tried to figure out how Princess Olga was maintaining her posture without tripping down the stairs.

The curtain closed and Katya waited.

"May I announce, Her Royal Highness, the Princess Yi Zhen of Shān." She tried to imitate the grace of Princess Olga by keeping her upper body still, abdominal muscles straining to hold her steady. She reached the edge of the stairs and waved, giving a small smile to the crowd.

She was not sure if she was unconsciously blocking out sounds or if the crowd had truly gone quiet. Everyone seemed stopped in time, and she felt as if she were the only one moving through it. Step-by-step, she descended the staircase. She tried to keep her gaze just above everyone's head. But as she neared the bottom, a face came into view.

Princen Alexis was staring at her, their mouth hanging open, eyes wide with shock. She set her feet down on the floor and thunderous applause broke loose. The musicians played a fast waltz, and she watched as couples formed and people paired off.

The princen bowed low, and as they rose extended their hand toward her. "My lady, I did not expect to see you here tonight. I had no intention of dancing, for no other partner could have pleased me as much as you. And here you are. I must ask: may I have this dance?" The shock was replaced with the suave charm that had so easily won Yi Zhen's heart a few nights before.

Katya curtsied and took their hand. "You may, my liege." They led her away from the stairs and couples parted for them to pass. As they found a space to dance, she decided to set aside her fear of messing up the steps. They seemed to know what they were doing, and the first few steps proved that so long as she followed their lead, she would be fine.

They twirled and spun and lost their breath. The princen had a grin, almost a smirk, across their face, and their eyes were filled with mischief. As the song ended and Katya started to catch her breath, the princen leaned in close and whispered into her ear. "How did you escape? And how did you get here so fast?"

Katya looked around, realizing that so many people were staring at them. She did not know how to respond to this question. Everything she had prepared, everything Ivan had told her, seemed to evaporate. She shook her head, feeling her face flush.

"My apologies, my lady. We should have some privacy for this conversation." They took her hand, pulling her behind them as they made their way through the crowd. They brought her to a small side door and opened it. She went in first and found a small spiral staircase. They closed the door behind them and ascended two steps at a time. Dizziness set in as she tried to keep pace with the Princen up these winding stairs, but she tried to put it aside.

At the top of the stairs there was another small door. Princen Alexis opened it and pushed aside a velvet curtain. It was dark. Katya tried to adjust to the lack of light, but as soon as she thought she had, a small torch blinked to life. Alexis made their way around the room lighting the torches.

Katya looked around. Small chairs were arranged in a half circle, music stands in a row along a wall behind them. Another velvet curtain lined the wall that the chairs were facing, and Katya walked up to it, found the edge, and pulled it aside.

She looked out over the ballroom, high above the dancers. She saw the giant chandeliers directly in front of her, glittering as the crystals reflected and refracted the light from torches, lamps, and candles. The view took her breath away. Below her, the dancers in their finery weaved around each other, fabric swirling, hair gems adding to the light show.

"We used to keep the musicians hidden away up here. The sound was so ethereal. We built a small stage on the floor itself once we became the patron of some well-known composers and musicians. The acoustics were worse, but everyone could see the musicians. Better visibility. I think the musician prefers it this way, too. She likes taking in and reading the energy of crowd. But now this room is all but forgotten."

Katya slowly closed the curtain overlooking the ballroom, fearful that another sudden movement might result in her being noticed.

"Tell me, princess, how did you escape? Is your companion safe? My mother is currently speaking with her guard—trained assassins. She is putting together a force for myself and Tatiana to lead. Were you followed? Is the sorcerer still alive?"

"You—you told your mother what was happening? Does she know who the sorcerer may be?" Katya said.

"Yes, my parents know. I think they may know who he is. Is the sorcerer still alive? We can still take a small army to capture him, hold him accountable for what he has wrought. Apparently my parents know of him, who he is. They said he has some grudge against my family."

"Does anyone else know?"

"My parents, myself, and the Mages Council."

She could not assassinate the entire royal family and an entire Council of Mages. No matter the magics she could call, it could not be done. But she reached inside of her anyway. She sought the well of aether inside of her core, ready to call it forth to immobilize the princen.

But it was nowhere to be found. Panicking, she kept trying to touch it, to call it. Desperate, she tried to call energy from nature, from the stars. In quick succession she tried conjury, thaumaturgy, sorcery, witchcraft. Every magical art she knew. But she could not call any magic. Her knees shook and sweat poured down her face, undoing the careful brushwork of powders and serums. The world spun around her and her vision stuttered and went dark. She knew what was coming next, as it had been happening so frequently. Her knees gave and she fell to the floor.

The knotted cord holding the hilt of the dagger to her thigh loosened and the knife clattered across the floor. Katya rose to her hands and knees as the world slowly blinked back into existence. Breathing slow and deep, she tried to make sense of what had just happened. She looked up to see the princen on the ground beside her.

"Do you need water? How can I help you?"

"I am fine," Katya said, the words forming with a sluggishness that should have frightened her. But the world still spun around her, snuffing out her concerns.

She lifted a knee to plant her foot on the ground and the princen helped her up. He led her to a chair and placed her in it. She placed her head between her knees, hoping for the spinning to stop, but her eyes fell on the knife.

She knew she should fear the princen seeing it, knew she should try to conceal it or find an excuse for its presence. But she could not muster the effort. She watched the princen walk over and inspect it. They were transfixed by it, reaching out several times as if to grab the blade and jerking their hand back as if stung. "Why did you have this?"

Words caught in her throat. She knew the words she should speak, but was unable to push them to her tongue. They burned as they fought to be released, but in doing so, they were consumed and turned to ash. Swallowing to clear her mouth of the taste, she began to panic. Her eyes cast about frantically, trying to make sense of what was going on as her surroundings wobbled and her thoughts slipped away from her like water through fingers. She could not hold on to anything, not her name, her purpose, or even herself.

"Zhen? What is wrong?" The princen abandoned their inspection of the knife and rushed to her side. "Zhen, breathe. Breathe in and out again, slowly."

With each series of breaths, the world wobbled less. It felt like both an instant and an eternity, but she righted herself. The hollowness where her magic had once been remained. As she took a final deep breath, she recalled the words of the tiger snake.

The curtains to the stairs moved, and after some fumbling, the woman Katya remembered as Tatiana entered the musicians' chambers. "Princen Alexis, your parents are looking for you. They heard that Princess Zhen was here!"

"How did you know to look for me here?"

Tatiana raised an eyebrow. "Alexis. This is where you bring all of your paramours."

The princen blushed and ran a hand through their hair. "Oh. You are right."

Tatiana crossed her arms and rolled her eyes, but halfway through her dramatic performance, her eyes landed on the knife. "What is that doing here?"

"I was just asking Princess Zhen, but my lady seems too ill to speak."

Tatiana crouched next to the knife. Without hesitation, she picked up the blade and turned it over in her hands.

"This is bespelled," she said with absolute certainty.

"How do you know?" the Princen asked, walking over to get a better look.

While the two were examining this curious object, Katya tried to take inventory. She was alive, but knew she was dying. She had no access to magic that might give her an advantage in killing the princen and Tatiana. She also had learned her number of targets had increased to encompass much of the royal family and however many people comprised a council. Her blade had been discovered, and if Tatiana was correct, it was laced with magics, magics she herself could not examine in her current state, magics that Ivan had likely concealed from her.

But for what purpose? Why would he enchant the knife, and why would he think sending her here was a good idea?

"Zhen? Zhen?" Her head jerked up to see the princen, almost overcome with worry. "Sweetheart, you keep drifting away. I want to know what happened, but maybe we should get you to a healer first." They sat at her side, taking her hand in their own and tracing small circles on her palm.

They loved Zhen, Katya realized. She knew Zhen was smitten, and she had guessed the princen was equally captivated, but the degree of concern in their voice told her the full extent of their feelings. She had come here willing to kill this person, to do so while wearing Zhen's face. The woman they loved would have been the last sight they saw as a blade tore through their throat.

She looked at the knife again, still in Tatiana's hands. Alexis caught her staring and motioned for Tatiana to come over. "Let her see it," they said to Tatiana. She held it out for Katya to inspect. Katya's stomach turned over on itself as she saw the runes inscribed upon it. Though they were not ones she had seen before, she knew the handwriting to be Ivan's. It then struck her that this was the knife he has cut her hand with when he first took Zhen captive.

He had not told her the blade was enchanted or held

ceremonial importance. Had he given her the wrong one, or had there been some magical purpose to this trip? Did he mean for her to take part in some spell, spilling blood onto a ritual knife, without her knowing?

Her mind did not want to entertain this thought, though he had done something eerily similar recently. He had cut her palm, spilled her own blood, without telling her what he was doing. With the very knife before her now. He had been lying to her by omission about his past, about his purposes in keeping Zhen, and about many things that she was sure he had not yet told her.

The years she had spent with him had instilled in her a sense of trust, a sense of safety and loyalty. He protected her and she returned the favor. But how many lies did it take for trust to break? How many half-truths could loyalty shoulder before it broke from the weight of deception on its back?

She did not know Alexis or Tatiana well, but she felt that she might be able to trust them enough to help ensure Zhen's safety. She could not stand the thought that Ivan might lie about Zhen being safe once Alexis was dead. She wanted to believe him, but this knife was proof of a web of lies. It was as if the knife had been plunged into her own soul, shattering any sense of trust she had. She knew his promise for the lie that it was.

Somehow, being hundreds of miles away from him had allowed her to see him up close, in all his deceitful detail.

"Zhen, is this how you escaped? Did you use some sort of magical knife to cut the ties that bound you to the lake?"

"I am not Zhen." She spoke those words first, knowing they needed to come while she still was resolved to protect Zhen at all costs. She would lose both Ivan and Zhen tonight, but Zhen alive and with Alexis was more bearable than Zhen dead. "I am Katya. Zhen is still trapped and the sorcerer lives. He sent me to kill you." As the words left her mouth, she felt the glamour she had cast begin to fade, slipping out of her control. Whether it was the truth or her weakness eroding it, she did not know.

The scraping of metal rang out as Tatiana drew a blade and held the point to Katya's neck. The princen scrambled away, nearly tripping over their own boots and catching themselves on another chair.

"I knew I could not trust you," Tatiana said through gritted teeth. "I knew your story did not add up."

"Please, let me explain. There is a chance to save Zhen, and that is all I truly want."

Alexis stood from the chair they had fallen into and approached Tatiana and Katya. They placed their palm on Tatiana's blade and pushed it down.

"What are you doing?" she yelled at Alexis. "We need to take her into custody. That is a magical knife. I do not know much about witchcraft, but by her own admission she means you harm."

"I want to hear her out. Zhen trusts her, and I want to at least hear why."

"She may be about to enchant you—do not fall for it. She is in league with a sorcerer, she is probably one herself."

"Tatiana."

"Fine, my liege." She sheathed her sword, crossed her arms, and backed away.

"I want to know *everything*."

"We do not have time for the whole of it, but I can try." Katya took a breath, the weakness still aching in her chest. She began the story of how Ivan had fooled her, sparing only the details of her parentage and its implications on her life. "When you discovered us, he sent me after you to assassinate you and anyone else who knew about him. I did not know the blade was enchanted, and I did not know why you needed to die. I was selfish. I fell in love with Zhen. He promised he would release her, and ensure she came to no harm, if I killed you."

A sob tore itself loose from Katya's chest, wracking her whole body as she grieved for all she was about to lose, was losing, and had already lost. "I just want Zhen to be alright. Happy and alive."

"You came here to assassinate me? And Tatiana?"

"Yes."

"Why?"

"He did not want to die, I think. I thought. There might be more to it than that."

"More how?"

"It's complicated, we do not have time."

She imagined the years Ivan spent imprisoned in the dungeons and wondered how horrible they would be. At least she knew that should they shut those bars on her, she would be dead soon after. Ivan's life was over, and hers would be, too. But Zhen could still survive this, and perhaps Zhen could forget about her and find a way to happiness with Princen Alexis.

When the next question came, she was not expecting the shortness of it. "Why?"

"I do not understand."

"Why are you cooperating? Why did you go along with the sorcerer? Was your fondness for Zhen not enough earlier?"

"I have been asking myself the same questions," Katya said, meeting their eyes. "I do not know why."

"Did he bespell you, too?" Alexis asked. "Some sort of sorcery to compel your cooperation?"

Katya did not want to think about this, what Alexis was implying. "Zhen is my priority now. My choice right now is to sacrifice my life to save her."

They stared her down, seeming to reach into her very core to check the veracity of her statement. She tried to keep her back straight, her chin up, and her eyes burning with determination.

They nodded and turned to Tatiana. "We need to alter our plans."

"I agree. Are you going to take care of the assassin first, though?"

They looked at Katya again, holding her gaze while addressing Tatiana. "She is going to help us. She knows the sorcerer and she can take us to him."

"She admitted she was here to kill you."

"She also admitted she was doing that to try to save Zhen."

"I don't like this."

"Good thing you are not paid to like my decisions." Their words were cold, and while they could have added an edge of authority as royalty, instead their words were laced with an anger that seemed to come from a wounded friend.

"If I have to play nice with the woman who wanted to kill you, fine. Let's get a move on investigating this knife. I don't like the look of these runes."

"Lead the way."

Katya rose to follow, but the sudden movement sent her wobbling again. Her vision faded out, her fingers tingled, and her knees tried to decide if they could hold her. She attempted to stay steady and felt a hand on her shoulder.

With an aching slowness, the world stopped churning and her vision returned. The hand belonged to the princen, and while the look they gave her was not friendly, it was also not abject hatred. Maybe she could get out of this situation alive.

"Better?" Alexis asked, their tone taking on formality and the distance that came with it.

"Yes, I can walk now." They nodded to her and let her go. They headed for the door, and Tatiana motioned to Katya to go next.

"You try anything," Tatiana said, "and I will not hesitate."

Katya nodded once and followed Princen Alexis.

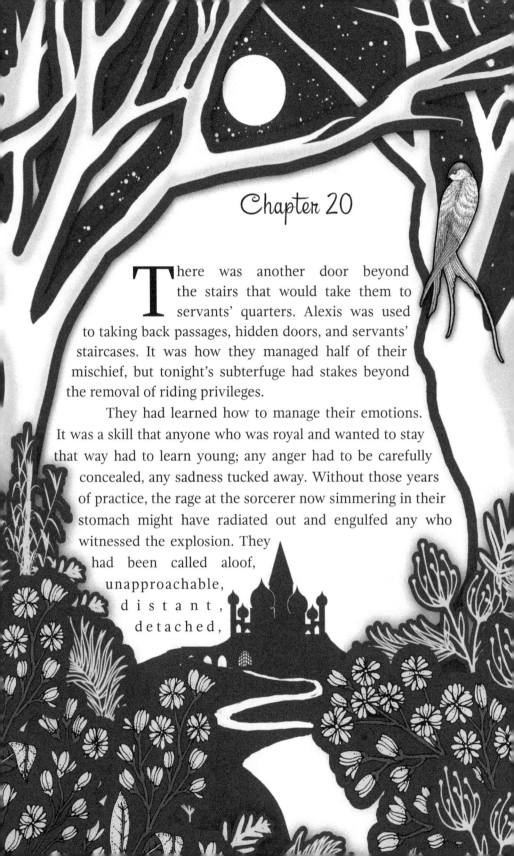

Chapter 20

There was another door beyond the stairs that would take them to servants' quarters. Alexis was used to taking back passages, hidden doors, and servants' staircases. It was how they managed half of their mischief, but tonight's subterfuge had stakes beyond the removal of riding privileges.

They had learned how to manage their emotions. It was a skill that anyone who was royal and wanted to stay that way had to learn young; any anger had to be carefully concealed, any sadness tucked away. Without those years of practice, the rage at the sorcerer now simmering in their stomach might have radiated out and engulfed any who witnessed the explosion. They had been called aloof, unapproachable, d i s t a n t , d e t a c h e d , and had cultivated that into an image of smug suaveness. It had the unfortunate side effect of making them look more desirable to half of their peers at court, and hated by much of the rest.

They had never had to practice containing love, for they showed it privately but freely to their family and close friends. And now they had shown it to Zhen.

They needed Zhen to live. They needed the sorcerer to die. They wanted Katya to hurt for her part in harming Zhen, but it sounded like Katya was already inflicting a punishment on herself. It also sounded like Katya was a victim of the sorcerer, too. They knew love could be infinite, and they knew it could be given in myriad forms. Zhen might love Katya, but Katya definitely loved Zhen. Zhen could love them both, just as their mother loved both of her partners.

Then why was this rotting seed of jealousy taking root in their gut? This question thundered in their head as they marched through the back halls of the palace. They knew the quickest way to silence these doubts, insecurities, and fears would be to follow Tatiana's advice and have Katya imprisoned or executed for treason and attempted murder, possibly attempted regicide if she truly had meant to kill everyone who knew about who was holding the princess. She had lied, spent her days deceiving Zhen, gaining her trust.

Their thoughts circled in a swirl of doubt and anger. When they neared the great library, they grabbed the handle of the door and threw it open with a force that knocked the door into the wall with a thud that reverberated down the hall.

"That was unnecessary," Tatiana told them as she pushed past and made her way to a large oak table. She unbuttoned her ceremonial doublet and looked around for other visitors while Alexis examined the walls for damage from their theatrics. Tatiana, satisfied that they were alone, deposited her jacket over the back of a chair and disappeared into the stacks while Katya and Alexis made their way to the table.

Alexis kept a close eye on Katya, but her jaw was slack and her eyes wide as she took in the sights of the library. "Tatiana will be back shortly with tomes on magic. I am going to go over there and look for books on weapons. Do you have any idea of other books that might lead us to some answers?"

"I'm not sure. Ivan's practices are eclectic. Maybe researching the forest itself? I'm curious why he chose that as his home."

"Do you know where he is from originally? There are different variations of magic depending on the region."

"He is from here."

"Lebedia is a large country," they said, exasperated. Katya was cryptic, and they got the sense she was still hiding something from them.

"He told me he was born a prince. I believe that would make him a distant uncle, if I have the proper understanding of family relationships."

That information made them pause. There had been a Prince Ivan. He should have been the second king in their dynasty, but he committed treason and was locked away for the rest of his life. Either the sorcerer was spinning tales or his magic was great enough to extend his own life.

"What do you think he wants?"

"I think he wants revenge. He told me some story about how your betrothal meant that he was found out and would be eliminated, that someone had figured out he was alive, still."

"I think that may be true. My father knew of a sorcerer, I am not sure if he was aware that the identity of the sorcerer was a former royal prince. He may have been, though."

"He is still angry, I think. He says he just wants to live peacefully, but looking back at his actions, I'm ashamed that I did not realize this earlier."

Tatiana arrived with an armful of books, two balanced on top of her head. "This one is on different types of runes, this one is on magical weapons, this one is on transformation spells, and here we have glamours. This one is basic enchantments, but I thought it might be useful still."

Alexis glanced at the different tomes. None stood out. "I am going searching for more. Katya, Tatiana, please try to get along with each other in my absence." Tatiana glared at them. Katya simply nodded, eyes still wide.

They stalked up and down the magical section of the library. It was odd. The sorcerer had great power and did not want a name attached to it. He had achieved a grand kidnapping, but did not want credit. If he had told Katya the truth and was in fact the damned ex-prince, why stay hidden? Alexis could understand waiting until a grand plan came to fruition. But maybe holding Zhen was not the end of his plan, but the start of it.

Was he holding Zhen to steal her life force? To keep himself young? That did not fit he would have had to been stealing people for years, and the people of Ignashino had reported no kidnappings, just scares. Katya seemed conflicted, confused, and betrayed by Ivan's actions. She might have gone along with his plan to hold Zhen for a few days, but this sounded like it was the first time she had been placed in a situation where she had to deal with questions of morality.

They picked books at random while musing on the questions of who and what and why. Some of the books they opened and flipped through, hoping that they would fortuitously land on the page they needed. Others they put back quickly after realizing they were in no language they could speak. Yet more books were picked up only to be taken to the end of the aisle and placed in a bin to be later collected and re-shelved by a librarian. How, Alexis thought, did one accidentally mistake a text on the use of torture devices for intimate purposes and place it in the magic section?

Arms full of a hodgepodge of texts, they made their way back to the table. Katya was staring at the pages of a book on magical forest creatures. Her eyes were unfocused, so Alexis assumed she was not really reading. Tatiana, however, was squinting at the footnotes of a dense book.

"I come with more gifts!" They set their stack down at the edge of the table and began to truly look at what they had picked up. There was a book on attempted magics to extend and preserve life, a book on generational curses, a book on healing magics, a book on forest monsters, one on the use of crystals, and one on divination.

Laying them all out, Alexis tried to decide where to start. The one on extending life played into their curiosity on the claim Katya had made about the sorcerer, but the one on curses might give them information on what the sorcerer was trying to achieve. "Katya, would you mind reading one of these?" they asked, motioning to the two books they were debating. Katya crumpled in on herself but nodded almost imperceptibly, reaching for the one on extending life. She took one careful look at the book she had been staring at before closing it and moving it aside.

Alexis sat down and opened the book on generational curses, glancing through the table of contents to see if there was a passage they could skip to. Nothing stuck out, so they flipped to the first page of the text.

It was boring and technical. Alexis read the same paragraph three times in a row, comprehending none of it despite their attempts. They were beginning to think they should swap books with Katya; Tatiana would not swap with them, even though she could read a book in an hour if given the chance, once she was absorbed in a book there was no taking it from her. They glanced at Tatiana, and sure enough, she was making her way through the pile quickly. Katya was drenched in sweat.

"Is everything all right, Katya?"

"Huh? Oh. It's just, I think I know how Ivan is still alive."

"And?"

"I think he is draining the life of the forest."

"That is not good at all."

"No, it really isn't," she said. There was a resignation in her voice, and Alexis wanted to prod her, but she seemed to keep retreating into some sort of internal shelter.

"Maybe we could get the princess out and burn the forest to the ground?" Tatiana suggested, somehow able to read and hold a conversation at the same time.

"That would probably work," Katya said, "but I think there is more to his draining of the forest than just wanting to extend his life. According to this book, he would only need a trivial amount of energy to prolong his life and retain his features."

"How do you know how much he is or is not siphoning?" Tatiana asked.

Katya chewed on her lip for a moment. "I don't know exactly, only that I have noticed the forest is dying. I didn't think this was related until just now." She looked down at her lap and flipped through the book.

Alexis was convinced now that there was more to Katya's story, but they doubted it was sinister, like Tatiana must have. They saw conflict in Katya's eyes, and they knew that if they looked at themself in the mirror, they would see the same fight: getting what you want at a morally disastrous price, or keeping a clear conscience, but living a lonely life.

They could have Zhen to themselves and not have to worry about sharing her with anyone else, but how would they sleep at night? Would Zhen even want to share their bed if she knew what they had done? They could not imprison or execute Katya to deal with their jealousy. Katya was helping them, and if they all survived this, surely that was more than enough for a pardon for a crime she had not yet even committed.

"I think I'll go check my father's personal library. The royal one is sorely lacking in some subjects," Tatiana said as she stood up, the chair sliding behind her. She bowed to Alexis and left the library.

"I hope she comes back with something useful," Alexis said. "We need to end this soon. We might be dealing with a war if we do not."

"That's what I have heard from Zhen, too."

"You do not seem to know much about politics or geography," Alexis commented.

"I suppose not," Katya said.

"If I remember my history lessons correctly, this war has been brewing for some time. It started under the first Czar Mikhail. The eldest prince was pushing hard for it—"

"The same prince Ivan claims to be?" Katya asked.

Alexis wondered, could this sorcerer be trying to ignite the war? Holding Zhen and not claiming credit could lead both sides to decide that the other had played them foul. It had almost worked; if their father had not already known about the sorcerer, then it would have.

"Do you think, Katya, that starting the war could be his goal? A war would decrease my family's standing. We would have to raise taxes, find soldiers, and send some of our own, maybe even myself, to the battlefield. A stray arrow could end my family's dynasty."

"I suppose so," she said, her brows squished together in thought.

"Sending you here disguised as Zhen to kill us would make our deaths look like a Shān assassination attempt."

"He told me the disguise would grant me easy access to the

palace," she pointed out.

"Katya, you have said yourself he has not been honest with you."

"I know, I just—this is difficult for me. I've known him my whole life. He took care of me when I was new to this world. Until last week, I had no idea who he was except a lonely mage. He protected me, sheltered me, and now..." Her lower lip quivered before she collapsed into her lap and sobbed.

Alexis chided themself for their unintended cruelty. They had not meant to provoke still raw feelings, and yet they had. "I am sorry, Katya. This must be so difficult for you."

"I'm throwing away what I thought would be a lifetime of happiness for a woman I can never be with. She will live, but she will live with you. I don't begrudge you your happiness, but I still ache."

It was Alexis' turn to chew on their lip. Katya was being honest with them about her feelings and fears. They had suspected that the sorcerer was her lover. They could not imagine would it would feel like to betray a lover as she was doing now, nevermind after realizing your lover had been betraying your trust all along.

"Can I ask why you do not think you two can be together?" Maybe, if they worked at it, the three of them could come to some agreement that they could all be happy with. They could work on their jealousy and insecurities. They had people they could learn from; after all, their parents had walked a path like this already.

"There are a lot of reasons, but she must marry you. Even if Ivan is gone, the tensions he may be stoking would remain."

"What if that was not a problem? She could marry me and still be with you some of the time."

"I don't know if that will work."

"It might, though. My parents make something similar work."

Katya looked them in the eye. A brief smile settled on her

face, just for a second, then vanished. "That sounds wonderful, but I don't think that would work."

"Why not?" they asked.

She sighed, shoulders sagging. "I can't tell you."

They felt anger simmering under their skin. They had just poured their heart out to her, suggesting a future that did not involve her paying for her attempted crimes. They had put aside their jealousy and envy to try to make a future where they could all fit together. They had recognized in her the type of conflict they were themself experiencing and had reached out a hand to help them. All this, and she had slapped that hand away.

They fell into an awkward silence, and Alexis tried to think of another approach. They were asking a lot of her; asking for trust they had not earned. Their willingness to offer her a different future was not enough to earn her trust, even if that future centered on Zhen. While building a relationship around another person was not the best way to develop trust, it would have to do for right now. They each had to trust that keeping Zhen safe was the lens through which they were making their respective decisions.

"I know you are going through a lot, but I want to help you," they said to her, their anger dissipating. "I cannot help you if you do not trust me. I saw how you looked at Zhen, and I know you care for her. We need to learn to trust each other, trust that the other wants what is best for Zhen. I am willing to believe in you."

"I trust that you have the best intentions, that on this, we are united. But there is more to it than that, and I have not yet had the courage to speak of it to others, let alone myself. It is personal."

Their shoulders sagged as they leaned back in their chair. They knew they should not press their luck any further. They stood up and stretched, twisting to unknot their back.

They took another tour around the library. They could not concentrate on the words on the pages anymore, and it would be pointless to force it. They passed by books on governance, economics, farming, trade routes, manners and etiquette, history, and myth. Things they were expected to know but could not always remember. Not that they did not want to learn; it was just hard to concentrate.

The only time they seemed to be able to focus was when they were doing something with their hands, or if they could watch the actual events happening, like when they would sneak away and drag Tatiana along. If they could watch their parents negotiating a new trade agreement or feel the crops in their hands as they were told about droughts and floods, then they would know it and always know it.

And now their inability to read some words on a page might mean a catastrophic loss of life. Alexis paused in the stacks. Catastrophic loss of life. Of course. They had read that line in a book of curses, they had read it a hundred times.

Katya had hidden herself behind her book on life-extending magics, and she did not bother to lower it from her gaze as Alexis thumped into the table. Without bothering to sit down, they flipped through the book on curses, looking for the illustrations they knew were on the page opposite the one they were looking for.

They jabbed their finger into the book. "There!"

"Excuse me?" Katya said, looking up over the top of her book.

"This is it! I do not know which of these five curses it is, but it has to be one of them!"

She put her book down, marking her page by folding the corner in. Alexis tried not to twitch as they watched this defacing of a priceless book. *She had lived in the woods her entire life,* they tried to remind themself. *She has no idea.* "How do you know?" she asked.

"These are the curses that require 'a catastrophic loss of

life.' Each curse requires many people to lose their lives, usually concentrated in one spot." They squinted at the page. "Most of them require the person or people you want to curse to be the first victim. I guess that is me, if the knife you brought was intended to start this process."

They finally sat down, pulling the book close to themself as they flipped back and forth between pages, trying to read all of it at the same time. "Whatever it is, it has got to be massive. They all require at least twelve sorcerers to complete the whole ritual."

"Let me see that," she said. "I see, yes. Most of these require a great deal of magic. Humans have a finite well inside, and it looks like these curses would deplete the wells of multiple people entirely. When a magic user depletes their well, they die." She hesitated before speaking the last word, and the sadness in her voice echoed in the empty library.

"So does he have, uh, friends? Disciples? A coven?"

"No, he doesn't. But he could use the forest. Some magic users can take magic from the ground, the trees, the earth. Some can drain animals, too. Even the stars."

"So he was not just draining the forest to extend his life, but to harvest energy for this curse?"

"Most likely."

"I wonder how long this has been going on. How much could he possibly need?"

"At least eighteen years."

"How would you know that?"

"The forest has been dying my entire life."

"I see." How, with her knowledge, had she failed to put this together? Alexis felt uneasy but decided to let it go.

"Why are you convinced this is a curse that requires a catastrophic loss of life?" she asked, and they could tell by her expression she was looking for any excuse to not believe them.

"This war that has been simmering. Taking Zhen ensured that both sides blamed the other, a catalyst to ignite the embers into flames. The war would create a crest of blood across the disputed territory, and your woods are at the heart of that crest." As they said it aloud, they felt the truth of it settle into their bones. Zhen was not a target but a pawn. Their marriage would delay war during their lifetimes, and maybe their children's lifetimes. This sorcerer had figured that out, and he either put his plans into motion now, or he would have to wait at least another century for his opportunity.

"That makes sense. When I told him that assassinating you to end the bethrothel agreement would not stop either side from seeking war, he said he knew that. That he still wanted the armies to come to the forest. I am trying so hard to accept that the man that I love can be capable of this violence. I don't mean to doubt you or your logic. It hurts so much right now." She held her hands over her mouth and nose, taking in giant breathes.

They let her cry. They let her exhaust herself as an onslaught of grief and anger consumed her. "I cannot love them both," she finally said. "To love one would be to betray the other. I cannot be loyal to them both, though even now a small part of me wishes I could find a way."

Alexis and Katya jumped as the door to the library burst open. Tatiana marched in with an armful of books, all with matching burnt-orange binding. She set them down with a thump on the oak table and let out an exhausted sigh.

"My father lent us these for the night. They are the complete collection of books on the Nribean magical order. They have magic unlike anyone else on this earth." She slumped into her chair and ran her hands down her face. "Sorry I took so long. Father did as he always does: recount every story he has that is even tangentially related."

"What makes this magic different from others?" Katya

asked, a curiosity lighting up her eyes.

"It apparently draws on a different source to fuel the magic. I have had little interaction with the people of the Order of Thea, but they say their order was founded when a woman outside of time and space—"

"Outside of time and space?" Alexis and Katya asked in near unison.

"Yes. Legend says the sky opened over a small village on the coast, and out of this opening appeared a tall woman with a headful of braids. She claimed to come from another world and was looking for shelter. She was sad, reserved. She wore her sorrow openly, but she was secretive with her story before her time in Nribo. The village took her in, and she taught the local hedge witches about a new form of magic. In time, her informal lessons became a more formal school.

"As the school grew, the Ezi offered her lands, titles, funding for her school. But she refused them all. All she said was, 'I came here because I could not go down that road, and I will not be tempted by it again.' She never spoke to him again. Many others offer her marriage as a means of alliance to grand houses with ample means to fund a larger school. But she said no to these, too.

"She found a pupil who taught her how to open herself to love again. They married. Legend says when she decided it was time to move on, she opened a magical portal and she and her wife stepped from this world into another.

"The Order of Thea are those who keep the school running, and these books were written by her and her first pupils. They are a mix of many magical forms, but ones that this sorcerer might not know. It does not sound like he has journeyed out of Lebedia."

"I hope she is happy, wherever she is now," Katya said, before looking back down at the book in front of her.

"What have you both learned while I was listening to my

father's tales?" Tatiana asked.

"We think he is draining the forest so that he can perform a ritualistic curse," Alexis started. "One that involves many human sacrifices. We believe he intends to get these sacrifices by instigating a war. Do you think that whatever spells or magic are contained in these books are doable by people who are not practiced in these ways? I do not have a shred of magical talent and neither do you."

"I could learn. At least, I think I can," Katya said, reaching over the piles of books for the top book in the pile Tatiana had brought. She carefully set aside the one she had been reading and opened the Nribean book to the first page.

Chapter 21

Katya was exhausted by the time they had a clear plan. At some point, Alexis had fetched the mages who would be going along with them. They each took turns reading the books Tatiana had brought, and they had all practiced the magic it contained. Some of those experiments had lead to small fires, others to loud bangs. At one point Tatiana had lead them all to the practice yards to prevent further damage to the library.

But they were all gathered back in the library now, and Katya had gone over the books multiple times searching for an answer she could live with. In the end, she resigned herself to the knowledge that she had been born to defeat Ivan. She might survive his murder, but she would still be irrevocably tied to her forest.

Ivan had earned her anger, her hatred, her wrath. When he had sealed Zhen to the lake, he had used Katya's own life force to bind the spell. It was her magic being used to conjure the items they had needed, used without her knowledge or consent. The degree to which he had made her complicit in his plans made her stomach roil. Yet, she thought, had his crimes earned him a death sentence?

The stars twinkled from the windows lining the far edge of the library. Katya closed the last book. "I think I have all that I need to know," she announced to Tatiana and Alexis. "We should go soon, though. Ivan is expecting me."

Alexis nodded and Tatiana got up from her seat. The plan was complicated. They had constructed it asynchronously as the night went on, as they struggled through their drowsy desire for sleep. They had reached a consensus and finalized the plan an hour ago, and now all that was left to do was double-check the spells while waiting for the Czarina's Guard to finish their own preparations.

Katya had found a spell in one of the Nribean books that could transport them to the edge of the forest in seconds. The spell did not rely on the magic inside of her or the aether of the earth, which was valuable, as she was running out of her own.

The doors to the library swung open as two dozen muscular women and individuals without gender marched into the foyer, Tatiana leading them, a steel helmet tucked under her arm. "We are ready, your Highness."

Katya stood up, unsure of what to do with herself, her hand resting on the table while she traced the swirls of the wood grain with her thumb. She had interacted with more human beings in the last several hours than she had in all of her life. Alexis looked back at her and flashed a confident grin. She tried to respond with a smile of her own.

"Are we ready?" Alexis asked everyone, hand resting on the hilt of their sword, the ceremonial blade replaced with one meant to see blood and flesh. The Czarina's Guard nodded as one, and Tatiana saluted. The mages shuffled their feet and tried to figure out what they were supposed to be doing. Alexis swung their hands behind their back and addressed the assembled forces. "This is Katya. She will be taking us to our staging point outside the forest. Katya," they said, turning to her. From their tone, she figured that she was to take the lead.

"Could everyone huddle around me? I need everyone to be close to ensure we all make it to the forest." As everyone gathered around her, she began to slowly focus on the air around her body. She closed her eyes and began to breathe in deeply, holding each breath for a beat longer than she normally did. The books had described the magic inside of tiny particles, so small that the eye could not see them, but were the fundamental materials of everything. In her mind's eye, she could find them, though. Find them and harness the massive power they contained.

She found one's center, she pulled it apart, and stretched it around them. She wished for the briefest of moments that she could see what this looked like to an outside observer, what looks the princen, or Tatiana, wore. But one misstep, one shift in focus, could destroy a city.

Once the energy surrounded them, she focused on using it to slip them through space, bending it around them so that the forest was beside them. Through the fog of her concentration she heard gasps and shouts. She let herself float back into the world and saw they were on the edge of her forest. She felt it call to her, sing to her soul as it welcomed her back.

Tatiana was already yelling out orders, and Alexis was backing her up. Katya saluted them and turned to enter the woods. She breathed in the smell of the soil, the flowers, and she listened for the sounds of her corvids welcoming her home. The trees seemed to straighten with each step she took, flowers un-wilted, and the sounds of a forest crying became a chorus of lively activity.

She was just past the point where the trees obscured her view of the guards when the tiger snake approached her, back arching up to take her measure. "You returned."

"I'm sorry I didn't want to listen before."

The snake nodded. Katya waited, wondering if a forest could know regret, if a forest felt anything like the sour pit in her own gut, the desire to find a way to turn back time and make a thousand small decisions all over again.

"Have you finished with your other business?"

Katya laughed. "My troubles and yours were one and the same."

"Oh?"

"The man who I've been living with here is the one who has been killing the forest and, I guess, killing me, too."

"What man?"

"Oh, that clever—" Katya screamed, grinding her heel into the ground. "How incredibly *stupid* have I been. It was right there, right there the whole time." Her sorrow swelled into a storm. A tumultuous tempest howled inside of her chest, demanding vengeance for her shattered dreams. She nursed the eye of the storm, the emptiness inside of it, into rancor.

How much of her origins had he known, guessed, and kept from her? He had hidden himself from the forest, and he had hidden her, too. He had to have known. How many nights did he catch her pouring over books for answers? How many times had she whispered the desire to know her origins into his ears? She had found it endearing that he loved her no matter what, but that was not truly the case.

Katya wanted nothing more than to lose herself in the fury that had infested her heart, but the steady gaze of the snake brought her back. She had to be calm. She would have her revenge on the man who had enchanted and dazzled and used her. She would find justice, and peace, but her burning passion alone would not be enough to aid her.

"The man who hid me from you played at being my friend, and I was foolish enough to believe him. I was away on a task he had set upon me, and in my searchings, I found him out. I have friends—" She hesitated. Alexis might be her friend. Tatiana could be, if Katya could find a way to make amends. Zhen, maybe, if she could find a way to explain herself and Zhen forgave her. This was not the time. No one could be her friend if they did not survive. "I know some people who are here to help. They want to rescue the princess who has been trapped here. He is using her as bait to lure hundreds of people to their death so he might use that crest of blood to seal a curse."

The snake nodded. "He has been siphoning our life away for a mortal grudge. Do you and your friends have a plan?"

"We do," Katya said.

"Good luck, child." The snake vanished as the last word was spoken, and Katya tried to make peace with the fact that she might never fully understand the strange entity that had birthed her. She was possibly losing everyone she held dear, but at least she knew she had a family. She transformed into a swan, took flight, and headed for Ivan's.

She arrived quicker than she expected to. Katya peered in the cabin's window and spied him passed out at his desk, his head pillowed on an open book.

As silent as she could, she entered her former home. She crept around him as she gathered dried herbs, her mortar and pestle, candle stubs, salts, and her own knife. With her own knife, she cut off a small bit of his hair, terrified the whole time that he would wake.

He looked so content, so serene for someone who had let revenge take over, someone so capable of manipulation and deceit. She had been happy here, once, though now she knew that happiness came from ignorance of his machinations. If she survived this, she wanted to at least try to find a true happiness. A happiness based on genuine love, and absent of any deception.

The knife Ivan had given her burned against her calf as she took one last look at him. She was not sure what to do with it. She could leave it here, a sign that she had completed her task, and hopefully buy some more time before he became suspicious. Or she could take it with her, possibly raising suspicions, but ensuring that he did not have the tool that was necessary to initiate his curse.

A scrap of paper and a quill caught her eye, buried under rubbish, but usable. She grabbed them and scrawled a quick letter. "I came back to tell you I succeeded and you were asleep. You looked so peaceful, I could not wake you. I will come to you tonight."

Short, nearly honest. She left her former home, knife still tied to her thigh, her ingredients and tools in a small satchel tied around her waist. She took off, repeating her next steps in her head. She needs to get Zhen safely inside of a protection circle, she needed to make that protection circle, she needed to assemble the components of the spells, and she needed to do it before—

Movement caught her eye. What looked like a procession of fire was moving toward her from the south. It was still some distance off, but surely it was a moving army. It appeared their anxieties about Shān had been correct, Katya thought, recalling Alexis' worries about them thinking that they had been played false.

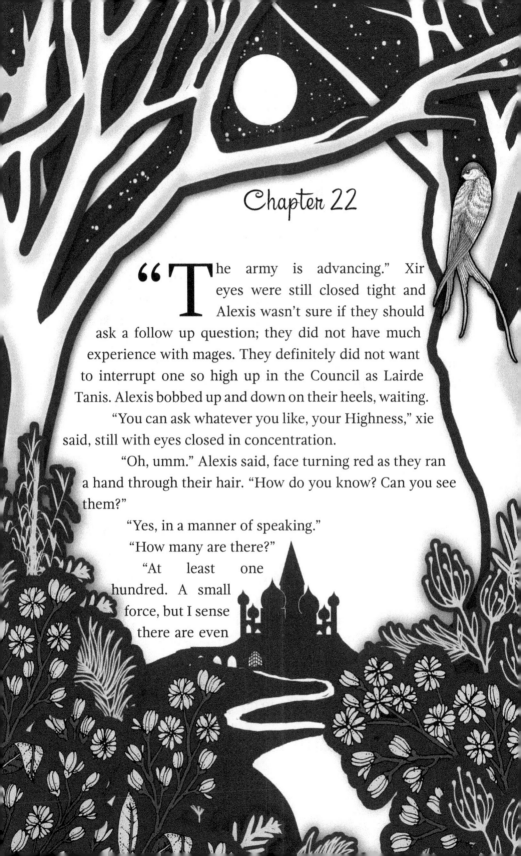

Chapter 22

"The army is advancing." Xir eyes were still closed tight and Alexis wasn't sure if they should ask a follow up question; they did not have much experience with mages. They definitely did not want to interrupt one so high up in the Council as Lairde Tanis. Alexis bobbed up and down on their heels, waiting.

"You can ask whatever you like, your Highness," xie said, still with eyes closed in concentration.

"Oh, umm." Alexis said, face turning red as they ran a hand through their hair. "How do you know? Can you see them?"

"Yes, in a manner of speaking."

"How many are there?"

"At least one hundred. A small force, but I sense there are even more waiting on the border."

An advance force, with more waiting for instructions behind them. Alexis looked around at the assembled Guard and mages. The odds were not good.

"How far off are they?"

"Not very. We have little time."

"Right. Can you keep us hidden from them?"

Tanis opened xir eyes, looking directly at Alexis, xir mouth a tight line and eyes knit in appraisement. Alexis felt as if xie was doing more than looking at them on the surface, but taking in all the unseen aspects of them, too. They felt very exposed under xir gaze. "Your Highness, we can keep you cloaked as we make our way through the forest. I do not know what surveillance magics or traps the sorcerer has laid down. The other mages have been attempting to figure that out without accidentally springing any, but once we are at the lake, and the fighting begins, it will be much harder."

"Is there something else we can do? I do not want to put us in a situation where we are fighting two fronts, and I would prefer to not have to kill any Shān soldiers. They are also trying to save the princess."

"I would have to think more about that."

"Do you think, maybe, you could direct the soldiers away from us?"

Tanis brought xir hand to xir chin, tapping xir lips with xir forefinger. "That is a possibility. We could probably weave some simple illusions to lead them in circles away from the lake."

"That would definitely work, if we could keep them away until we have defeated the sorcerer, and then we could explain things to them."

"It would take all of us to do that, though."

"All of you?"

"Yes, and it would take a lot of magic, especially as we would be unable to draw from the earth."

"That is not so good."

"No, it is not. It is up to you, your Highness. We will follow your orders, we will be wherever you want us to be."

Alexis wished that Tanis had told them what xie and xir force would be doing. They did not want to be the one who shouldered the weight of decision. If something went wrong, if they asked xir to distract the Shān army and then they needed the mages in the battle, if the battle was lost because of that choice, Alexis did not want to have that on their conscience. "Thank you, Tanis. I will let you know what I decide."

"Your Highness, a leader never runs to choices that can have grave consequences. It is never a decision that a good leader wants to make. There is more at stake here than most of the choices you will be faced with as Czar. It is unfair, but I doubt your parents would have entrusted you with this if they did not believe you were a good leader."

"How did you—" Alexis said, eyes wide. But Tanis shrugged and headed towards the tree line, eyes already closed in concentration.

"Mages. They are incredibly frustrating, aren't they?" Tatiana came up behind Alexis, putting her arm around their shoulders.

"They are all like that?" Alexis put their arm around Tatiana and let her lead them to the fire that the Guard had built. They were boiling water for coffee, double checking their weapons, sparring with each other to warm up and get acclimated to the terrain, and waiting for their orders. A few people from Ignashino had noticed them, and luckily they were able to answer questions with chat about "routine survival drills" and "practice sessions." A few had asked if they could look into the beast in the forest while they were there. Some of the children had gotten sticks and were play-fighting nearby, some of them hoping to catch the eye of the Guard, dreaming of being whisked away for an adventure.

"Most of them, yes. I think it comes from spending so much time reading. Or maybe it's the magic stuff." Tatiana sat down on a stump and took out her knives, holding them up to the light one by one.

"Did you overhear the conversation?" Alexis sat next to her, hunching over and resting their chin in the hands.

"Yes," Tatiana said, somehow finding a small blemish on one of the knives and trying to buff it out on her skirt.

"What do you think I should do?" Alexis could feel their stomach churning as they thought about the way that lay ahead. They'd made sure to eat and drink to help keep them strong, but right now they wanted to vomit into the nearest pale, dignity be damned.

"I do not think the Guard can fight a hundred Shān soldiers while also taking on a sorcerer."

"I led us both into so much danger earlier. I do not want to make that same mistake again."

"You cannot let this paralyze you, though." She put down her knives and turned to them, taking one of their hands in hers. "You are a good person who wants to do the right thing. You do not want others to hurt because of you and your choices. Everyone here signed up knowing they might get hurt, though. This mission is important; they believe in it."

"You are right. I am getting very wrapped up in 'what if.' What if we need the mages and they are not around? What if we have them with us and the Shān army is closer than we think? What if they-"

"Alexis. You are doing it again."

"All right. Decision time. I can do this. Deep breath. The mages will try to keep the Shān soldiers away from the lake."

"Want me to go tell Tanis?"

"No, I think xie should hear it from me. This is my responsibility."

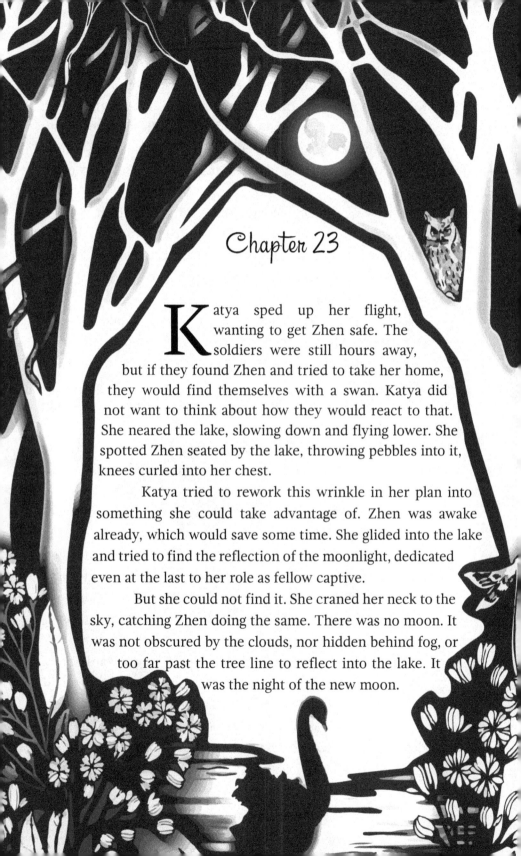

Chapter 23

Katya sped up her flight, wanting to get Zhen safe. The soldiers were still hours away, but if they found Zhen and tried to take her home, they would find themselves with a swan. Katya did not want to think about how they would react to that. She neared the lake, slowing down and flying lower. She spotted Zhen seated by the lake, throwing pebbles into it, knees curled into her chest.

Katya tried to rework this wrinkle in her plan into something she could take advantage of. Zhen was awake already, which would save some time. She glided into the lake and tried to find the reflection of the moonlight, dedicated even at the last to her role as fellow captive.

But she could not find it. She craned her neck to the sky, catching Zhen doing the same. There was no moon. It was not obscured by the clouds, nor hidden behind fog, or too far past the tree line to reflect into the lake. It was the night of the new moon.

"Katya!" Zhen cried out, reaching the same conclusion. "Oh, Katya!" She ran into the lake, her *aoqun* trailing in the water, looking up at the sky, seeming to plead with the heavens to realign themselves. She stumbled, slipped, and fell. Without hesitation, Katya transformed, lunging forward, her arms extended to catch Zhen.

There was no time to contemplate her predicament.

"Katya—how?" A thousand lies waited behind her lips as Zhen looked up at her, her head nestled in the crook of Katya's elbow, water weaving through her hair. One by one, the lies died, leaving only ashes behind.

"I lied to you." The unadorned truth. Katya helped Zhen up, but as she regained her balance, she pulled away from Katya.

"Lied about what?" Zhen asked, each word was a dagger, sharp and short.

"I had been helping the sorcerer," Katya began, but already Zhen was turning away.

"You were *what*?" called Zhen over her shoulder as she sought a place to escape. But there was nowhere to run. Zhen was still a prisoner.

"I'm not anymore, I promise, please. I am sorry! I brought Alexis and Tatiana. They're preparing to come rescue you. I'm getting ready to fight Ivan, to free you. I am trying to make this right, Zhen." Katya stood in the middle of the lake, her hair a tangled and wet mess clining to her face. Her throat was tight and she could feel the itch of magic under her skin, telling her to transform and run.

"You pretended to be trapped with me? For what purpose?" Zhen cried as she circled back to the lake, marching toward Katya. "I gave you my confidence. I loved you even though I knew it could not last." The decrescendo in her rage as it moved into regret was palpable, and Katya was sure that it was not water dripping from her still wet bangs. "Was that a lie, too? Was that an act for you?"

"No, that was not a lie. I know you do not trust me right now, but I do love you. And right now, I need to kill the sorcerer. Princen Alexis and Tatiana are coming with soldiers, and I need to get you safe before I can start casting the spell that will destroy him."

"How can I believe you right now? How do I know you are not trying to kill me instead?" Her face was red and splotchy, and her movements articulated and staccato.

"I don't know. I stayed all night in a library trying to find a way to destroy him, and I have spent most of my life as his partner. But he betrayed me." Katya choked on the words. She heaved as she tried to put to words the damage he had done to her. "He violated me in ways I cannot even begin to explain, and I can not let him hurt you anymore. Please, I am going to make a protection circle, and then I am going to prepare for what I need to do. I would like it if you were inside of the protection circle, instead of outside."

Zhen hesitated. "Where are Alexis and Tatiana now?"

"I brought them to the edge of the woods. They are preparing, although by now they are probably about ready to march here."

"Brought them here from where?" Zhen crossed her arms, still skeptical.

"Kristallicheskiy."

Zhen took a quick breath in, her eyes wide. "How did you bring them here?"

"With a spell from a book Tatiana's father had."

Her voice was barely louder than a whisper. "So you have magic beyond what you have let on?"

"Yes and no. If I'm here in the forest, yes. Not much outside of it. And Ivan sealed the spell on you with my magic without telling me that was how he did it."

"Every time you got weak, it was when—" There was a spark of sympathy in Zhen's voice as she said it.

"Yes. He did not tell me that, either." Katya looked down at her feet, trying to rein in another wave of anger.

Zhen scrunched her face, her eyes far away, lost in thought. "I have not forgiven you, and I do not know how to trust you anymore. But it sounds as though Alexis has trusted you in this plan." She wrapped her arms around herself and turned away from Katya. "Cast the protection circle. I shall stay inside of it."

Katya nodded, the sting of Zhen's words finding all the wounds she had inflicted on herself for being so oblivious to what had been happening. The words were salt, but she could not hold them against Zhen. Katya unpacked her supplies and made preparations: placing crystals, pouring salt, lighting candles, and burning the hair she had stolen from Ivan.

Zhen sat on the ground near her, watching. She would sometimes get up, look around, and then go back to fidgeting. She sighed and asked, "Is there anything I can do?"

"I don't know. Alexis and Tatiana should be en route. Shān's soldiers will be, too." Katya hurled a crystal she had been trying to imbue with magic to the ground. "Dammit, I need more time."

"My soldiers, my parents' soldiers?" Zhen sat up.

"Yes, they apparently heard you did not arrive, as you feared."

"You know for certain?" Her hands clasped together under her chin, eyes filled with anxiety.

"I saw them advancing." Katya brought a flame to her hand, ready to light more candles, but her nerves were getting the better of her and she burned herself.

Zhen got up and walked to Katya, carefully stepping over the magical accoutrements Katya was organizing. "I cannot grant you more time, but I can conceal you."

"What?" Katya jerked up from her preparations, eyes wide at Zhen.

"My thread magic. I could weave a shroud to hide us."

"Zhen, that is brilliant," Katya said, wanting to get up and kiss her, forgetting for a moment that their lives were all in danger, and that Zhen was still angry. Zhen smiled back at her before she tore out the hem of her gown.

Nothing could be constructed from nothing; there was always a price for magic. The magics she had known involved taking from your own reserve or using a sacrifice. Katya had been Ivan's sacrifice, nothing more to him than a source of magic. She had read the night before about such arrangements where a mage and a source were bound: partners, companions. Maybe if Ivan had asked her permission, maybe if they had discussed it, she would have consented to being a source of power for him if what he had wanted to do was positive. But he had never even asked.

She had read about taking power from the earth beneath her, but it was a tricky business. The earth, the surrounding terrain, influenced the results; and if too much was taken, the earth around could be killed. But this new magic she had learned about, where one took magic from anything, was exciting. All objects had substance, and therefore, power. Even the air was made up of something. She could focus on the tiny grains that made up the air, and at their centers was an impossibly compact but infinitely powerful source of magic. She could crack the shell open and harness it.

Although she had read explanations repeatedly and had practiced it with the mages, her nerves kept getting the better of her. To err was to bring about a cataclysm that Ivan could only dream of or hope for. But now she had to do it. She cast her protection circle, watching from the corner of her eye as Zhen continued to pick at her hem, moving from the hem of her skirt to the ones on her blouse.

She used the magic she was used to, weaving in strands of the new magic she had learned, amplifying the effects and hopefully doing so in a way that Ivan could not quickly undo. Sweat dripped down her brow. She was not used to doing such intricate magic, especially for such long periods of time.

She infused the last of the crystals with the pulse of her heart and watched as cloaked figures emerged into the clearing, shaking the shadows of the forest from their shoulders. Tatiana and Alexis rode at the front, but they were heavily cowled and hooded, only their eyes showing.

Zhen gasped as she saw the riders, almost dropping the knotwork she had been working on, and soared to her feet. She took two giant strides to the edge of the circle, outlined in salt, and then fidgeted while she waited for the princen to come to her.

"You are here!" she cried. Alexis approached the circle, but did not remove the robes hiding their features.

"I told you I would come back for you. I never break my promises." They held their hand up, hovering it over her cheek. "I suppose Katya should disguise us. Though we rode shrouded, I do not want any whispers to get back to the sorcerer. The mages have kept us concealed to the best of their ability so far, we were an invisible force coming through the forest."

Katya stood up, but the sudden movement almost landed her on the ground again. The world lurched, black spots appearing in her vision. She tried to steady herself, but her hand finding nothing on which to gain purchase, she slid back down. "A moment, please. I am a little overworked right now."

"Katya," came Zhen's voice through the blackness that swirled in Katya's vision. It contained none of the harshness of their earlier conversation. It was full of concern. "I can do it. I can weave an illusion."

"You should not have to. I should be strong enough."

Alexis cut in. "Our mages are also a little worn right now, but I can get one of them to do it."

"I *said* I could do it," Zhen huffed. "A princess must cooperate in her own rescuing somehow. Alexis, what are you being disguised as?"

Katya nodded. She did not have much ability to argue.

"Any face but my own, same for Tatiana. He's seen our faces already. If you could conceal the rest, too, then relieve our mages."

Zhen nodded and got to work. Katya remained seated and tried to watch as Zhen tore out more threads from her dress and hummed. Katya wished she had the strength and knowledge to really pay attention to what Zhen was doing as she combined thread and song magic. If Zhen still talked to her after all of this, she would have to ask.

Though her vision was still hazy, she could see a glamour settle over the princen and their champion, and then over the Guards and mages. They all wavered in and out of clarity, sometimes disappearing all together.

She smiled up at Zhen, who only seemed a little winded from her exertions. Zhen caught her eye and smiled back. The smile was hesitant, full of apprehension, but it was there. She scrambled to her feet, still dizzy, but getting better.

Alexis took off their cowl, and their entire face was different, subtly so in some places. A larger nose, smaller ears. Something was different about their eyes and chin, but Katya could not place it. They did not look like Alexis at all when all the changes were synthesized.

The four of them stood there for the space between a heartbeat, putting aside their doubts, their uncertainties, and their mistrust of each other. They needed to be united.

"I shall lead the attack against the sorcerer when he arrives," Tatiana said. "I shall have half of the Guard with me. A small group of three will keep you two surrounded, and Princen Alexis and the rest shall guard against any minions the sorcerer might call. The mages will try to hold off the advancing army, keep us concealed so that they do not see us, slow their advance with mirages and the like. A few of them will try to provide back up to Katya, if they can."

"I don't think he has any minions, though," Katya said.

"How do you know? He seems to be far more powerful than you thought. How can you be sure that he does not?" Tatiana pressed.

"You're right. I do not know for sure what he is capable of, and we can't take the chance," Katya replied.

"Are you ready?" Princen Alexis asked Zhen and Katya. They both nodded. "I suggest you start your spell. I am sure we have attracted the sorcerer's attention by now."

Princen Alexis drew their sword and raised it above their head. Tatiana followed suit, giving hers a flourish as she raised it. The Czarina's Guard let out a cry, raising their own weapons and marching toward their leaders. Tatiana twirled on her heel and marched toward her advancing troops, sword still aloft.

Katya did not have a chance to sit down before she heard the screech of an owl. Zhen's hands again worked complex knots as she hummed a song under her breath. She paused for but a second to nod to Katya. Katya understood. Zhen was finishing the shielding spell.

She focused her attention on the flame of a candle before her and let everything else fall away. She did not hear the shouts as an abomination of a creature landed in the lake. She did not hear the gasps as that creature shed its feathers and became a looming and menacing man. She did not hear the rallying cry as Tatiana screamed, "To me! To me! For Lebedia!" She did not hear the haunting song that Zhen sang to keep them safe.

She could, however, hear the buzz of invisible motes, vibrating in nervous energy. She closed in on one and plucked it from the air. It sat in her outstretched hands. It looked like a tiny model of a solar system. She had seen drawings in the books Ivan kept, but this was so much more. At the center was the tiny sun, the source of fuel she needed. With great care, she sliced it open and held it to her mouth, pouring the energy into her very core.

All sound ceased. The buzzing that had been background noise vanished. The world crept back into her awareness, but it was quiet, muted, dull. She saw commotion around her, but heard none of it. She saw Ivan binding *leshy* to his will, bidding them attack the Guard. She saw him summon her own crows and force them to harass the soldiers. He stole her bees and set them upon the horses. He used the creatures she had nurtured and cared for as weapons. She screamed, but she did not hear it. She could feel the forest trying to revolt against him, to shake his hold on it and its children, yet she heard nothing.

She tried to not let this bother her; she needed to finish what she had started. She saw Ivan near the edge of the lake, Tatiana trying to clear a path to him by taking on the giant *leshy* that surrounded him. Her soldiers attacked with equal passion as increasingly more creatures descended from the tree line.

Zhen tore out another thread from her tattered dress, and as she wound her knots, *leshy* fell. They were not defeated, but for the time being they could not attack. Tatiana took advantage of the opening and leapt over the *leshy* trying to get to their feet. Her sword swung with precision and grace as it sought Ivan.

She could see the mages shimmering and floating around the clearing, she could almost feel them pluck at the forest, weaving in their own magic. She could feel the vibrations of the army as they marched across the forest, one way and then another as the mages tried to corral them away from the battle, away from unnecessary harm.

But then the vibrations of a scream hit her. And then another. One by one, she felt each mage fall. A gasp of breath, a cut off scream, and then their magic winked out of existence.

She felt the army charge into the clearing all at once, the

crash of their steps reverberating down her spine.

All of the parties involved in the battle turned at once to the opposite side of the clearing. Katya saw the torches glimmer in the forest as soldiers of Shān broke through the tree line and into battle, torches thrown to the ground. She saw Tatiana's mouth open wide, horror etched in her eyes. But then the closed her mouth into a tight line and waved her soldiers on again.

Katya and Zhen were now the only ones with magic in this fight.

Chapter 24

Alexis had not accounted for this situation; in all of their anxieties and worries, they had not considered that the mages would fail. No, they did not fail, they were killed. They were murdered by the sorcerer. And now the Shān army was advancing on them. Alexis swung their sword hard onto the skull of the bear that was attacking them and then turned to meet the army.

They made eye contact with the leader, the plumage on the helmet bright and tall. The leader ran toward them, sword raised, a scream tearing from her throat. Alexis screamed in answer.

Their swords clashed together, the Shān leader's sword was thin and light and curved. She swung it like it was an extension of her own arm, g r a c e f u l and elegant but gorgeously lethal. Alexis was a clumsy apprentice compared to her, their broad sword clunky and inefficient. Still, they had to try.

"This is not what it appears," they said, gritting their teeth in pain as they struggled to keep her sword at bay. She used momentum to her advantage, each blow more heavy than it should be for a sword so small.

"And how is that?"

"The sorcerer, he has her. We're here for the same thing, we can work together to overtake him!"

She leaped backwards, laughing, bringing her sword in front of her. "That is not what it looks like to me."

"What does it look like to you, then?"Alexis advanced on her, trying to keep her from getting too much distance, wanting to keep her unable to use her speed and agility to her advantage.

"You are here to murder her, you have kept her here for weeks. Trying to get information from her. That's what our scouts have told us. That is what they have seen." She parried each of their blows, knocking their sword back over and over, as one might swat at a fly.

"They saw wrong! Or it was a trick!"

"You think we would not know what we saw? What we heard? You think we would misunderstand?"

"That is not what I am saying! The sorcerer, he has been the one keeping her! He has tricked all of us! I love her, I would not murder her!"

"You are not so tough for an heir." She advanced on them. They stumbled and nearly lost their footing.

Alexis felt their stomach drop. They had exposed themself. They shook their head, and raised their sword again.

"You promised to keep her safe, was that a lie?"

Alexis kept fighting, but was losing ground.

"You promised to eliminate all the threats to her, were you excluding yourself from that?"

Alexis could feel their muscles on fire, a mix of rage and exhaustion. They kept parrying.

"If this sorcerer is truly real, and he truly has been the one holding her, why did you not eliminate him earlier? How could Lebedia forget about a powerful foe that might steal our princess? If your story is true, did you not care? Did you have so little regard for our princess?"

Alexis took a step forward. She raised her eyebrows but blocked their swing.

"You claim you love her, you claim that you would not murder her. So is this neglect? Or are you lying about the sorcerer? Which is more likely, heirling?"

Alexis' eyes bulged in anger, they wanted to let loose, they wanted to swing their sword and viciously cut their tormenter down.

"Can you not see him? Can you not see the sorcerer over there?"

"You are pathetic, resorting to tricks and distractions. I can see you losing control on your emotions. You're becoming sloppy. You think you can call yourself a monarch one day? What weak rulers the Lebedians have. I almost feel sorry for them."

Alexis could feel the sword slipping from their grasp, they were sweating heavily. They could feel it forming on their brow, collecting in their palms, sliding down their back.

"We will save our princess and bring her home, find her someone more *worthy* of her."

"I AM WORTHY," Alexis cried. "I am here to save her. I have planned this rescue mission, and I will save her from the sorcerer with or without your help."

They brought their sword above their head, then brought

it down, pommel bashing the Shān leaders helmet. She collapsed, knocked unconscious. Alexis' heart was racing. They looked around. The Guard were taking on the soldiers three or four at a time. They raised their sword to rally their own. "Do not kill them," they cried. "Knock them out, disable them. But do not kill them." Then, they rejoined the fray.

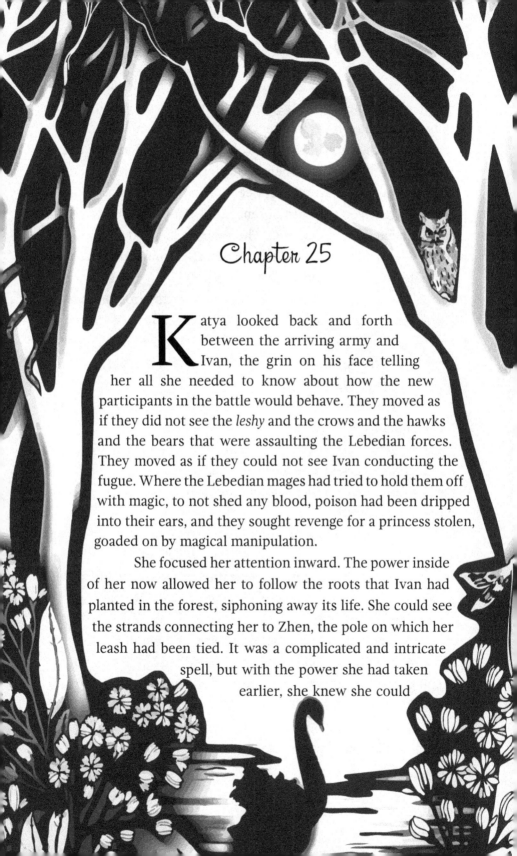

Chapter 25

Katya looked back and forth between the arriving army and Ivan, the grin on his face telling her all she needed to know about how the new participants in the battle would behave. They moved as if they did not see the *leshy* and the crows and the hawks and the bears that were assaulting the Lebedian forces. They moved as if they could not see Ivan conducting the fugue. Where the Lebedian mages had tried to hold them off with magic, to not shed any blood, poison had been dripped into their ears, and they sought revenge for a princess stolen, goaded on by magical manipulation.

She focused her attention inward. The power inside of her now allowed her to follow the roots that Ivan had planted in the forest, siphoning away its life. She could see the strands connecting her to Zhen, the pole on which her leash had been tied. It was a complicated and intricate spell, but with the power she had taken earlier, she knew she could end it.

She formed the energy into a powerful blade, glowing golden in her hands. Precision was unnecessary, and with inelegant chops, she severed the connections between herself and Zhen. She did not pause more than a second before turning her attention to Ivan.

Where her sword was a column of light, he was a void of nothing. His being was an absence, not darkness, not black, but the complete lack of anything. The roots he had planted to sap the forest were a swirl of liquid gray, a molasses converting the blood of the forest into a force for destruction.

Sound returned to her as she felt the first drop of blood hit the ground. She could not tell who it belonged to or if the wound was fatal, but the reverberations shot up through her head, breaking her concentration. From the way Ivan jerked, a predator suddenly on the scent, she knew he had felt it, too.

She refocused. The din of the fray echoed in her mind, threatening to pull her back from the half-world she had walked into. She needed to act quickly. Her anger and bitterness and sorrow and regret and grief were clawing at her mind. She took a tentative step toward him, and then another, until she was at the edge of the circle she had cast.

She knew she would lose the protection of the circle as soon as she stepped out of it, but she was unsure about Zhen's illusion. Ivan appeared to be deep in concentration, muttering to himself, his hands in front of him, palms facing the heavens. Maybe he would not notice her, anyway.

She bolted toward him, weaving in and out of fighters who did not even see her. She watched as blood pooled on the ground, seeping into the soil of the woods; whatever cataclysm Ivan was conjuring was feeding on it. Despite her momentum, she could make out various hubs of magic around the lake begin to awaken and glow. She watched as the blood in the ground crept toward these points with methodical determination. Her stomach lurched as she recalled the night he had bound Zhen here; he had placed those points that night. She wanted to vomit, but instead she she held her blade low to the ground and neared him, ready to strike at the roots he had planted into her forest. She swung the sword over her head, gathering momentum before plunging it toward the ground.

The blow struck a barrier, materialized in a honeycomb pattern around Ivan. It was nearly as clear as glass but it was as hard as steel. She swore as her sword ricocheted off the shield, flinging her to the ground. When she looked up, Ivan was bearing down on her.

"My family sent a more competent mage with them, too? You shall die as the others did all the same." Contempt dripped from each word, a temper that Katya had only ever caught glimmers of, always threatening to flare.

"No, they did not," she replied, realizing he did not recognize her. Zhen was protecting her still. She scrambled to her feet, pulling her blade up with both hands and pointing it at him.

"Then who are you, and why are you here?" His full attention was on her, squinting at her as he looked her up and down.

She took a deep breath, letting it out slowly, and then concentrated again on sinking into the very essence of the forest. She found the small motes that made up the shield he had protecting him, and with her magic, she plucked them out, crushing them. Each crush created a contained explosion, taking out more of the shield with it.

He looked around him, eyes wide with shock as he realized what she was doing. She kept at it, her brow wet with sweat. The work was delicate, and he started to repair it almost as quickly as she was breaking it apart.

But one of the reactions got out of hand, and she could not

contain the explosion.

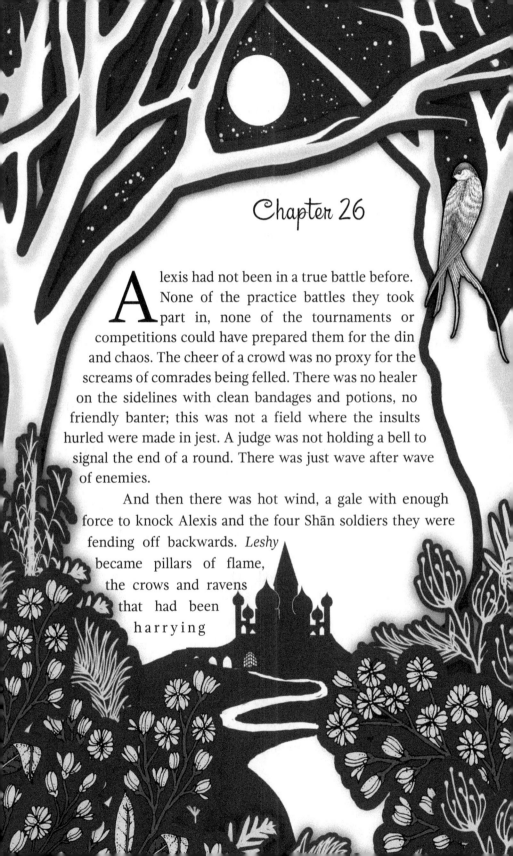

Chapter 26

Alexis had not been in a true battle before. None of the practice battles they took part in, none of the tournaments or competitions could have prepared them for the din and chaos. The cheer of a crowd was no proxy for the screams of comrades being felled. There was no healer on the sidelines with clean bandages and potions, no friendly banter; this was not a field where the insults hurled were made in jest. A judge was not holding a bell to signal the end of a round. There was just wave after wave of enemies.

And then there was hot wind, a gale with enough force to knock Alexis and the four Shān soldiers they were fending off backwards. *Leshy* became pillars of flame, the crows and ravens that had been harrying them fell to the ground. The soldiers of both sides were knocked into trees, and the orchestrated chaos of battle became all out entropy.

Alexis turned over from their back, getting on all fours, using their sword to prop them onto their legs. They saw the soldiers they had been fighting laying, unmoving, on the ground, side by side with members of the Guard. Tatiana was was getting to her feet again, rallying the troops again, her sword waved as one might a flag.

They could not see Katya or Zhen, which meant that Zhen was still working her magic. Unhurt, hopefully.

They raised their sword, ready to charge in again, but there was another rush of searing wind, another painful collision with the ground. From behind their closed eyes, they could still see a flash of bright light at the center of the lake.

This was it. This was failure. This was the end; for them, for the Guard, for Tatiana, for Zhen. All of the people that had trusted them, believed in them, would now meet their end. They had let them all down. They felt something warm, something thick, trickling down their forehead.

The responsibility had been too much. They had not been smart enough or strong enough to save Zhen. They had been too rash, too impulsive.

"I'm sorry, Zhen. I tried." They wanted to open their eyes, just one more time. Try to see if they could find her, look at her. They wanted her to be the last thing they saw. But they couldn't, they were not strong enough for even that.

"No, not yet. You made me a promise." The voice was far away, muffled, but there. Alexis tried to place it, tried to figure out who it belonged to, where it was coming from.

"Alexis, you have to get up." It was in their head, they were hearing things, they thought. They'd heard that dying people sometimes saw or heard things, visions of their past, spectres of what their future could have been. It was the brain misfiring, some doctors said, or the mind expanding, the mages postulated.

"Alexis, please get up." The voice was desperate and full of sorrow, be insistent and pleading.

"Zhen?"

"Please get up." They could hear her, her voice strained and high-pitched.

"Where are you?" They said it aloud, hoping that she could hear them.

"I am still safe. I am not that great at healing larger injuries; I have tried my best. Please. Get up." As the words reached them, they realized they ache of their head had lessened, the throb in their side had dissipated. They no longer felt as if they were floating, they felt more solid. Grounded. Alive.

"Thank you," they said. All of their muscles still screamed at them, protesting as they again stood up.

They saw her across the battlefield, she was no longer in the protection circle that Katya had created, and had been knocked back in the second explosion. She was no longer hidden, and, Alexis realized, neither were they. Her glamour had been broken, and she was on the ground searching for something. Further away, Katya lay prone against a tree. They had no one to protect them.

All the complaints their muscles could have lodged vanished. They wiped the sweat and blood away from their forehead on their sleeve and ran. They sliced through the fauna and flora that the sorcerer had set upon them. They wove in and out of the soldiers and Guards as they resumed the battle. It became a scherzo, almost choreographed as they switched battle partners, traded blows, and made their way across the stage.

And then they were there. They threw themself in front of Zhen and Katya, determined to keep them safe.

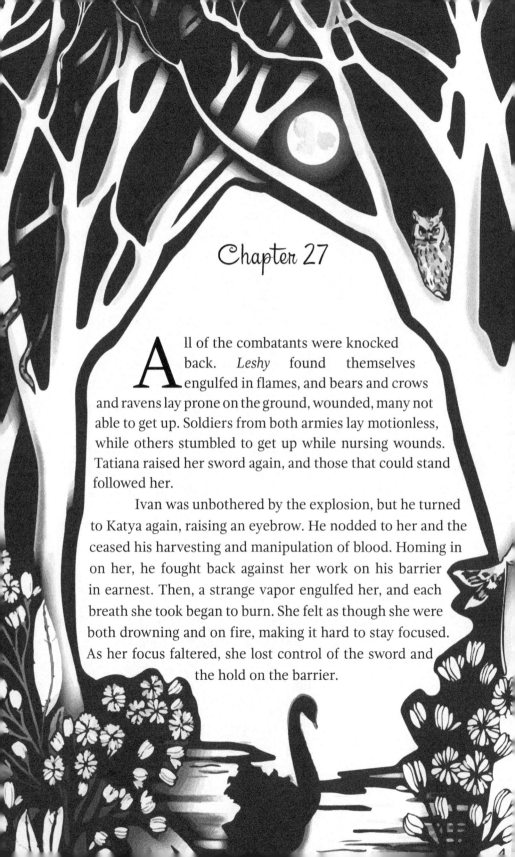

Chapter 27

All of the combatants were knocked back. *Leshy* found themselves engulfed in flames, and bears and crows and ravens lay prone on the ground, wounded, many not able to get up. Soldiers from both armies lay motionless, while others stumbled to get up while nursing wounds. Tatiana raised her sword again, and those that could stand followed her.

Ivan was unbothered by the explosion, but he turned to Katya again, raising an eyebrow. He nodded to her and the ceased his harvesting and manipulation of blood. Homing in on her, he fought back against her work on his barrier in earnest. Then, a strange vapor engulfed her, and each breath she took began to burn. She felt as though she were both drowning and on fire, making it hard to stay focused. As her focus faltered, she lost control of the sword and the hold on the barrier.

The sword evaporated in a blaze of hot energy, an explosion of pain and force all that remained. Katya was knocked back, landing hard against a tree on the edge of the clearing. She struggled to keep her eyes open, looking for Zhen. The haze of heat made it hard to see, but she could make out Zhen in the distance.

"Ah, there you are," Ivan said, rounding on Zhen. Zhen looked up at him. Katya realized too late that Zhen was no longer in the protection circle, and her threadwork must have been lost as she was hit by one of the explosions. All of her protection and glamour were gone.

And so was Katya's.

She leapt in front of Zhen before she could even think about what was happening. She flung her arms to the sides, trying to bring up a temporary protective barrier. As the last words left her lips, a shadow fell over them. Opening her eyes, she saw Princen Alexis, also without glamour now, sword ready, standing in front of her and Zhen.

"I will hold him off. Do whatever it is you need to do, and, please, do it fast. Zhen, I will not let you down," they said, a roguish grin spreading across their face before they winked at Zhen and charged Ivan.

"Zhen, I need your help with this part," Katya said. Behind her she could hear the clink of swords meeting, but she could not be distracted.

"Do you need another illusion?" she asked.

"No," she said. "He knows we are here now. Let us hope Alexis and Tatiana can keep him distracted enough that he cannot raise his shield again."

She began pulling threads from her gown again, the ends frayed and tattered. "What are we doing?"

"Hold my hands and concentrate with me." Katya hesitantly held out both of her hands, palms facing upward. With trepidation,

Zhen placed hers in Katya's, her stray threads falling to the ground. Katya began breathing in and out slowly, and Zhen soon followed her lead. Katya reached the in-between space, the strange place where magic could be seen, not just felt, and where the world seemed sharper, clearer, and brighter. She opened her eyes and saw that Zhen had followed her.

"I have never done this before. It is different than when I do song or thread magic, but somehow similar."

"If we survive this, I should like to learn more about the magics you do."

"We will survive this." Zhen smiled, her words a promise.

"Right," Katya said with a smile. "Follow my lead." Katya plucked a mote from the air and again opened the center. Zhen raised her eyebrows, but then did the same.

"Is this what you learned while at the library?" Zhen asked, her eyes fixated on the impossibly small yet vast glow of power in her cupped hands.

"Yes, it is incredibly dangerous. I think that blast I set off is only a small demonstration of what could go wrong."

"A toast," Katya said, raising her hands, "to our freedom."

Zhen raised her own hands, touching them with Katya's before they threw back their heads and drank the pooled energy. Katya was prepared for the odd sensation as it ran down her throat, but Zhen was not. She coughed a few times, hunching over as she fought to control her reaction. "This feels strange," Zhen said as she righted herself, her gaze finding the shine of Alexis' sword in the battlefield.

"I need you to bind him, if you can, enhancing your thread magic with the power you just consumed. Hold him so that he cannot reach for his own power or the power of others. Can you do that?" Zhen turned back to Katya, and their eyes met. Zhen nodded, picking up the threads that had fallen earlier. With eerie precision, she began weaving them while her focus remained locked on Ivan. As she braided, knotted, twisted, and twirled the threads, Katya saw glowing ropes begin to settle over Ivan.

At first, he seemed unphased. Ivan had fashioned his own sword out of aether and was making what looked like a half-hearted effort to keep his attackers at bay. His focus remained on Tatiana and Princen Alexis as he toyed with them, showing off flairs and lunges. He moved like a predator, who fancied some fun before striking his prey. Katya wondered if he had been a skilled fencer back when he had been a prince, or if this was something he had learned after his escape.

The thread magic, amplified, entwined him without his notice. It became clear that he had been relying on some form of magic in his swordplay, whether for strength, grace, agility, or skill. He stumbled, his parries became slower, his aim less true, his moves less elegant.

Katya knew the exact second he realized that he had been cut off from his external sources of magic. His eyes widened in shock. She watched him as he tried to muster what little he could from his own life force, and in horrific slow motion, he transformed into his owl form, taking flight and hovering above the battlefield, searching with his now keener eyes for his magical assailant.

"I'll take it from here," Katya said, before leaping into the sky herself. She flew up in a blaze of power and embers, her black wings taking on the appearance of burning coal, the energy she carried a flame, brightly burning.

She hovered there, smoldering above the center of the lake, a star reaching zenith. Softly, in the wordless language they had shared, she called to him. He ceased his circling and flew to her.

She felt him touch her mind, a tumult of emotion. A torrent of worry, concern. "Where have you been?" he ask, "Are you all right? Are you hurt? I have been looking for you. It seems as though the princen managed to survive. I have been so scared for you. One more time, please, will you help me?"

Apparently he had not noticed her earlier. She faltered. Before this wordless means of communication had been intimate, but now it felt intrusive. No, she had to destroy his curse and force back the spell he had written in the earth with blood, and then she had to kill him. Or did she? Here, in this moment, was an opportunity to turn back.

She could tell him she was unharmed and would help him, turning her back one more time. She could tell him she was weak, unable to help, but she would be waiting for him at home. She could—

No. She had been here the whole time, but his eyes did not want to see her. They had never wanted to see her for who she truly was. She focused her will, shaping her wings into two sharp blades, and plunged to the ground, gliding in and out of the fray. She slashed at the veins of power in the ground. She was no longer a physical entity; she was rage and power and grief and hope. She was a being of pure magic, a daughter of the forest, and she existed on a plane of aether.

He followed her, calling to her, begging her. Ivan was telling her that he was right all along, that Zhen was a threat to them, that Zhen had destroyed the most important thing to him: their relationship. But she ignored his cries as she severed the last cords of his spell. She felt the dull background hum of the forest roar into a full-throated howl, jubilation on the wind. The denizens of the forest that he had conscripted ceased their attacks. The rivers of blood in the earth dissipated.

She touched down on the lake, transforming back into her human form. Ivan circled above her. She began the last bit of magic, not wanting to wait, not wanting to think about it anymore. Katya took out the same knife he had handed her not so long ago.

The blade drawn, she stepped from the physical plane and fully into the world of magic.

He was standing before her, waiting for her in aether. They were alone, apart from the rest of the chaos unfolding on the lake. "Katya, why?" He was not begging. His shoulders sagged in defeat. His hands kept twitching. He brought his hand up, a gesture so familiar and intimate that she almost leaned in, she could feel his palm against her cheek. There were thousands of words she wanted to say to him, dozens of reasons why she was betraying him.

Katya looked him in the eyes, those eyes she had looked into so many times with love and devotion. In them she did not see confusion, bewilderment, or puzzlement. She saw betrayal, but he knew what he had done, he just did not know how she knew.

Yet, she did not owe him an explanation, she realized. He had taken so much from her, had deceived her in so many ways, so much so that to demand an answer from her seemed grossly presumptuous. He had shattered their partnership, if she could even call what they had had a partnership, and had no right to protest her lack of loyalty now.

She had come ready to kill him, to execute him. But an idea came. A punishment that was far worse.

She raised her knife as if it was a sword, and then brought it crashing down, slicing the aetherial tether that joined him to his magic. He rushed toward her, a cry lodged in his throat. But she sliced and hacked and sawed and destroyed his ability to wield ever magic again.

Chapter 28

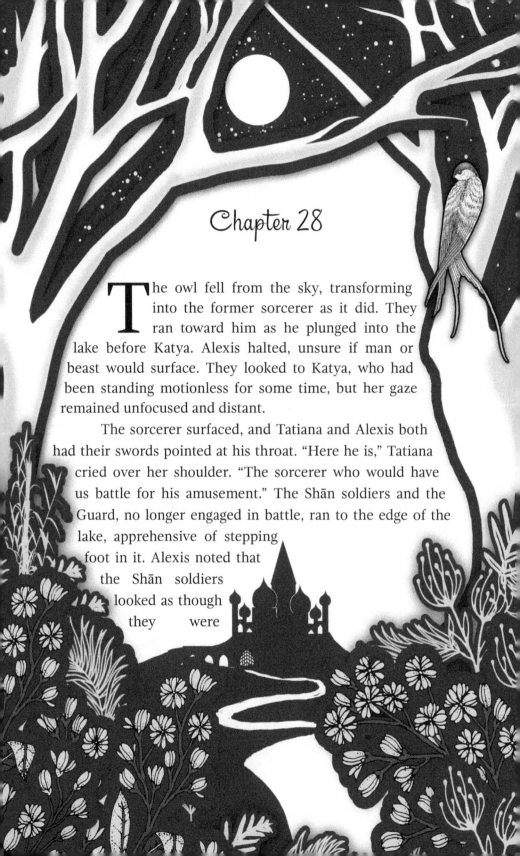

The owl fell from the sky, transforming into the former sorcerer as it did. They ran toward him as he plunged into the lake before Katya. Alexis halted, unsure if man or beast would surface. They looked to Katya, who had been standing motionless for some time, but her gaze remained unfocused and distant.

The sorcerer surfaced, and Tatiana and Alexis both had their swords pointed at his throat. "Here he is," Tatiana cried over her shoulder. "The sorcerer who would have us battle for his amusement." The Shān soldiers and the Guard, no longer engaged in battle, ran to the edge of the lake, apprehensive of stepping foot in it. Alexis noted that the Shān soldiers looked as though they were waking up from a dream. Their leader had woken up, and with Katya occupying the sorcerer, Princess Yi Zhen approached her.

Now, the would-be warmonger was before them. Ivan glanced between Tatiana, Katya, and Alexis. With a gulp of air, Katya came out of whatever magical trance she had been in. Alexis met her eyes, and she nodded to them, "he can't do anything anymore." Then backed away.

The sorcerer was helpless, it seemed. They could kill him here, now. They could show their decisiveness as a leader, prove themself before veteran soldiers of the two nations they were trying to bring peace to. The fickleness of their past, the sneaking out, the rashness, the impulsive decisions they had made that had brought worry to their parents' eyes—all could be wiped away with a single slash of their sword.

But would that be just another impulsive decision? Could they show both strength and wisdom in this moment? A trial would be a more definitive way of proving their commitment to peace, officials from both kingdoms able to attend and demand answers and interrogate the sorcerer.

Zhen came up behind them, putting her hand on their shoulder. She still glowed slightly, and Alexis caught sight of a glint in her hand. Removing her hand from their shoulder, she tied complicated knots, and as she did so, steel bindings wrapped themselves around Ivan's wrists, securing them together behind his back.

Alexis knew what to do. "As princen and heir of Lebedia, I find you guilty of kidnapping a member of the royal family, attempted assassination of members of the royal house, and treason. You shall be brought with us to the royal dungeons where you shall await a interrogation and sentencing."

Tatiana grabbed him by an elbow and hauled him to his feet. He resisted and turned back to Katya. "I loved you, Katya," he said, a mixture of devotion and sorrow in his eyes.

"No, Ivan. You loved the idea of me," she said, looking deliberately away from him. Tatiana dragged him to a horse and chained him to the saddle. Alexis, Yi Zhen, and Katya followed behind her, wading out of the lake. "Ana, Vera; I want you two to keep an eye on him," she ordered. The two women snapped to attention and took up positions to stand watch over the sorcerer.

Alexis turned to Zhen and Katya. "Are you two able to leave here now?"

"Zhen can leave. No more of his magic should remain to tether her to this place," Katya said.

Alexis ran their hand through their hair and grinned at Zhen. "I promised I would save you, my lady," they said as they got down on one knee. Yi Zhen radiated happiness as she approached them. They took her hands in their own, overjoyed that they had managed to not only foil the plans of the sorcerer, but also had done it for a woman they were in love with.

"I helped a little," Zhen said.

"You helped a lot. I did not know you were so good with magic," Alexis said. They had been told she could do a little, enough to entertain guests, but her skill had surpassed their expectations.

"I have always wanted to learn more, though my parents would not let me."

"I shall make sure you are introduced to all the finest scholars we have. The library is yours to explore."

"My parents had a specific vision for me. They had this image in their head of who I was, who I would be. They had expectations, and it seemed so unimaginable that I could escape the box they wanted me in."

"You can be whoever you want. I will never try to change who you are."

"Say I want to be a mage today, and tomorrow I want to be a

fencer. What about that?"

"Then I shall love a fencer."

She smiled at them, her thumbs tracing circles on the tops of their hands. They were relieved that they did not somehow bungle the conversation. They could not have hoped for more, and they suspected that she would continue to surprise them.

"I cannot wait to get back to the palace and introduce you to my family for real," they said. "We shall have a proper celebration."

Zhen flashed a glowing smile at them, and they felt their heart flutter in response. "I look forward to meeting everyone and planning our wedding together."

"Yes. We shall have hundreds of flowers, dancing, the best musicians in the land, and the best food and entertainers—"

"And we shall have each other."

"Exactly." They wanted this future, but they also wanted to savor this moment, this joy and excitement. Their body was still overloaded from the rush of battle, and the anticipation that had been building finally had its release. They never wanted to forget how it felt.

But there was something gnawing at the back of their mind, something about what Katya had said.

Zhen figured it out first. "You said I could leave, but what about you?" she asked as she turned to speak to Katya. But Katya was already striding past the tree line, walking away from the battle alone.

Alexis ran toward her, Zhen following behind. "Wait, Katya!" they called as they approached her. "Where are you going?"

"I am not sure yet. There was a cottage I shared with Ivan. I suppose I can stay there for a few days while I find another spot to build a new home."

"You do not want to come with us?" Alexis asked. She had been guarded and secretive in the library, but surely she would not continue to live in the woods. She had been trapped here, too, in some sort of way.

"I cannot."

Zhen reached out for Katya's hands and took them in her own. A pang of jealousy jolted through Alexis. This was supposed to be *their* moment, but with effort, they crushed the jealousy. This was also Katya's moment. They had worked together to bring about this victory. They could not claim ownership over something that they all were entitled to.

"Why not? I know that it will take time for us to rebuild our relationship. But I want to try. I recognize that you were in a difficult spot, too. You hurt me, but I do not think it is something we cannot get past. If Alexis is all right with it, you are welcome to come with us."

Alexis knew this was the toughest battle they would fight today. They wanted to be understanding and show Zhen that they trusted her, that they wanted her happiness. Their parents had raised them to accept that love was infinite, and the look on Zhen's face told them she had feelings for Katya.

"I do not mind," they said. "You are my bride, Zhen, but I cannot keep you from loving others. If you and Katya—"

"I cannot leave this forest," Katya said.

"You do not have to do this to yourself," Alexis said.

"No, I mean," she chewed on her lip, considering her words. "I am bound to this forest, even with Ivan gone. To leave it is to die."

"There has to be a way," Zhen started. Alexis could feel the desperation coming off Zhen in waves.

"I have figured out where I am from, and it is here. This is my home, and the forest is my parent and I do not want to leave it. It needs me, to undo all that he did."

"How did you leave the forest to get Alexis?" Zhen asked.

"At the risk of my life, if I had not come back when I did I might not have come back at all."

An idea came to Alexis, and they knew to freely offer it would be the right thing to do, the unselfish thing. "What if we could arrange for Zhen to visit you?"

Both Zhen and Katya looked at him in shock. "Maybe once a month, Zhen could have a small escort, and she could stay here for a few days or a week. Whatever amount of time would work best for the two of you."

Zhen took their hand and then grabbed one of Katya's. She looked between the two of them. "I would like that very much," she said to Alexis. "Katya, what do you say?"

Katya's eyes watered. An inkling of a feeling bubbled in Alexis, seeing Katya and Zhen happy, together, made them feel happy, too. They would miss Zhen when she was away, but if this brought her joy, and if it brought Katya joy, how could they deny that? Katya nodded at them both, wiping away a tear as it welled. "I would also like that," she said.

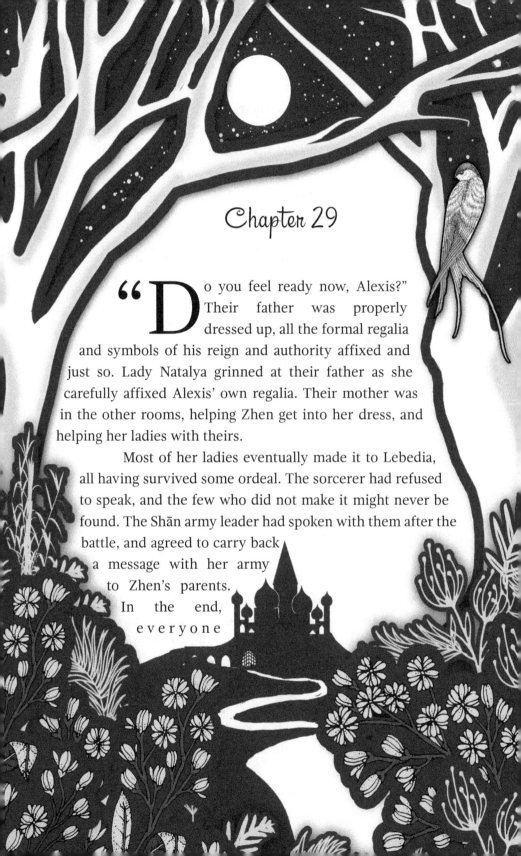

Chapter 29

"Do you feel ready now, Alexis?" Their father was properly dressed up, all the formal regalia and symbols of his reign and authority affixed and just so. Lady Natalya grinned at their father as she carefully affixed Alexis' own regalia. Their mother was in the other rooms, helping Zhen get into her dress, and helping her ladies with theirs.

Most of her ladies eventually made it to Lebedia, all having survived some ordeal. The sorcerer had refused to speak, and the few who did not make it might never be found. The Shān army leader had spoken with them after the battle, and agreed to carry back a message with her army to Zhen's parents. In the end, everyone agreed that the wedding should still take place.

So here they were, on their wedding day.

"I do not think so," Alexis told their father.

"I thought you would say that. But I think you are."

"Why do you say that?"

"You lead a force on a rescue mission, you minimized casualties, and you have managed to find an agreeable arrangement with a metamour"

"I stumbled into what could have been a trap, then I went back, I nearly died, I got half the Council of Mages killed, and many of the soldiers on either side, too."

"Alexis, you cannot blame yourself for that. They all went in knowing what would happen. Lairde Tanis managed to get many of them out of there before the full effects of that sorcerer's spell could be wrought. Xie has told you xirself that there was nothing you could do about that. All of them signed up for the mission voluntarily."

"I know, you are right. I just cannot stop feeling guilty about it."

"There are days I still feel guilty for decisions I have made. A good ruler should always have empathy and compassion. If you felt nothing at all, I would be very afraid, and probably asking one of your siblings to be heir instead."

"I am still nervous about this marriage, about the arrangement I have with Zhen's girlfriend. I'm going to trip going to the altar, and then I am going to fall on my face during the first dance."

"Alexis, you are going to be wonderful. For all of it."

"You only say that because you have to."

"You owe me five gold, Mikhail," Lady Natalya said, not looking up from the medal she was attaching to Alexis' doublet.

"What? That should not count," the czar huffed.

"I told you they would be too flustered to accept any of your well deserved pride."

"They were refusing my compliments, not my pride."

"I'm with Natalya on this one, father. You owe her that gold."

"Did I miss anything?" Tatiana said, coming into the rooms.
"Minor betting."

"No, I didn't miss that," Tatiana said to Alexis before turning
to Lady Natalya. "Have they complained about their skirt and pants
not being the proper lengths yet?"

"Twice. I've let both in and hemmed both up again. I told
them to deal with it the last time they complained."

"Okay, this is incredibly unfair. How do I get in on some of
these bets? You cannot be the only ones who make money off of me
being 'so predictable.'"

They all just laughed. Alexis crossed their arms and scowled.
"I hope none of you are taking bets on Zhen."

Lady Natalya looked scandalized. "Of course not, but she did
place one of her own on you."

"What? What did she bet on?"

"You'll have to ask her that."

"I will!"

"You better!" Tatiana said. "Speaking of, I was sent to get
you. The ceremony will be starting and we need to get you to the
hall now, unless you want to be late."

"Almost done, give me just a minute," Lady Natalya said. She
opened a small box and pulled out another medal, one that Alexis
had not seen before. "A medal of honor and valor, for your service
to Lebedia, and your efforts to ensure peace." She placed it above
all the others, pinning it in place and stepping back. "We are all
very proud of you. We will have a ceremony to present it properly,
to you and everyone else who fought, but we wanted you to have it
for today."

Alexis was not one to cry, but they almost wished they were

in this moment, because they could feel themself blushing. "You should not, I mean, I do not—"

"Alexis, we're wasting daylight," Tatiana said.

They allowed themself to be led down to the great hall. At some point their father and Lady Natalya split off, and it was just them and Tatiana.

"I am so nervous."

"You are going to be fine!"

"Thank you for being there for me, Tatiana. I mean it."

Alexis expected one of her usual quips, but instead she stopped and turned to them. "I know you do. I'll always be here for you, as long as you want me to be."

"And I'll always be there for you, it's what best friends do."

"It is what they do. I could not be more happy to be your best woman today. So I have to ask, will you be my best gentleperson at mine and Inna's wedding?"

"You are getting married? You are doing it?"

"I think! I have not asked Inna yet! But I plan to! Soon! I think she will say yes."

"Of course, of course. I could not be more happy for you!"

"Okay, okay, enough sap for now, we got to finish this wedding first."

They approached the hall, and many assorted staff descended upon them, leading them and telling them how to stand and when to walk. They had practiced this last night, and it was all still fresh in Alexis' mind. But, they still feared messing up.

"Stand right here," someone told them. "I will tell you when to go. The door will open, and it will stay open and you need to pause before you start walking, so do not walk until I say go."

The door opened. There were three aisles of seats and everyone stood in unison. Alexis knew that one door over the doors had opened on Zhen, too. At the front of the hall they saw the altar.

Tatiana and Ying Yue, Zhen's sister, were already there. They took a deep breath in and let it out.

"Go," they were told.

They walked down the aisle, looking straight ahead but hoping they were lined up perfectly with Zhen as she walked down the next aisle. Each step felt less difficult, each breath quelled some of their nerves. When they reached the altar, they turned and walked directly toward Zhen. She smiled at them, her hair pulled away and a phoenix coronet of gold and rubies perfectly situated on her head. She was in all reds and golds, silks and satins embroidered with gold. She looked radiant.

They reached her and took her hands in theirs.

"What did you bet?" they asked her.

"Excuse me?" she whispered back.

"The others said you placed a bet on me."

"Oh! Yes, I will tell you later, after I have won." She winked at them.

The priestess began her speech, addressing those assembled and asking them to sit. The ceremony was a blur to Alexis, speeches and songs about love and commitment sprinkled with humorous advice. They presented each other with rings, each etched with the symbols of their countries and their families.

"Princen Alexis, do you swear to love and cherish and trust Princess Zhen?"

"I do."

"Do you promise to always communicate with her in perfect love and perfect trust?"

"I do."

"Princess Zhen, do you swear to love and cherish and trust Princen Alexis?"

"I do."

"Do you promise to always communicate with them in

perfect love and perfect trust?"

"I do."

"You may read each other your vows."

Alexis unfolded a paper they had stashed in their doublet and cleared their throat. "I am sometimes rash and impulsive." They heard more than a few people in the audience laugh. "Except when it comes to love. I never have loved easily, but I easily love you. I hope that I get to spend all of my days loving you. I hope that we can help each other grow as people, assisting each other in overcoming any obstacles. I promise to always respond to you with kindness and respect, to always listen to what you have to say, and cherish you as you pursue your own dreams."

"Was I supposed to have something written up ahead of time?" Zhen whispered to them.

They ran their hand through their hair. "Uhh."

She winked back at him. "When my parents told me about the betrothal, I cried. I thought my life was over, but when you secretly started exchanging letters with me, I realized it might not be as terrible as I feared. I love very easily, and very freely. It was not hard to fall in love with you. I promise to always be honest with you, even if it means I am telling you that you are about to do something incredibly foolish. My love for you means that I trust you, and I promise to be deserving of your trust in kind."

They both smiled at the priestess. "I now pronounce you married!"

Everyone rose to their feet and clapped as Alexis and Zhen ran hand in hand back up the aisle that Alexis had come down. "Now let's party!" Zhen cried.

They raced to the ballroom and flung open the doors.

"Which dance should we start with?" Alexis asked, spinning around the empty ballroom. As if on cue, a waltz began to play, drifting from the hidden musicians galley. "Will this do?" Zhen asked.

"I do not think we practiced a dance like this."

"So?" She grabbed their hands and began dancing, leading them through steps they did not even know. As the rest of the guests trickled in, they applauded and shouted and joined in.

"What did you bet? Can you tell me now?"

"I bet that you were not so bad at dancing."

"I wish we could do this forever," Alexis said.

"We can," Zhen replied.

Chapter 30

The cottage still smelled like him. He was alive still, probably not for much longer, and yet his shade seemed to occupy every shadow in the home they once shared. Katya kept expecting him to appear over her shoulder to ask her if she needed anything, or offer her tea. Every creak of an old table as she piled objects on it, every howl of the wind against the walls could be him.

It had been a month since she had watched him be taken away in chains, a month since she had kissed Zhen goodbye with promises of a visit soon. She had built herself a new cottage on the lake, and she made sure that there was space for Zhen and whatever she might need while visiting. She had moved her bees, leading the hive while gently guiding the queen through the forest. All that was left was to pack the last of her things, and then she would burn this cottage and everything inside.

"Daughter," came a voice

from behind her, ringing like a bell. She shrieked as she turned to face the intruder. A woman stood in the doorway. She had honey-brown eyes, neat bangs, and flowing warm blonde hair that fell to her waist in loose curls. Her outfit was almost all in shades of black, a loose dress and velvet boots. A lace shawl made of cloth-of-gold hung around her shoulders. "Daughter," the woman repeated.

"Yes?" Katya asked.

"I wanted to say thank you, and I am sorry."

"Oh." Katya said, unsure of what else could be said.

"I would like to help you. There are old spells on this dwelling. They are deteriorating, but we should take precautions."

Katya nodded and then hoisted the box of her belongings onto her hip. The woman followed her lead, picking up two of the other packed boxes and following her out. "There are a few more boxes I want," Katya told the woman as they set down the boxes inside of a small cart.

When the last of the belongings were outside, Katya inspected the cottage one last time, searching for any tokens or mementos she might want, or books she had forgotten. Her eyes lingered on her favorite tea mug, and then on some knick knacks he had gifted her. She stared at the small wood carvings on the windowsill in the main room, miniature bees, crows, and a small swan. "This was my whole life."

"This was a lie."

"I know that now."

"We should get started. There are complex workings here," the woman said. Katya followed her back outside.

The woman pulled out a wooden wand with a rose quartz affixed at the top. It looked like it might be a conjury tool, but then Katya noticed the small markings etched in the wood. It looked like a small star map was inscribed, such as was used by celestians. Katya watched as she drew in power from nature, the stars, the elements and then gathered power from her own inner source of aether. She cast a circle of salt like she was a witch, and then she channeled that power toward the cottage. Her eyes were closed, but after a few moments, she lifted one eyelid to glance as Katya and gave a lopsided smile.

Katya closed her eyes and began her own spell to dismantle the cottage and whatever strange workings Ivan had placed on it. She fell back into that space between particles and destroyed them one by one. She knew of the woman beside her, combining sorcery with witchcraft and melding conjury to celestialism. Together, they undid years of magic.

The sun was rising when they had finished their task, and Katya was exhausted. "Well done," the woman said. "Did you want the honors of burning it?"

"Of course," she said. She had used the sorcery rune for lighting a fire hundreds of times; to light a candle or to kindle a hearth. She had never lit anything of this size on fire. A month ago she could have said there were many things she had never done before. And yet.

She visualized the rune for fire, directing her will through the mental image, with no need for a rod to direct her power. The power welled inside of her, pooling before the rune. With a thought she released it, and the cottage blazed resplendent.

The woman nodded her approval. They both watched, silent, as the remnants of her life before she found herself burned. Dozens of questions ran through Katya's head, and there were times she almost blurted them out and broke the silence. But she had a lifetime to ask her parent questions, and for now it seemed best to not tarnish this moment. She was glad the woman was here to witness this moment, this catharsis.

When the last embers grew cold, the woman smiled once more to Katya. "I will always be here," she said. Then she transformed into a skylark and took to the skies. Katya watched her until she could see her no more, then picked up the handles of the cart and began walking to the lake.

Her coven of crows followed her, some flying ahead and waiting in the bushes, others staying back a little way before rushing forward. The forest felt more alive than it had a month ago, as though a hundred springs were happening at once. Katya noted each new sproutling on the forest floor, each new nest in the trees.

The lake sparkled in the late morning sun. Katya slowed down as she approached, and set the handles of her car down. Although she had been living in the new cottage by the lake, today was the first time it was actually home. Her first homecoming, she let this new reality settle into her core. She wanted to remember this moment in perfect clarity. She wanted to remember everything from the formation of her crows in the trees, to the smell of the lake as a breeze brushed past it. This was no longer a prison, and never would be again.

She picked up her cart again, and sang a small melody as she marched towards her cottage. She set her cart down outside the door, picked up a box, and went inside. The light streamed in from the windows, and a breeze played in the curtains of an opened window. She set the box down on a table, and went to go back outside to grab another.

She heard the footfalls of a horse and looked up. On the other side of the clearing, a chestnut horse was galloping toward her. The rider pulled on the reigns, strands of dark black hair flying around her face. "Katya," Zhen called. "Katya!"

Zhen leapt from the horse before it had even stopped and ran, arms outstretched, into Katya's embrace. Katya inhaled the scent of Zhen's hair, floral and sweet. "You're here!"

"I am! I am here!"

Katya held her close, and then whispered, "may I kiss you?"

"Please?"

Time became irrelevant. Katya knew that this week with Zhen would be one of many for years to come, but that did not mean she could not kiss Zhen slowly, that she could not take her time. The two created a new language together, one that only the other could understand. A language comprised of slow kisses, quick pecks, and gentle bites. A language Katya could use to welcome Zhen to her second home.

Acknowledgements

This book started out as a half-remembered mid-night scribble. Maybe a cat woke me up, maybe something outside was loud enough to rouse me. I reached for my phone to check the time, and instead wrote three pages about a forest-spirit racing through the woods with a coven of crows. Those three pages became twenty in the coming days, and then coalesced into the story that it is today. None of those initial scribbles are still in this book, but that spirit still haunts the pages.

I wanted to say thank you to Mike, my spouse, for reading draft after draft and being an amazing sounding board as I tweaked and kneaded and sculpted the shape of the story. Thank you for being patient as I grew further and further behind in Final Fantasy XIV and still being kind enough to run now weeks-old dungeons with me for the first time. Thank you for believing in me and this story and for providing me the space I needed to complete it.

Thank you to Kat, for believing in me and this story and for cheering me on as I sent you picture after picture of Haruka Tenoh, Utena, and other sword wielding gender-bending anime bad-asses trying to describe some of the characters. Thank you for squeeing with me as I sent WIP cover art. Thank you for that super chill week I spent at your place under the kotatsu and thank you for the super chill week you spent at my place eating arepas and sushi. I needed both of those to hammer out large portions of this book.

Thank you, Liz, for all the support. Especially for lending me some very good books that got me thinking about my own. I always appreciate hanging out with you and screaming about books!

Thank you to all the wonderful people I met at Madcap Retreats Writing Cross Culturally. A weekend in beautiful Tennessee was not enough time. I wish we could have all stayed there another week. I learned so much from every single person I met and I will never forget the advice I received from the faculty.

Thank you to Ana Mardoll, Benjanun "Bee" Sriduangkaew, Katherine Locke, and so many more writers who have been amazing on and offline support. I love cheerleading your books and I hope I can pay back the kindness and support you've given me with interest.

Thank you to Louisa Smith of Juneberry Design, Laya Rose, and Dane Low for amazing cover art. I've changed the art for this book a few times, but all of the covers are special and amazing and dear to me.

Thank you Jen Anderson of Clearing Blocks Editing for an amazing edit! Seriously, thank you! You understood what I was trying to accomplish and helped me execute more clearly on that vision. I learned so much from your comments, and I feel like such a better writer now.

Thank you, Aurelia Fray of Pretty AF Designs, for the beautiful interior design! I tried to do formatting of the interior myself and failed very spectacularly. This book would not be as beautiful as it is without your fantastic attention to detail.

Thank you, Stuart Thaman, for your advice and encouragement, it helped me go the extra mile and was exactly what I needed to hear.

Thank you, Jenny of Seedlings Designs, for the amazing promotional materials. The headers and bookmarks you designed are amazing, and I cannot wait to put those bookmarks in as many hands as I can!

I devoured everything Swan Lake as soon as I realized where this book was going, including a spectacular performance by The Russian

Grand Ballet at the Warner Theatre in DC. It was technically a presidential debate night, and as my day job was a developer for the DNC, I should have been frantically watching our servers and spinning up rapid response pages. But my fantastic and amazing boss let me have a night off! Thank you, Mike, this book might not have happened without that time off!

Thank you to my friends in #supersecrettechfeminist slack, I appreciated it each time yall let me get off topic and talk books instead of Javascript in the #hustle channel. Special thanks to Tessa, Heather, Angelina, Coraline, and Nicole who all provided amazing feedback on a few of my requests for comment.

Thank you to my pets, Tom, Didi, Stormy, Melusina, Calcifer, and Luna. You all were very good companions. Even when you were not.

This is a first novel, so I have a backlog of people who helped me onto this path, even if they did not help directly in this book. Thank you to my high school teachers who made me realize I liked being creative: Ms. Glunt, Mrs. and Mr. Mummert, and Mr. Lane. My high school friends who my have read some early writings and (probably bad) fan fiction; Hunter, Melissa, Shannon, and Ashley. To my college professors who helped me thrive: Professor Tamashiro, Doc Hepler, and Chief. To my ADPi sisters who helped me survive: Nico, Ashlee, Christina, Hannah, Meg, and Sarah. And of course, thank you to my mom, my sister, my aunts and uncles and cousins for letting me ramble for hours.

Thank you, awesome reader, for reading this book! It is a deeply personal thing to share a story with the world, and a deeply personal thing to read someone else's story. Thank you for making a spot for my story in your probably ever overflowing TBR pile. I hope you enjoyed it. Please leave a review on Goodreads, Amazon, or you blog!

About the Author

Dax writes positive queer fantasy and science fiction; worlds where being LGBTQIA is normal, accepted, and celebrated. Fey enjoys creating new magic systems, blending science and magic, and building kingdoms that ask to be torn down. Fey pays homage to fairy tales by inverting them, subverting them, and making them very, very gay.

Dax grew up in Fairview, PA, where fey spent their days playing flute for the band, spinning flags for the winter guard, being wild in the school plays, taking medals in the speech and debate team, and falling into streams and creeks and lakes with feir friends. In ninth grade the pastor of a local church declared fem a witch during a Sunday sermon, claiming Dax was converting the entire marching band into a coven. To this day, that accusation still haunts fem.

Dax completed an undergraduate degree in Political Science at Allegheny College in Meadville, PA. While there, fey also took courses in music, poetry, and astronomy. Fey are a member of the Alpha Delta Pi sorority, Eta Beta chapter. Fey completed feir senior thesis on the on-going belligerent and illegal occupation of the Kingdom of Hawai'i by the imperialist forces of the United States. Do not ask fem about this unless you want to see Dax screaming about the evils of fruit companies.

When not writing bisexual witches, Dax can be found playing music or writing code, exploring Eorzea, petting cats, or ranting on Twitter. Dax is owned by three cats, and calls the DC metro area home.

Let's Connect

daxmurray.com

@DaxAeterna

@DaxAeterna

Sign up for Dax's twice-monthly newsletter for bonus deleted scenes, book recommendations, adorable pet pictures, updates on projects, exclusive first looks, and monthly book giveaways: newsletter.daxmurray.com

An excerpt from
The Resignation Letter,
the origin story of the Order of Thea

Spring awakened slowly in this part of the world, bearing flooding rains and a mist that hung over the thaw from winter. When the gray lifted, the sun again cast warmth upon the land, and the flowers began to unfold themselves, the Empress would invite her closest friends to a picnic.

The miasma of pollen left a certain glow on the entire event, and Amalthea wasn't sure entirely to what she should attribute the daze in which she found herself. She was, as she called herself, a scientist. The mages mocked her, yet a roll of scented parchment had found itself into her small dark hands. Did the Empress wish to get to know the most scandalous woman at court? The woman who took the vows of a mage just to break them? Who invented titles for herself, who cloaked herself in an air of scientific supremacy over the superstitions of sorcery? The woman from that far-off conquered land who never should have been allowed in the Academy of Mages to begin with, and yet, despite her braided hair, was here?

The picnic was not the last time Amalthea found herself with a scented scroll. Spring became summer, and still the Empress sought out her company. At first it was a procession of small gatherings, where the intimacy was subtle, and sometimes Amalthea swore she imagined it. But steadily the Empress sought her out more. Earls and duchexxes gave her confused looks, seeking to know why the places of honor they once occupied were now given to a wayward and obstinate mage. A mage who wasn't a citizen by birth but by conquest. But, all else aside, she was a mage: mages were tools, weapons sometimes, but always resources, never friends.

The looks never turned into words. After all, who would critique the Empress's choice of friends? The Empress was nothing like either of her fathers, her birthing-father a taciturn tyrant who oversaw the governing of the realm and her seed-father a hungry expansionist who oversaw their military conquests. She did not behead those who disagreed with her, reduced the size of military, and stopped the invasions. But she could turn cold, and those who were touched by her chill found themselves frozen out of her warm gatherings.

At one such gathering Amalthea found herself to suddenly be one of the last of the guests excusing herself, and in doing so, found the Empress asking her to stay. Another hour passed, and the Empress continued to be interested in soliciting her opinion. Soon it was just her, the Empress, and some rude but high ranking duke. The duke was clearly vying to be alone with the Empress, and Amalthea was convinced she was here now to prevent just that. Another quarter hour passed before he got up and indicated that he and Amalthea had overstayed their welcome, and he would be happy to escort her to her chambers.

"That won't be necessary, I have a few more questions I would like to ask our scientist. Thank you for joining us this evening. Give my regards to your father."

A dismissal. There was no way he could tarry any longer. A heartbeat passed after the soft click of the door shutting, and then the two women turned to fully face each other, and Amalthea knew there would be no turning back.

An excerpt from
Birthing Orion, a novel in verse
Coming Fall 2018

The Creator

From the miasma
I become

making and breaking
our beautiful children

my stars and planets and
asteroids and meteors

careening through me.
Incandescent radiance
you and me and us
my darkness, yours

holding you
in my center,
my very core
my infinitesimally infinite

heart--

The Destroyer

I am hunger
I am all of everything that ever will be

condensed
to a single point

all futures happening at once
and never happening at all

except the future
we hold

together: our galaxy
we are equilibrium
you are the only thing that sates me

Proto

We were denser than some of the rest,
we accumulated, we shared gravity -
We were many atoms all compressed
We collapsed into stars, majesty

But we burned too brightly, too fast
We were gone before we could even start
It was all too good to last
But we continued on, rather than depart

Collapsing, dying, a globular cluster
and rotating disk, attracting evermore-
We were not lackluster
repeating all that had already happened before

gas, dust and dark matter: a protogalactic cloud
we wore our newness as a shroud

Binary stars

I made them for you,
they share a common center

just like me and you
two stars, one orbit

always so close
to each other

I had not considered
that these twin stars

would only touch each other when they explode

perhaps this was not the romantic gift I envisioned for you

Eternity

A gravitationally bound system:
a conglomeration of component parts,
in no particular order or prescribed quantity,
but all unhurriedly drifting apart.

Stars and their remnants, dark matter and dust,
solar systems and interstellar gas,
planets with memories too young:
all orbiting this dense center of mass.

Too fondly have I loved these stars;
all these galaxies we once called ours.

CPSIA information can be obtained
at www.ICGtesting.com
Printed in the USA
LVHW090210280921
698854LV00007B/673

9 780692 142431